Crime In The Tower

ALSO BY CATHERINE MOLONEY

CRIME
IN THE
TOWER

CATHERINE
MOLONEY

Detective Markham Mystery Book 22

Joffe Books, London
www.joffebooks.com

First published in Great Britain in 2024

Cover art by Dee Dee Book Covers

ISBN: 978-1-83526-909-1

For Rev Grahame A

PROLOGUE

It was shortly after six o'clock on the evening of Saturday 2 December as cleaner Pam Appleton worked her way through the offices in the basement of the Queen's House, the governor's residence at the Tower of London. Mechanically emptying waste-paper bins and wiping computer screens in the outer office, she reflected how it was funny the way people imagined working in the Tower to be romantic and spooky, like starring in one of those paranormal shows that were all the rage nowadays. The truth was that for most of the time, it was just like any other job and she had come to take the ancient surroundings almost for granted.

Mind you, at this time on a cold wet winter's day, the vast stone walls and ramparts seemed vaguely clammy and menacing, as if some baleful humidity had broken out on them like a disease.

And then there were the ghosts . . . She hadn't been able to avoid hearing about *them*.

Her favourite was Lady Arbella Stuart, known as the White Lady, who was supposed to go flitting about after dusk wringing her hands in the approved tragic style. A cousin of James I and niece of Mary Queen of Scots, she ended up being imprisoned in the Queen's House after some plot or other and promptly set about starving herself to death. The assistant curator Margaret Esdaile had done a special study of Arbella, telling Pam that she most probably suffered from porphyria like Mad King George and might even have been clinically certifiable.

To think of the royals having all these nutters in their bloodline. No wonder Prince Harry and Meghan kept banging on about mental health!

Pam liked it when Dr Esdaile told stories about all the folk who had suffered in the Tower or showed her antique books containing 'contemporary sources'. She'd even memorized some lines a poor young Catholic scribbled before dying for his part in a conspiracy to free Mary Queen of Scots:

> *My tale was heard and yet it was not told, My fruit is fallen and yet my leaves are green, My youth is spent and yet I am not old, I saw the world and yet I was not seen; My thread is cut and yet it is not spun, And now I live and now my life is done.*

That was just how Pam felt at times. Like life was passing her by and she hadn't made the most of her opportunities, so the pressure was on to make up for lost time. Mind you, Dr Esdaile had said not to be daft and the world was her oyster, even writing a reference to help her get into the History programme at St Mary's Twickenham. Pam was willing to bet snooty Benedict Ryan and Daniel Locke, the joint chief curators, would have given her short shrift if she had dared approach *them*, but Margaret Esdaile had no airs and graces and was never too busy for a chat about Pam's long-term ambitions. She even made time to show Pam the carved graffiti that laced the walls of the Beauchamp Tower and recount stories about famous prisoners like Sir Walter Raleigh who kitted out a cell as his study and had a converted chicken shed where he conducted all kinds of weird and wonderful experiments on treasures plundered from the

New World. Then there were the legends about Elizabeth I and Robert Dudley having clandestine meetings in the Bell Tower, through that was probably 'a load of tosh'.

Pam knew Dr Esdaile had a new and exciting research project on hand. Something to do with the Princes in the Tower and hidden relics. It had put Dr Locke's nose properly out of joint, her moving in on what he regarded as *his* patch. And word had it that Dr Esdaile's ex-husband Steven Winders, now a curator at Hampton Court, was none too happy either, seeing as he and second wife Lucy (HR manager) planned an exhibition on Richard III and were afraid she might steal their thunder. Academics were a right bunch of prima donnas in Pam's opinion, but Dr Esdaile was different from the rest.

The assistant curator was no pushover though, Pam thought with a wry smile, as she recalled that business with Beefeater John Whittingham. Thanks to Dr Esdaile reporting him for fluffing his spiel to the tourists, he'd had to mug up on his history and do some kind of oral exam in front of the deputy governor. He was hopping mad about that, and her complaint that he'd been overly familiar with a group of Italian exchange students just poured oil on the flames. Pam didn't much care for Whittingham herself — too leery by half — but he was popular with his colleagues, and the episode left Dr Esdaile in the doghouse with the small Tower community. Just as well she didn't live in the palace . . .

Pam supposed it must be a feather in one's cap to give the Tower as your home address. The black and white timber-framed Queen's House was something else, though stuck-up Clare Hunter, the events co-ordinator, took good care to ensure the facilities staff had little opportunity to linger and marvel at its treasures. The cleaner pulled a face as she recalled how Hunter practically threw a fit when she came across Dr Esdaile giving her a guided tour of the Council Chamber where they'd interrogated Guy Fawkes. The Tower's chaplain, the Reverend Bernard Doyle MBE, wasn't much better, she reflected sardonically, despite all that blather about them being one big happy family. It seemed like any time her team was on shift in the Chapel of St Peter ad Vincula, where Anne Boleyn was buried, the padre hovered around like he suspected they might pinch the candlesticks or something. And he'd been a bit standoffish when she asked about taking a look in the little crypt where Thomas More was buried. 'His head isn't there, you know,' was the quelling response to her enquiry, as though she was a ghoulish philistine looking for cheap thrills. 'It's kept in a vault at St Dunstan's Church in Canterbury,' the chaplain pronounced, ushering her firmly towards a memorial plaque to the left of the main altar.

Doyle was the kind of bloke her mum described as a long drink of water, and she supposed he wasn't *too* bad if you liked the half-starved and hollow-cheeked look. There was a rumour that he'd made a play for Dr Esdaile before she married Steven Winders and still carried a torch for her even though she was now happily remarried to stockbroker Charles Esdaile.

Pam couldn't imagine Doyle had ever stood much of a chance with Margaret Esdaile. There was just something so buttoned-up and bloodless about him . . . Mind you, Winders was one of those cadaverous brooding characters too, so maybe when she was younger Dr Esdaile leaned towards a preferred type . . .

Somewhat shamefaced at her own prurience, Pam justified it with the reflection that the Tower was . . . well, if not exactly a hotbed of romantic intrigue, certainly home to some interesting personalities. And gossip had it that Bernard Doyle wasn't the only one to have a thing for Margaret Esdaile. If Sophie McGrath was to be believed, stiff and stuffy Daniel Locke had a crack at his colleague too, only to be rebuffed.

Even though she was just an intern, Sophie's intel was usually bang on the money. Pam wasn't sure she really liked the pert blonde twenty-seven-year-old, though the Beefeaters had predictably fallen for her to a man. Pam had the impression that Dr Esdaile kept Sophie somewhat at arm's length.

It was the same with the new apprentice conservator Elena Rogers, a well-spoken thirty-something brunette who had previously worked for English Heritage. The curator was perfectly friendly but never let either woman get too close — as if there was something which made her wary. Given Sophie's reputation as a snoop, it was probably sensible to be cautious.

The basement quarters were orderly, sleek and well-tended as befitted their situation in an historic landmark, with pale oak floors, oriental rugs and trellised bookcases of dark-red wood where gold-tooled almanacs were ranged behind gleaming glass. Dr Esdaile's office was at the far end of a vestibule, and Pam never begrudged dusting its spindle-legged furniture nor the mahogany lectern and book plinths because she felt they somehow brought her close to that mysterious realm where great wars had been fought, with blood feuds leading to murder in high places and the heads of traitors rotting on pikes above London Bridge.

Unusually on this occasion, however, Pam felt strangely uneasy as she stood in the thickly carpeted little hallway.

Everywhere was very quiet, the usual background hum of tourists finished for the day.

Through the corridor's oriel window she saw cottony white flakes floating down and suddenly felt very tired. What was that poem about woods being lovely, dark and deep and a traveller having 'miles to go before I sleep'? Her mum would be bustling round in Tower Hamlets getting a chippy tea ready round about now, and she felt an unexpected acute yearning to be away from all this history and antiquity and back in her everyday cocoon, her safe shell.

The silence was like a thick pall.

What the heck was wrong with her? she wondered, shaking the sweaty fringe out of her eyes. She wasn't one for superstition and fairy stories and all that jazz. Always felt quite superior when some of the others banged on about White Ladies and wailing spectres and the rest of it; she liked to think she was too sophisticated for nonsense like that . . .

Only now, despite the central heating being on full blast, it seemed as though the temperature had suddenly dropped and she felt icy cold.

Again, she was conscious of the profound hush.

Neither the governor nor the deputy governor was in residence. The same went for the senior administrative staff and curators who generally hightailed it at weekends. The yeoman warders would be doing their rounds but hadn't yet got round to the Queen's House.

Normally Pam wouldn't have welcomed the Beefeaters' over-loud galumphing presence but now felt a strange yearning for that reassuring patrol.

Get a hold of yourself, girl! she told herself. *You can't stand here forever.*

Gently, respectfully, she turned the handle to Dr Esdaile's office.

The curator was sitting at her desk, looking towards the door as though to greet Pam.

But her eyes were filmed over and her mouth frozen in an agonized 'O'.

A pool of blood coagulating stickily in front of Margaret Esdaile showed that she had been the victim of a savage attack.

Strangely, it never occurred to Pam to imagine that she herself might be in any danger. She sensed that the tsunami of murderous rage had spent itself and moved on.

Margaret Esdaile's handsome bony face and Joan of Arc dandelion bob weren't disfigured by her death throes, but it seemed somehow more of a sacrilege to Pam that the curator's desk and papers should have been despoiled.

Afterwards, she couldn't say what had made her move all of the books and documents to one side. It just seemed the right thing to do at the time.

'Contamination of the crime scene,' a forensics officer had snarled once the flashing lights brigade descended on the place, but DCI Knevitt with the kind creased face and soulful eyes told him to button it, questioning Pam kindly and patiently until she had given them everything she could think of.

Seeing her distress, he made a feeble joke about the historic environs and no one taking any tombstone seriously if it began with the words *Here I Lie*. But she knew obscurely that this man was a terrier who would follow the trail wherever it led.

The notorious Crime in the Tower investigation was underway.

CHAPTER 1: THE CALL

DI Gilbert ('Gil') Markham and his partner Olivia Mullen were ensconced with the Sunday papers in the living room of Markham's apartment at the Sweepstakes, an upmarket complex off Bromgrove Avenue, when the telephone call came.

The weather was fiercely wet and windy, but they were toasty warm, the trusty wood burner inducing a feeling of soporific lassitude made all the more pleasurable by contrast with the tempest that raged outdoors.

This was their favourite room, with baroque red and gold vintage wallpaper, thick carpet of the same hue, comfortable wingback armchairs and a Chesterfield sofa upholstered in tartan check. Carefully chosen walnut antiques and a certain old-fashioned ambience gave it the air of a gentlemen's club, but Olivia's ballet prints and figurines (she was a serious balletomane) lightened the décor and offset the subdued colour palette.

'Only a fortnight till school breaks up!' she exulted, plonking a pile of magazines on to a gate-leg coffee table.

'There's still the carol concert to get through,' Markham laughed.

'Oh yes.' She grimaced. 'Can't wait to sing ten choruses of "Holly and the Poison Ivy"!'

She looked nothing like a schoolteacher in that cling-ing sloppy joe number, he thought admiringly, with the side-parted (and fashionably highlighted) dark-red bob that skimmed her shoulders a striking contrast to the pale com-plexion, high cheekbones and starry grey-green eyes that glit-tered in the soft light from the Tiffany lamp at her elbow. He noted with relief that she had regained some of the weight lost when they separated briefly for a time, while the old mischievous smile played once more over her full lips.

If Olivia hardly resembled the traditional schoolmarm, still less was Markham anyone's idea of the average police-man, his commanding height, thick dark hair (lightly streaked with silver), sensitive chiselled features and keen dark eyes combining with a reserved, almost donnish demeanour to give the impression of something unusual; a copper with undoubted star quality. He lacked personal vanity, however, and was notoriously aloof, relaxing only with Olivia and a tight-knit group of confidantes.

He was looking forward to a cosy Christmas with just the two of them, having worked hard to clear his caseload and plough through a blizzard of paperwork before the hol-idays. Aware that his workaholic tendencies had damaged the relationship with Olivia and contributed to their recent break-up, he now kept Sundays sacrosanct, so was startled when their peace was interrupted. 'I'll take it in the study,' he murmured, slipping away to pick up the extension.

He was gone for a long while and looked preoccupied when he rejoined Olivia, who saw at once that something unexpected had occurred.

'*Go on!*' she urged. 'Don't keep me in suspense, Gil. What's going on?'

'That was DCI Len Knevitt,' he said slowly. 'He was based up here for a time before moving to Tower Bridge and wants my help with something.'

'What kind of something?'

'Murder at the Tower of London . . . the victim's a curator who was researching the Princes in the Tower. It was a frenzied stabbing apparently.'

She scanned his face intently. 'There's more, isn't there?'

'Yes.' Markham sat down heavily, his gaze turned inward as though he no longer saw his partner. 'A short time ago this same curator, one Dr Margaret Esdaile, contacted Knevitt's colleague DI Gordon Morrissey to say she might have information about an unsolved case connected to the Tower: the disappearance of two children who went missing in May 2008 during some kind of procession — "Beating the Bounds", I believe it's called. Morrissey arranged to meet with her yesterday afternoon—'

'Only she never showed up.'

'Correct.' Markham's expression was grim. 'Someone got to her first.'

He returned his gaze to Olivia, his expression guiltily apprehensive.

Before he could resume, she said quietly, 'They want you in on this . . . down in London?'

'If I can scramble the team, yes. Knevitt read about our art gallery investigation—'

She shivered, remembering. 'That one with the missing child . . .'

'He thinks there are some parallels. At any rate, reckons my lot might be a useful addition to his resources.'

Her mouth twisted ironically. 'Can't imagine the gang passing this one up, sweetheart.' Then suddenly she had a flash of inspiration. 'Look Gil, why don't I come with you . . . It's only a few days to the holidays and the English department would be able to sort cover. Plus, everyone's demob-happy, so it shouldn't be a problem. I'm sure Mat can swing it for me.'

Markham tensed imperceptibly at this allusion to the deputy head with whom Olivia had been briefly infatuated during their separation. But she didn't appear to notice. 'Come on,' she pleaded softly. 'It can be my pre-Christmas treat.'

'You may not see much of me,' he warned, clearly weakening.

She flashed a radiant smile. 'No worries, Gil. I *adore* London . . . nowhere better for a spot of retail therapy . . . and all the heritage stuff,' she added sheepishly. 'Palaces and museums and the rest of it . . . I could offer to do a project on the Princes in the Tower next term,' she suggested piously. 'Richard Crookback would go down a storm with my Year Eight.'

He grinned. 'You're incorrigible, but if you can square it with the school, why not?'

Indulgently, she waved a hand towards the door. 'Go on, I know you'll be wanting to round up George and the rest of the gang.'

But once in his study — its cool minimalism in marked contrast to the cluttered living room — Markham did not immediately reach for either his laptop or the telephone. Instead, his thoughts turned to the members of that same 'gang' and Olivia's history with them.

First up, George Noakes . . .

Markham's austere features softened as he thought of his oldest friend.

Noakes had now been retired from CID for three years. Not a minute before time, was the opinion of the former sergeant's long-suffering superiors who had never exactly warmed to his uniquely iconoclastic brand of humour and intergalactic tactlessness.

Noakesy still turned up at all the retirement bashes and police social events, to the ill-concealed chagrin of Bromgrove's high command and widespread mirth amongst the lower ranks. Most recently, he had caused mortal offence to the po-faced wife of Chief Superintendent Ebury-Clarke after she overheard him commenting in a loud voice that the raffle prizes were so rubbish that folk with the winning tickets probably wouldn't own up. Matters hadn't been improved when Ebury-Clarke opened his speech with the immortal words, 'Let us consider Bromgrove as a whole,' after which things rapidly deteriorated, Noakes's poorly suppressed hysteria bursting out afresh when his well-refreshed former boss concluded with a tribute to the town as a 'monument to posteriority' and a toast to 'our gaseous Queen'. It had all undoubtedly left a legacy of ill will.

DCI Sidney had been apoplectic when, at the same dinner, in response to the toastmaster's injunction to 'Pray, all be upstanding', the former sergeant was heard sniggering, 'Them that are able', before telling his neighbours that on such occasions he always felt there was something to be said for the likes of Rishi Sunak and Donald Trump being lifelong 'teetotalitarians'. Whereas Markham had always enjoyed his friend's notorious malapropisms — or Noakesy-isms, as Olivia affectionately called them — such sallies invariably made Sidney's eczema flare up to an alarming degree.

Oh yes, it had been a bright day for Sidney when Noakes collected his carriage clock. Mind you, Markham thought with a reminiscent chuckle, it was a miracle his friend had managed to scrape through that last fitness test, a passion for junk food and fry ups invariably getting the better of all his virtuous resolutions. And how he had finagled a positive medical review was anyone's guess. 'The quack spouted a whole lot of guff about lifestyle an' body mass ratio an' histo-pathology whatsits,' he confided cheerfully to Markham afterwards. 'At the end of it all, he said I had between twenty-five an' forty per cent chance of having a morbid coronary episode in the next ten years . . . Thank chuff for that. *Back of the net!* I honestly thought he was going to tell me the odds against having a heart attack!'

Olivia simply adored the piggy-eyed, paunchy Yorkshireman whose appalling dress sense and capacity for gaffes were alike legendary. As far as Noakes was concerned, Kipling connoted cakes and Hamlet cigars, while Socrates was a world-class sweeper. She had gradually converted him to 'High Culture', however, and he had been touchingly thrilled to discover that Shakespeare and the Romantic poets were full of quotations from Markham's partner. Her colleagues in the English department at Hope Academy (popularly known as Hopeless) were equally fond of Noakes, whom they had got to know over the course of sundry investigations involving the school, and delighted Bromgrove CID's *bête noire* by presenting him with a special limerick in his honour:

> *The men that come from Yorkshire are poets to a man, And when they curse and swear at you, they make it rhyme and scan. (With apologies to G.K. Chesterton.)*

Mrs Muriel Noakes was less charmed by her husband's enthusiasm for Olivia, regarding the teacher as a neurotic poseur and nowhere near good enough for the handsome inspector whose grave courtesy and old-fashioned gallantry were greatly to her taste. Bossy and an inveterate social-climber who had met Noakes (most improbably) on the amateur ballroom dancing circuit, she softened somewhat after her brassy perma-tanned beautician daughter Natalie — formerly the doyenne of Bromgrove's less salubrious nightclubs — became unexpectedly pregnant only to suffer a miscarriage. Now the proud possessor of a degree in History to boot, the prodigal daughter was affianced to Rick Jordan, proprietor of a local fitness centre whose hard-featured mother was seemingly in no hurry to see her precious son and heir walk his on-again off-again girlfriend down the aisle.

Olivia had never really got on with Natalie who, despite being his blue-eyed darling, was not in fact Noakes's natural daughter (the discovery of which fact sent him temporarily off the rails), but tried to smother her antipathy 'for George's sake'. She liked Muriel even less, finding the woman's arch affectations and pretentions a perpetual source of annoyance. But there was pity mixed with her irritation, and she had come to see the vulnerability and social insecurity which lay beneath the other woman's brittle veneer. Besides, Noakes was immensely proud of his wife, regarding her as the oracle on pretty much everything — from 'free pea sweets' to foreign monarchs (she was a dedicated royalist). And Olivia understood how much Noakes meant to Markham, she and the burly Yorkshireman being the only two people who knew that he was the survivor of childhood abuse by an abusive stepfather, a trauma he had somehow survived but his brother Jonathan — long since lost to drink, drugs and suicide — had not.

Noakes had fallen on his feet after retiring from CID, landing a cushy number as the security manager at Rosemount, an upmarket nursing home. This hadn't prevented him having a finger in every CID pie, however, leading to his retention by Markham as a 'civilian consultant', another development that didn't do much for DCI Sidney's blood pressure. Of course, Olivia — no fan of 'Slimy Sid' (as he was known by the troops) — was tickled pink by the notion of the DCI's nemesis hovering in the wings as a sort of honorary copper, but it had made for some decidedly sticky moments. At least with Sidney himself not far off retirement (something he had deferred in the wake of an acrimonious marital separation), things should be less fraught. There were rumours that Sidney nursed ambitions to become some sort of TV pundit in the mould of John Stalker, which had sent Oliva and Noakes into paroxysms of laughter at the prospect of 'The Rhinocerboss' transforming himself into 'The People's Peeler'. But stranger things had happened, and such a reinvention might be precisely the development which would bring Mrs Sidney (aka 'The Valkyrie' and an even bigger snob than Muriel Noakes) back to the marital home.

But there was no question that Sidney had mellowed in recent times and, whatever his resentment of Markham's good looks and Oxbridge credentials, he had fought his DI's corner where necessary. It was unlikely he would object to this secondment to London, especially with it being the run-up to Christmas, traditionally a fairly quiet time in Bromgrove.

Noakes had now resigned his position at Rosemount to set up as a private investigator, so would be an invaluable asset to any enquiries that Markham undertook, quite apart from the fact that wild horses wouldn't keep his friend from being part of such an intriguing case. An armchair historian and avid consumer of true crime documentaries, the whole

Princes in the Tower angle was right up his street and guaranteed to set him off like a truffle hound. Sidney and the high command might prove prickly about Noakes coming on board, but Markham was reasonably sure he could swing it for his former wingman to join the team. And of course, DI Kate Burton could always be relied upon to pour oil on troubled waters.

Burton, still engaged to Professor Nathan Finlayson of Bromgrove University's criminal profiling department, appeared no nearer making it to the altar than Natalie Noakes. A psychology graduate and fast-track detective, it had taken a good while before she and Noakes warmed to each other. Eventually, their fierce loyalty to Markham and shared fascination with true crime brought about a rapprochement. Outwardly somewhat earnest and indefatigably politically correct, Burton in fact possessed a mischievous sense of humour which was apt to take the unwary by surprise. And, like Noakes, she was never fazed by Markham's cultured intellectualism and use of 'Big Words' (which had led to him being dubbed 'Lord Snooty' by the rank and file and regarded with darkest suspicion by his superiors). Her colleagues nearly fell off their chairs when Noakes quoted from Macaulay's *Lays of Ancient Rome*, only for her to observe slyly that she'd always loved the story about how Horatio made a fourth at bridge not to mention that line 'How can man die better than facing fearful sods'. It was possibly then that Noakes recognized here was a kindred spirit.

Burton, whom Markham now regarded as a dear friend, had proved strangely unreachable in recent months, as if she was struggling with some kind of emotional log-jam that left her unable to open up. He knew that the death of her father had hit her hard and that there had been 'blips' in the relationship with Finlayson (nicknamed 'Shippers' by Noakes on account of his startling resemblance to the serial killer Harold Shipman). He wondered too if feelings for himself had proved an obstacle in her romantic life and remained unsure if his own emotions — a mixture of respect, tenderness and protectiveness — were entirely irre-proachable. Noakes believed Burton carried a torch for him, while Olivia had picked up on the complexity of his feelings towards his colleague and never warmed to Burton in con-sequence. Markham's fellow DI had resolutely turned down opportunities for advancement elsewhere and remained attached to his special homicide team, causing him to worry that their affinity might somehow have worked to her pro-fessional detriment.

Still, he knew that like Noakes she would be keen as mustard to seize this opportunity of working with the high-ly-regarded Knevitt and Morrissey on a case that was bound to put them all through their paces.

DS Doyle and DS Carruthers would likewise want their share of the action, he thought with a wry smile.

Doyle and Noakes were old friends, the veteran sergeant taking an avuncular interest in the easy-going auburn-haired youngster's romantic dilemmas — now happily resolved with the advent of teacher girlfriend Kelly — and sharing his pas-sion for Bromgrove Rovers. When the formerly ambitious Doyle appeared distracted by domestic bliss and somewhat apathetic regarding his inspector's exams, Noakes nagged him from the sidelines about career progression despite him-self having never been remotely interested in rising higher than sergeant.

DS Roger Carruthers (or 'Roger the Dodger', as Noakes had christened him), on the other hand, needed no urg-ing to make the most of himself, being highly driven and what his colleagues called 'ace at brownnosing'. The fast-track detective was nephew to Superintendent 'Blithering' Bretherton and initially hard to warm to, with his peculiar pallor, slicked-back hair, horn-rimmed specs and a penchant for leather trench coats which heightened his resemblance to an officer of the Third Reich. It didn't help matters that he was rumoured to spy for Sidney and the high command. However, over time he had bedded into Markham's fabled 'Gang of Four', proving that he was his own man and nobody's cat's paw. An obvious respect and admiration for Markham had appeased even Noakes whom Carruthers now called 'sarge' like the rest. The fact that Carruthers was football mad ensured that he made a rapid conquest of Doyle, while his passionate interest in forensic psychology gradually won over Kate Burton. Quick at repartee, he gave as good as he got. On Noakes informing him that he was the spit of Joseph Goebbels, the younger man merely replied deadpan that many considered the Nazi propagandist to be the most influential broadcaster of the twentieth century. On another occasion, listening to Noakes complaining loudly — with a sidelong glance in his direction — about 'poshos' who said '*hice*' instead of 'house' and were generally incomprehensible, he punctured the tension with an amusing anecdote about Bristolians who put 'el' on the end of any words ending in a vowel, which led to West Countryman DI Les Jago calling the chief constable's wife 'Normal' for the duration of a police federation dinner. Oh yes, there was no doubt that Carruthers was able to handle Noakes!

There *had* been a time when Markham suspected him of being too close to journalists at the *Gazette* (in particular, one Gavin Conors), but he had tipped Kate Burton the wink and she now kept a discreet watch on her colleague. Nobody had ever detected Carruthers engaged in anything slippery and Markham sincerely hoped it would remain that way.

His study's large picture window looked out on to the neighbouring municipal cemetery but, swivelling round in his office chair to look, he saw that the landscape was pitch black, monuments and obelisks invisible in the darkness. Only his reflection, wan with concentration, gazed back at him.

Through the enveloping winter gloom, he was aware of all the graves out there in the wild, wet storm. That was why he had wanted the apartment.

Timor mortis conturbat me.

The cemetery was a permanent reminder of all his murdered dead and the insatiable gnawing urge to avenge them, to bring those shrouded victims out from their 'palace of dim night' into the light so that they could at last find peace.

He could just imagine how Sidney would react to such fey musings, the DCI having little time for anything that smacked of 'romantic moonshine'. Best to play down the whole Princes in the Tower side of things and emphasize the potential kudos for Bromgrove CID if they helped to crack a murder *and* child abduction.

The whole Tower connection, however, meant that this case would be quite unlike anything the team had encountered before.

He reached for the telephone.

Time to set wheels in motion.

CHAPTER 2: GREEN LIGHT

It was traditional for Markham to spend some time before the start of each new investigation gathering his thoughts in the tranquil terraced graveyard of St Chad's Parish Church round the back of Bromgrove Police Station.

The morning of Monday 4 December was no exception, though wreathes of fog and a crackling carpet of hoar frost weren't conducive to protracted meditation on his favourite bench. Unusually, there were no squirrels about, which suggested that nature too was battening down the hatches.

While savouring the peace and Gothic ambience, he kept a wary eye out for the Reverend Simon Duthie (whose vocation to the priesthood came late in life, after a career as a bank manager), feeling disinclined for his somewhat forced brand of pastoral bonhomie.

Mercifully it was too early for the clergyman to be about, he reflected glancing at his watch and breathing in lungfuls of the sharp, pine-scented air which invariably helped to clear his head before the rigours of the day.

Eventually, regretfully, after saying a silent prayer for the soul of the curator whose murder they were to investigate, he headed for the station.

The stale fug of CID and garish, half-hearted paper decorations trailing drunkenly across the computers and work surfaces weren't exactly the epitome of Christmas cheer, the DI thought wryly as he walked towards his own office. And the sparsely decorated white twig tree was what Noakes would call a poor show.

Talk of the devil!

Opening the door to his corner cubbyhole (with unrivalled view of the car park), it was no great surprise to find his ex-wingman installed like a portly genie in the chair opposite his own, ferociously bashing the desk pendulum that he was prone to abuse in moments of high excitement despite an avowed contempt for such executive toys and gadgets.

The former DS was attired in an extraordinary combination of novelty plum pudding sweater and baggy purple cords the colour of which almost matched his corned beef complexion. Wiry grey hair sticking out in every direction like prongs gave him a somewhat wild aspect that an overflowing stomach and stubby poorly shaven chin did nothing to mitigate. Markham could only hope the DCI wouldn't take it into his head to attend the morning briefing. The spectacle of this 'civilian consultant' apparently masquerading as some sort of dishevelled Santa lookalike was virtually guaranteed to send Sidney's blood pressure through the roof.

Aloud, he observed mildly, 'I take it you're not working undercover today, Noakesy?'

The sarcasm was water off a duck's back.

Giving the pendulum one last swipe, the other beamed complacently. 'I cleared the diary soon as I knew about this Tower thing. Mr Shah from downstairs said he'll keep things ticking over.'

Noakes now rented a minuscule office above a Tandoori in the Medway Centre, a move not at all to his wife's taste, since she regarded his departure from Rosemount's manicured surroundings as a definite comedown. Markham, however, knew his friend missed chasing 'scrotes an' scumbags' and had helped reconcile Muriel to the situation by valiantly talking up Noakes's new enterprise and stressing his continuing association with Bromgrove CID. He had already helped to put a couple of jobs his friend's way while Olivia had sorted the office stationery. Meanwhile, kindly Mr Shah sent many a free takeaway upstairs to his new neighbour. Moreover, Noakes was still a welcome visitor at Rosemount, staff and residents having become very fond of their unconventional security manager.

'How's your campaign to poach Kevin coming along?' the DI enquired, referring to Noakes's young apprentice at the retirement home. 'Any chance of him becoming your Man Friday?'

'He ain't sure yet,' Noakes replied gloomily. 'His mum reckons he should stick where he's got *prospects* . . . better pay an' all.'

'Oh well, at least you can always use him for freelance jobs.' Markham's tone was bracing.

His friend brightened. 'Yeah, thass true . . . An' he's sound is Kev, says he's gonna see if they c'n get a picture of Captain Cook for the library, one showing him fighting the aboriginals . . . summat *inspiring*.'

Noakes had taken a hands-on role when it came to refurbishment and décor, his history as an alumnus of 2 PARA making him desirous of surrounding Rosemount's retirees (including many an ex-serviceman) with suitably patriotic heroes on which to feast their rheumy eyes.

'So you've switched loyalties from Horatio Nelson then?' the DI teased. 'No longer flavour of the month is he, even despite "England Expects" and all that?'

Noakes pursed his lips. 'Nelson's a bit . . . *flamboyant*,' he said thoughtfully.

Markham suppressed a grin as he recalled his friend's reservations about the whole 'Kiss me, Hardy' episode.

'An' when all's said an' done, Captain Cook's a *Yorkshireman*.'

'*Ah*,' Markham said in a deep tone of comprehension, long familiar with a world view which considered Yorkshire as the backbone of England while London was somewhere to the south.

'Cook's a bit controversial these days though, Noakesy,' he was unable to resist pointing out, thinking that in the current climate Noakes's paragon was more likely to be called Captain *Crook*.

'He were 'xactly what you'd want alongside if it were a case of life an' death,' was the squelching reply. ''Sides being good at trigonometry an' charts.'

Markham could think of no adequate response to such a magnificent non-sequitur.

'Right,' he said hastily. 'The main thing is that you're gloriously available for this London case.'

Noakes nodded vigorously. 'There might even be a bit of publicity for "Medway Investigations",' he said hopefully (for such was the name of his new business venture).

For some reason, the grizzled veteran's eagerness brought a lump to Markham's throat.

'Absolutely,' he agreed with more confidence than he felt. 'Olivia plans to wangle some leave and join us.'

Noakes was looking cheerier by the minute.

'I think Liv's going to sell it to Hope as a fact-finding exercise for some project on the Tudors,' Markham continued. 'She tells me she's had it up to here with colleagues banging on about the Industrial Revolution and evil capitalists.'

Noakes sympathized heartily with this point of view, seeing as he claimed Bromgrove was known to have had some of the most revolting industrialists in England, especially when it came to building and infrastructure. 'Mind you,' he concluded evilly, 'it ain't as bad as some places. I mean, jus' look at all them statues of Queen Victoria sitting on a throne, holding the orb an' whatnot, with her legs straddling the signs for "Ladies" an' "Gents".'

'Olivia always insists Bromgrove has pockets of great historical romance, though,' Markham qualified.

'Romance my backside,' Noakes snorted. 'What she means is some bugger like Thomas Cromwell knocked half the churches down or a manky poet snuffed it from cholera or one of them other nasties.'

Entering the room as Noakes offered his pearls of wisdom, Kate Burton looked almost as though she wanted to reverse back out.

'Morning sarge,' she offered weakly.

The small black eyes were riveted on Burton's brown paper bag and tray.

'I thought we could use muffins and coffee from Costa.'

'Nice one,' Noakes approved, losing no time in getting stuck in.

Burton was followed in short order by Carruthers and Doyle, the trio as well-groomed and dapper as Sidney's heart could desire, Markham thought gratefully.

Actually, his fellow DI now cut a far more striking figure than the rather frumpy, homespun picture she had presented on first joining CID, her sleekly streaked geometric bob and well-cut trouser suit the epitome of corporate chic. But the expression of loyal devotion in the hazel eyes had never changed, and she still persisted in calling him 'Sir' despite the fact that they were now the same rank.

The Noakesian preoccupation with commissary and 'fuelling up' was legendary. 'I look all right from the back,' he retorted when twitted about his expanding girth. Even Sidney's acid comments about 'the seeming inability of DI Markham's team to go five minutes without a pit stop' failed to dent his insistence on proper rations. And Markham had come to like the collegiate, almost cosy, atmosphere this engendered (the more so, seeing as his refractory office radiator appeared finally to have given up the ghost). His little unit *Contra mundum*. Even Burton joined in, though he noticed she swiftly substituted a granola bar for the double chocolate pastries she had brought for her male colleagues.

'Have we got the go ahead for this Tower investigation then, sir?' she asked politely as the others guzzled their way through the Costa offerings.

'Indeed we have, Kate,' Markham said warmly. 'So long as we keep the DCI fully briefed, of course.'

'An' make sure he gets to share the glory when we crack the case,' Noakes observed beadily through a mouthful of muffin.

Markham was unruffled. 'That too,' he agreed easily.

'What's with the whole Princes in the Tower setup?' Carruthers wanted to know. 'Has it got something to do with this woman being murdered?'

Markham took a last sip of coffee and got down to business.

'Dr Margaret Esdaile's research interests centred on the legend of Richard the Third and the Princes in the Tower,' he confirmed.

'They've always thought highly of Crookback in Yorkshire,' Noakes weighed in with no small satisfaction. 'Apparently the snooty brigade down south decided northerners were savages — more or less running around with their faces painted in blue woad — until Tricky Dicky showed them we knew what's what.'

'*Plus ça change*,' Carruthers murmured. Then, observing Noakes squinting suspiciously at this lapse into French, he added, 'I imagine the chatterati still feel the same about anything north of Watford.'

Noakes was duly mollified. 'Too right,' he said fervently before continuing, 'Dicky were a brave soldier despite having a wonky spine.'

'So what happened to the Princes then?' Doyle enquired. 'Did Richard *really* murder them?'

Burton piped up, delighted as ever to be afforded a pedagogic opportunity. 'There's various theories about it,' she told them, having clearly gone into the subject with her usual thoroughness. 'Some sources say they were walled up in a room and left to starve to death. Others insist they were buried alive in a large chest. And there's a body of opinion that thinks they were drowned in a vat of red wine like their Uncle Clarence.'

God, why does she always come across like some boffin from Time Team, Doyle thought. *She's even made bleeding* notes, he groaned inwardly, eyeing the jotter Burton had whipped out. However, he was intrigued despite himself.

'But their skeletons eventually turned up, right?' he asked.

'That's right.' Burton beamed at him, as though he was a promising student. 'In the reign of Charles the Second some workmen found two skeletons in a wooden chest buried about ten feet below ground while they were digging at the base of a staircase which led to the Chapel of St John the Evangelist in the White Tower. The taller child lay on its back, the smaller face down on top of it.'

As his colleague said this, Markham had an unwelcome flashback to one of their earliest cases at St Mary's Cathedral choir school. With an effort, he suppressed the intrusive memory.

'The bones had pieces of rag and velvet on them,' Burton continued after a swift, uneasy glance at Markham. 'The velvet was a crucial clue because it wasn't made in England until the sixteenth century and in the 1400s the wearing of imported velvet was restricted to the nobility.'

'So the skellies had to be toffs,' Noakes said trenchantly.

'Exactly.' Burton ducked her head submissively. 'It was a fair assumption that these *were* the Princes. Charles the Second eventually arranged for the bones to be reburied at Westminster Abbey, apart from a few which went to the Ashmolean in Oxford and ended up getting lost.'

There was an eloquent sniff from Noakes at this. *Typical academics!*

'Though not before an antiquarian had seen them and recalled them being very small, especially the finger bones,' Burton added hastily. 'George the Fifth later allowed an examination of the remains in Westminster Abbey. There were all kinds of bones mixed in with them including animal bones, but the doctors eventually established they had the incomplete skeletons of two children aged between twelve to thirteen and nine to eleven. They couldn't be sure of the sex, but the older child had a chronic bone disease of the jaw

— probably osteomyelitis — which would have been very painful and might explain why people said Edward the Fifth suffered from depression before he disappeared.'

'As if being locked up an' scared for his life weren't enough to be going on with,' Noakes pointed out, his expression darkening.

Markham felt a sharp stab of unease at this. Olivia had been badly scarred after undergoing an abortion before he met her. This had temporarily unbalanced her during the course of their relationship, to the point where she had actually entertained mad ideas of adopting Natalie Noakes's unplanned baby. Natalie's miscarriage had put paid to those schemes, but now Markham wondered if it was really such a good idea to have Olivia accompany him down to London for an investigation that involved missing children. On the other hand, she had seemed in excellent spirits the previous night, talking without any apparent self-consciousness about Natalie's decision to start a family with Rick Jordan and disappointment that she was having difficulty conceiving. 'Only George could come out with such gems as his daughter being "impregnable" and inconceivable",' she laughed blithely, though Markham wondered what pain lurked beneath the apparent insouciance.

Burton resumed her disquisition with characteristic punctiliousness.

'The medics worked out that there was a familial link between the skeletons and that a red stain on the facial bones of the older child indicated suffocation. Later on, experts concluded that dental records supported the theory that these were pre-pubescent relatives. Of course, we still can't be sure because Queen Elizabeth refused permission for further testing of the remains on the grounds that they should be allowed to rest in peace.'

There was a respectful silence at the reference to Elizabeth II whose framed portrait adorned the open plan CID workspace.

'Quite right an' proper,' Noakes said finally.

'Though it looks as though King Charles might be up for further investigation,' Burton continued, 'given his interest in archaeology.'

Noakes blew an irreverent raspberry. 'Yeah, with him being a crank an' all.'

Burton bit the inside of her cheek at this interjection but continued earnestly enough. 'Well, it would be good to know one way or another,' she told them. 'A couple more bodies that could have been the Princes turned up in St George's Chapel at Windsor Castle in the 1700s, but some people are convinced the older boy was let go by Richard and ended his life in Devon as a park ranger. All very *Da Vinci Code*,' she added apologetically, 'but intriguing nonetheless. There's carvings in the church where he's buried showing a woman with a snake-like tongue that historians think might be a veiled attack on the mother of Henry Tudor, the one who deposed Richard the Third after the Battle of Bosworth . . . and all kinds of occult messages,' she finished hesitantly, aware of her colleagues' scepticism.

'What about the younger lad?' Noakes demanded.

Burton frowned. 'Some academic at the university of Leicester thinks he was smuggled out of the Tower to live with his mother when the elder boy died of natural causes . . . ending up as a bricklayer after Bosworth. And there are people who've made a case for various so-called imposters actually being the lost Princes.'

Doyle was growing restive.

'So, *what the heck* . . . Are we saying some nutter with a thing about the Princes in the Tower went after this curator woman 'cos they didn't like where she was going with her research?'

The DI smiled, mindful of DCI Sidney's frequently expressed irritation that 'Markham's unit does nothing but *talk* . . . like some outpost of the Open University'. Personally, he found such 'talk' invaluable in terms of understanding the context for murder.

'I don't know as yet whether there was anything particularly controversial about Margaret Esdaile's research interests,' he admitted. Even as he said the words, however, he felt this legend of the Princes in the Tower gnawing away at his subconscious, as though some twisted medieval pathology was insidiously poisoning the present.

'And there's some unsolved kidnapping or whatever with two kids who went missing from the Tower?' Doyle persisted.

'Correct.' Burton took over crisply. 'Annie and Dominic Sullivan aged nine vanished during the Beating the Bounds procession in 2008. It's a centuries' old affair — people from the Tower tapping the ground with willow wands . . . something to do with marking boundaries . . . kind of like a great big street party—'

'Only with kids being snatched at the end,' Carruthers interjected drily.

'Properties and gardens along the route were extensively searched at the time,' Burton retorted stiffly. 'But no one found hide nor hair of them. Apparently Margaret Esdaile contacted DI Gordon Morrissey at Tower Bridge the day before she was killed to say she had information about the children's disappearance, but when he made an appointment she never showed.'

The team digested this.

'So her murder's got to be tied in with the kids' disappearance?' Carruthers pressed.

'It would seem so,' Markham replied cautiously. 'The fact that Dr Esdaile contacted the police about an unsolved abduction surely *has* to be more than pure coincidence.'

'So who's in the frame then?' Noakes wanted to know.

'Well . . .' Markham's mouth twisted ironically. 'It appears the governor and deputy governor can be ruled out, since they're both currently visiting Fontainebleau as part of a cultural exchange programme organized by the British Council.'

Before Noakes could say anything sarcastic about leeching off taxpayers — his wingman's screwed-up expression appearing to herald a polemic on the subject — Markham continued, 'That being the case, we can confine our enquiries to the Tower community . . . those who had a connection with Margaret Esdaile either professionally or personally.'

The DI paused and looked down at his hands, mentally marshalling the roster of suspects.

'Here goes,' he said calmly. 'Dr Esdaile was on her second marriage to stockbroker Charles Esdaile. Her first husband Dr Steven Winders is based at Hampton Court and also happily remarried to the HR manager there.' Aware that Noakes was always keen to uncover a juicy crime passionnel, he added swiftly, 'By all accounts it was a highly civilised setup and they were both hands-on parents to their daughter Antonia.'

'Any blokes sniffing around Esdaile?' Noakes demanded, ignoring how Burton winced at such bluntness.

'She was apparently on friendly terms with the Reverend Bernard Doyle, the chaplain,' Markham replied. 'Sounds like he was an admirer . . . Dr Daniel Locke, one of the joint chief curators, was another . . . though he and Dr Esdaile were academic rivals since he also had Ricardian research interests. I gather the other joint chief curator Dr Benedict Ryan wasn't enamoured of Dr Esdaile — it had to do with them crossing swords over relics or artefacts or something of that sort.' He continued trawling his mental rolodex of potential suspects. 'There'd been some unpleasantness with John Whittingham, a Beefeater Dr Esdaile accused of unprofessionalism, and relations were fairly cool towards two other women in her office — the intern Sophie McGrath and an apprentice conservator name of Elena Rogers . . . Oh, and she didn't really get on with Clare Hunter the Tower events co-ordinator.'

'So Esdaile was standoffish then?' Carruthers asked interestedly.

Markham was thoughtful. 'Not according to DCI Knevitt,' he said. 'Apparently junior staff adored her . . . the cleaner who found her body was in bits.'

'Any chance it could've been random?' Doyle asked. 'I mean, the Tower must attract all kinds of oddballs . . . maybe there was a security breach, so that's how they got in? And the thing about missing kids isn't connected . . . ?'

The DI considered this. 'Security at the Tower is tight,' he pointed out. 'Difficult to see how an intruder could have made it to Dr Esdaile's office undetected, plus, the fact that she was murdered the same day DI Morrissey was due to meet her strongly suggests a link with the Sullivan case.'

'Whatcha reckon to Knevitt an' Morrissey then, guv?' Noakes asked. 'D'you rate 'em?'

'Very much so,' Markham replied. 'Knevitt's got no side despite an impressive solve rate . . . genuinely humble and just wants fresh pairs of eyes on this. Gordon Morrissey's the same, absolutely on the level.'

'And Sidney's on board?' Doyle enquired with a hint of incredulity.

'No objections in principle,' the DI answered with a thin smile. 'I've got a meeting with him straight after this, so I'll make sure he signs off on it.'

'When do we start?' Carruthers was all business.

'You four can catch the two fifty-three to Euston and get yourselves booked in at the Tower Hotel, St Katharine's Dock. I'll follow later this evening. Then tomorrow morning we meet up with Knevitt and Morrissey nine a.m. sharp at the West Gate. I'm operating on the basis that we'll be away at least a fortnight. Don't forget to keep receipts for everything,' he warned before adding casually to Noakes, 'your expenses are sorted, Noakesy, just swing by the desk sergeant before you head off.' Not for worlds would he have had his friend aware of the that he was personally subbing him an advance, though a sidelong glance from Kate Burton told him that his fellow DI had a shrewd idea.

'Champion.' Noakes was delighted. 'Mind you, I wanna go in the Quiet Coach, otherwise all we'll hear on the way down to London is dickheads shouting, "I'm on the train!"'

Doyle and Carruthers exchanged grins as Burton shuddered delicately.

'I were on the Trans-Pennine Express this one time an' the train kept stopping,' Noakes continued happily. 'The last time it happened, we were stuck in Milton Keynes an' this announcement came over the tannoy.' Noakes affected his best Jamaican accent. '"Ladies and Gentlemen, I apologize for the delay to your journey. The reason is . . ." Then there were this pause that went on forever. "Human cock-up."'

As Burton cringed, Carruthers chuckled. 'It'll be great, sarge. You know you like train journeys. Aren't you always going on about that politician bloke on TV.'

'Oh aye, *Portcullis's Great Railway Journeys*,' was the laconic rejoinder.

'He means Michael Portillo, ma'am,' Doyle explained observing Burton's puzzlement.

They lingered a while longer, engaging in inconsequential chat about plans for the festive season. There was a tricky moment when Noakes announced he was getting a new coat for Muriel for Christmas and Doyle quipped, 'A good swap, I reckon,' but Carruthers diverted the conversation into safer channels — football and the awfulness of in-laws — and the awkwardness passed.

After the other three had departed, Burton lingered.

'Shall I come up to see the DCI with you, sir?' she offered shyly.

'Could you bear to, Kate?' He smiled, reflecting that senior management invariably responded well to his colleague's respectful earnestness that was unmixed with servility or sycophancy.

'Of course, boss.' She grinned puckishly. 'I'll get him on to the heritage angle. If we play our cards right, he'll see it as fodder for a TV spot — something along the lines of those Jack the Ripper programmes with Emilia Fox and Professor David Wilson . . . though I'm not sure he's quite so photogenic.'

Too right, Markham thought ten minutes later as they sat in Sidney's sanctum listening to the DCI drone on about British history, a subject on which he suspected his superior was decidedly less well informed than culture vulture Burton. How was it, he wondered idly, that Sidney's strictures seemed to require chronic adenoids as well as chronic sinusitis, but he supposed he was now more or less reconciled to the strident honk.

At least the Princes in the Tower angle was catnip to the DCI, he reflected, glancing at the Hall of Fame, as the photomontage in Sidney's office was irreverently dubbed by the lower ranks. Yes, there was HRH The Duchess of Edinburgh, Sidney's all-time favourite 'celebrity', prominent in several pictures of civil shindigs, with his boss's bald bonce bobbing away unctuously over the royal shoulder.

He suddenly became aware of Sidney's basilisk gaze skewering him.

'Quite remarkable that Knevitt should suddenly have thought of you, Markham,' the DCI said suspiciously. 'I mean, it's not as though you're a habitué of historic palaces.'

He spoke as though his DI was a presumptuous peasant capable of nicking the silver.

Markham had long experience of holding on to his temper.

'Oh, it's just that he remembered the art gallery investigation, sir, and thought we might be useful . . . the experience of being around academics and museum types—'

'Curators and conservators,' Burton interjected owlishly.

'We don't have any homicide investigation on hand right now,' Markham continued smoothly.

'And DI Carstairs says he's available to deal with those outstanding burglaries in Old Carton, sir.' Burton duly picked up the baton.

We make a good double act, Markham thought in amusement as Sidney looked from one to the other.

'So it's just yourselves along with Sergeants Doyle and Carruthers on this . . . assignment,' Sidney said after a long pause.

God, he makes it sound like we're off on a massive skive. But Markham kept his charming smile nailed firmly in place.

'Any other personnel involved?' As in civilian consultants. Time to bite the bullet.

'As you know, George Noakes has set up as a private investigator, sir,' Markham began.

The DCI's countenance suggested he did not regard this development with any particular enthusiasm.

'It just so happens that he's got a window in his diary,' Burton said brightly.

Sidney's expression was highly sceptical, as though he found it hard to imagine the former sergeant being exactly overwhelmed with business.

'And of course he was part of the art gallery enquiry, sir,' Burton continued bravely, trying hard not to remember her former colleague's sacrilegious denunciations of Western art. 'You'll recall that case involved child abduction as well as—' she groped for suitably impressive terminology — 'a cultural foundation . . . so, with that kind of experience . . .'

'It's understood that Noakes has no official remit.' Sidney's tone was flinty, but his two subordinates could see that they had won the day.

'Absolutely, sir.' Burton nodded fervently.

'And I want receipts for everything,' the DCI rapped.

'Naturally,' Markham murmured, having already generously ensured that his friend wouldn't have to wait until some hard-faced auditor should cough up expenses.

'Noakes just can't keep away from CID,' Burton said with a polite cough. 'But he knows his place, sir.'

That should appease Sidney's seigneurial streak, Markham thought as they salaamed their way out of the Presence.

'I always feel a bit disgusted with myself after one of those sessions,' Burton said ruefully once they were safely back in his office. 'Feel as though I'm laying on the obsequiousness with a trowel.'

'You were note-perfect, Kate.' Markham wanted to ask about her own plans for Christmas, but something in his colleague's expression suggested it might be dangerous territory.

'Right,' he said. 'You need to push off and clear that in tray if you're going to catch the two fifty-three . . . London here we come!'

After she had gone, he wandered across to the window. The skies outside were grey and bruised looking, but a powdery sprinkling of snow softened the outlines of the town centre beyond.

Despite the tedium of his self-flagellation before Sidney, Markham felt a stirring of excited anticipation. This case promised to be the most unusual challenge of his career.

Bring it on!

CHAPTER 3: FIRST ENCOUNTERS

The West Gate entrance was picture-postcard perfect on Tuesday morning when Markham's team arrived for the rendezvous with their London counterparts. Earlier snow flurries had lifted, but the castle's masonry sparkled beneath a crisp patina of frost which gave it an appearance of being fashioned from spun sugar — disconcertingly Disney rather than a prison designed to strike fear into the hearts of traitors, Markham thought as they made their way across the drawbridge.

DCI Len Knevitt was a short, broad-chested but handsome man with greying hair, keen brown eyes, swarthy complexion and an engaging smile. His DI Gordon Morrissey was tall and fair with a soft Devonian accent and air of placid stolidity that belied his impressive CV. After cordial introductions, the team was whisked past gawking tourists into the moat.

'*Hey*, isn't this where they planted all them flowers for the Platinum Jubilee,' Noakes exclaimed. 'An' the ceramic poppy whatsit for Remembrance Day.' He stared around him, taking in dozens of Christmas trees dripping with decorations and interspersed with strikingly realistic full-size figures in Tudor costume. 'Looks a bit different today, mind.'

Knevitt smiled at the former DS. He knew all about the fabled 'bromance' between Markham and the pug-featured Yorkshireman, not to mention the consternation it engendered in Bromgrove's high command. But the DCI had never underestimated Noakes, despite the other's blunt speaking and eccentric exterior (today's red and blue donkey jacket and navy cords, an unconscious echo of the yeoman warders' undress uniform, were in sharp contrast to the others' sharp tailoring). He also admired the disdain for 'buttering up' and 'brownnosing' which, together with his fierce commitment to the underdog, had made Noakes stick out like a sore thumb amongst the careerists in CID.

'It's an installation of famous historical figures,' he said. 'There's Anne Boleyn with her famous "B" necklace . . . and Walter Raleigh with the pipe he brought back from the New World—'

'And Thomas More with his Chancellor's gold chain,' Burton interrupted eagerly. 'They're incredibly lifelike.'

'Yeah,' Doyle agreed. 'As good as Madame Tussauds, if you ask me.'

'Chuffing Nora, there's *Crookback*.' Noakes was excited to spy Richard III looking suitably malevolent. 'He ain't properly hunched over, though.' This was said with a distinct note of disappointment. 'You c'n tell it's him 'cos it looks like all them pictures they showed after he were dug up in that carpark . . . an' they've made one shoulder higher than the other.' He still sounded dubious.

Knevitt laughed. 'Yes, I believe technicians worked from the famous red portrait which was designed to make him look sinister and unattractive . . . If you look, you can see a crown at his feet — a reminder of how it fell off and rolled under a bush at the Battle of Bosworth.'

'Presumably the two little blond boys on either side are meant to be the Princes in the Tower,' Carruthers said, something in his supercilious tone suggesting he found it all a bit naff.

'Not sure about them,' Noakes opined. 'Look like they belong in a boy band with all that wavy hair.'

'Artistic licence,' Knevitt chuckled. 'When it starts to get dark and they're backlit, I promise you the effect is quite eerie.' Observing Burton's avid expression and the guidebook clutched in her hand, he added, 'Look, the Tower closes at four thirty in winter. Once the hoi polloi are gone for the day, I'll get one of the yeoman warders to give you a personal tour, that way you can soak up the vibes without having to stand in line. In the meantime, I'm going to take you over to the Queen's House where Dr Esdaile was based.'

There was barely time to register the matrix of ancient alleys, towers and quadrangles, as though through a view-finder, before they arrived at Tower Green and the black and white timber-framed building that was the governor's official residence.

'Shouldn't it be called the *King's House*, on account of Charles the Third's accession?' Burton didn't like anomalies.

'Technically yes,' Morrissey said in his quiet country-man's burr. 'That's the official title now. But apparently the community here still call it the Queen's House amongst themselves . . . Anne Boleyn was kept here before her execution, so I guess that's why the name kind of stuck.'

'That's Lady Jane Grey over there,' he said, pointing to a striking installation on the cordoned-off square of lawn.

It was another life-size figure in Tudor court dress, with burgundy-coloured draperies trailing on the ground . . . like a pool of blood, Burton thought uneasily.

'The cleaner who found Margaret Esdaile said she was enthusiastic about all the other installations,' Knevitt told them, 'but she took a real dislike to this one for some reason . . . called it creepy and a "whey-faced monstrosity".'

Burton was puzzled. 'It's not that bad really . . . and, after all, Jane Grey *was* a prisoner here.'

Morrissey shrugged. 'Maybe Dr Esdaile thought it was bad form putting it here right next to the church.'

'That seems most likely,' Markham agreed, mentally filing away the information that something about this particular figure and her history had unsettled the curator, since even the most trivial, seemingly insignificant character trait might hold the clue to why she was murdered.

'Actually, Lady Jane probably didn't even die on the Green,' Knevitt said. 'Most likely it was opposite the Waterloo block where they keep the Crown Jewels.'

'But this is more picturesque,' Burton observed, biting her lip.

'Yeah, and just wait till you see her lit up,' the DCI said. 'It's like she's a vengeful ghost or something.'

Seeing Burton shiver, Knevitt ushered them into the Queen's House and led the way down to the basement.

'As you know, none of the bigwigs is currently in residence,' he said cheerfully. 'And this building isn't on the tourist trail, so there's been no difficulty about preserving the crime scene. I'm using the chief curators' office as an incident room — they've shifted to the Cradle Tower for now.'

The chief curators' domain was impressive, its walls panelled in oak up to halfway and a cluster of heavy maroon-upholstered armchairs arranged around what was clearly an original Adam fireplace. No expense spared, Burton thought beadily, taking in the expensive oriental carpets, flock wallpaper, antique redwood bookcases and Queen Anne chairs. Books and papers spilled across every surface, the majority being piled high on a walnut console table next to the large sash windows. There wasn't much of a view, just a small enclosed courtyard, but the lush décor was ample compensation. Burton eyed the oil paintings which had the dim, rarified look of Old Masters — she was willing to bet one Venetian landscape was a Canaletto — thinking that the room might have belonged to an Oxford don or well-heeled academic. For all the expensive accoutrements, however, there was something anachronistic about the overall effect, old-fashioned wooden filing cabinets contrasting oddly with Apple PCs on top of Edwardian kneehole desks and creating a strangely disjointed atmosphere, as though the room couldn't quite decide which era it belonged to.

Still, it was comfortable and welcoming, with floor-length, maroon drapes keeping out draughts and a fire supplementing the warmth from discreetly concealed radiators.

There was nothing antique about the palace switchboard, moreover, and in no time at all a staffer arrived with a trolley of hot drinks, biscuits, savouries and freshly made cake from the New Armouries Café.

'This is Justine Campbell, married to one of the Tower's longest serving Beefeaters,' Knevitt said, endeavouring to reassure the apprehensive looking woman by the warmth in his tone, though with her drooping demeanour and straggling flaxen chignon she looked almost as much in need of a restorative pick-me-up as the visitors.

Noakes's eyes followed her thoughtfully as she served them their refreshments before disappearing as unobtrusively as she had arrived.

'That one looks like a frightened rabbit,' he observed.

'They're like a family here,' Morrissey told him. 'The murder's hit them hard.'

Some desultory chit-chat followed as the detectives took each other's measure.

'How's DCI Sidney?' Knevitt asked politely. 'He must be coming up to retirement now.'

'Thinking about a media career,' Doyle answered through a mouthful of sausage roll. 'Police talking head . . . pundit . . . that kind of thing.'

'He's got the right face for radio . . . literally no beginning to his talents,' Morrissey commented deadpan, causing Carruthers to smirk appreciatively and reinforcing Markham's impression that there was more to the mild-mannered Devonian than met the eye.

After a time, feeling increasingly at ease, they got down to the matter in hand.

'So, Dr Esdaile was researching the Princes in the Tower,' Markham began. 'We know different academic camps can get pretty intense about their theories,' he went on, thinking of their previous investigations in museums and colleges. 'Do you know if there was anything particularly *controversial* about her work . . . anything that might have triggered her killer?'

Knevitt thought for a moment. 'I'm not across all the academic stuff, but apparently she was particularly interested in rumours that Richard and his niece Elizabeth of York conspired to do away with his wife Anne Neville who eventually wasted away—'

'Not a Ricardian then, I take it,' Markham observed wryly.

'Well, according to Dr Daniel Locke she wanted to "reframe history in the light of modern psychological discourse", focusing on Richard's marriage and personal life as stepping stones to the Princes' murder—' his lips twisted ironically — 'along with promoting "trendy ideas about coercive control and gaslighting".' His air quotes told the detectives that Knevitt hadn't particularly cared for Dr Locke. 'Apparently she was heavily into psychoanalysis. As well as this notion of Richard being some kind of medieval abuser, she went a bundle on the idea of him killing his nephews because of suppressed rage that he'd always been in their father's — his brother's — shadow.'

'Edward the Fourth was this six foot athletic blond hunk that women couldn't get enough of,' Morrissey chipped in. 'A massive lad really . . . like those rugger bugger gilet-wearing types who always steal your girlfriends at college,' he added ruefully, as though he had personal experience of such manoeuvres. 'So Dr Esdaile fancied the idea of sibling jealousy boiling up over the years and Richard making his brother pay by wiping out the next generation . . . kind of settling accounts if you like. The fact that his own child was sickly made him even more venomous towards his nephews. And then after he had murdered them, there was karma when his own son died.'

Markham could see how more traditional academics might have disliked such an approach, but as a motive for murder it was pretty thin.

Burton clearly felt the same. 'Okay, so maybe her research interests were a bit left field,' she ruminated. 'But I can't imagine anyone wanting to *kill* over it.'

Noakes wasn't so sure. 'Museum people are a pretty rum lot,' he grunted. 'They don' think the same way as sensible folk . . . right loonies some of 'em.'

'Was there anyone apart from Dr Locke who might have been upset by the academic stuff?' Carruthers enquired.

'Well, she was on the trail of a psalter,' Knevitt said. 'An illuminated prayer book that supposedly belonged to Anne Neville but went missing from Middleham Castle sometime in the eighteenth century. That put Dr Benedict Ryan's nose out of joint because he was researching the Neville family artefacts and it was kind of raining on his parade. Her ex-husband Dr Steven Winders is arranging an exhibition at Hampton Court and wasn't too happy either by all accounts, in case she stole his glory.'

'Did she find the prayer book or whatever it is?' Doyle asked.

'Well, Pam Appleton who found her body says she seemed really happy and excited about something in the weeks before her death, like she was hugging a secret . . .'

Noakes's dour expression suggested that keeping secrets rarely ended well.

'What was so special about this psalter thingy anyhow?' he demanded. 'Is it jus' 'cos it's dead old?'

Morrissey consulted his notebook. 'The conservation team said Dr Esdaile mentioned a local tradition in Middleham that Anne Neville had inscribed graffiti in the margins,' he told them. 'Coded messages about her despair over the loss of her ten-year-old son and the way she was being treated. People got the impression Dr Esdaile was fascinated by Richard despite his wickedness — found him strong and compelling like some kind of Bluebeard but thought Anne Neville was a bit of a milksop, which is why he ended up being attracted to his niece.'

'What was so special about *her* then?' Noakes grunted.

'Well, apart from being Edward the Fourth's daughter, she was a great beauty with an eye to the main chance,' Morrissey shot back.

'Okay,' Doyle said briskly, never keen on historical blind alleys. 'So Dr Esdaile could've tracked down this book and . . .' A thought struck him. 'Presumably it's valuable?'

'Priceless,' was Morrissey's laconic reply.

'And then someone found out and killed her for it,' Doyle pursued. He frowned. 'But they'd hardly be able to sell the thing or explain how it had turned up without landing themselves right in it . . .'

Markham had to agree this seemed unlikely.

'Maybe they just wanted it for themselves . . . some kind of obsession,' Carruthers hazarded.

'Had there ever been any issues with artefacts or valuable items going missing?' he asked.

'Oddly enough there *was* some sort of altercation between Dr Esdaile and a trainee conservator.' Morrissey again consulted his notebook. 'Name of Elena Rogers. Something to do with her taking an item from the display case in Dr Esdaile's room, but that was just a misunderstanding and they cleared it up between them.'

'Any other "misunderstandings"?' Noakes wanted to know.

Knevitt grinned. 'Dr Esdaile had a run-in with one of the Beefeaters . . . too cocky by half. And she wasn't wild about a couple of female staff. But look.' He came to an abrupt halt. 'Why don't I let you make up your own minds rather than colouring your judgment in advance.' He glanced at his watch. 'I've arranged interviews here and over at Hampton Court Palace where Dr Winders and his new wife are based—'

'The ex-husband.' From the hopeful tone of his voice, it was obvious Carruthers fancied a crack at Winders.

Knevitt took the hint. 'If DI Markham's agreeable, why don't you and DS Doyle take Hampton Court,' he said easily. 'Winders' wife Lucy is based there as well,' he added.

'Fine by me,' Markham confirmed.

'And in the meantime, yourself and DI Burton can take the joint chief curators, events manager and chaplain . . . the conservation woman and Dr Esdaile's intern should be around too,' Knevitt went on, ticking them off on his fingers. 'They're making a room available over in the Cradle Tower.'

'What's the intern do?' Noakes asked to cover his anxiety that he hadn't been allocated an assignment.

'She's a history graduate from Goldsmiths College doing unpaid work experience here,' Knevitt replied. 'The Tower only offers a few slots each year, so competition's pretty fierce. In this case,' he added sardonically, 'I gather the young lady had contacts in high places.'

Noakes frowned. Nothing like nepotism to sour his mood.

'We thought *you* could take the Beefeaters, sarge,' Morrissey said politely. 'Seeing as they're all ex-services and you'll know the best way to handle them.'

The other visibly brightened. *Now that was more like it.*

Markham was touched by the use of his wingman's 'honorary title' and the respectful deference that accompanied the request. It made perfect sense of course that Noakes should be chosen to fraternize with the guardians of the Tower, since they would be far more likely to open up to a former serviceman than to anyone else on his team.

'Do they still do that thing every night . . . the changing of the guard whatnot?' Noakes asked gruffly, aglow from the compliment he had been paid.

'Oh you mean the Ceremony of the Keys,' Knevitt replied. 'That's just before ten p.m., so I'll make sure you get a ringside view. The keys'll be delivered to the chief yeoman warder with the governor and deputy governor being away, but it's still well worth a look.' He consulted his watch once more. 'Look, why don't I show you Dr Esdaile's room. And then you can get stuck into the interviews . . . They're laying on a buffet lunch back here at one p.m. and I've arranged the same for Sergeants Doyle and Carruthers over at Hampton

Court. Later on, you can all have a tour of the Tower and finish up at the Keys for a drink.' He smiled. 'It's the yeoman warders' private boozer, so I'd say we're honoured.'

Noakes nodded approvingly. Knevitt certainly understood the importance of creature comforts.

'What about the unsolved abduction?' Burton said anxiously. 'Do we say anything about what happened in 2008 with Annie and Dominic Sullivan?'

'I was just coming to that.' The kind face was suddenly very sombre and Markham recalled that both the DCI and Morrissey were parents.

'There's not been a whisper about the kids' disappearance in connection with what happened to Dr Esdaile,' Knevitt continued. 'So she was playing her cards very close to her chest.'

Burton turned to Morrissey. 'How did she seem when she rang you?'

'It was just after four p.m. She was very polite, apologized for bothering me and said she'd seen one of our flyers about reopening the Sullivan case . . . it was most likely nothing, but something was niggling her and she felt maybe we ought to know . . . Her tone was a bit preoccupied perhaps, but she didn't give the impression that it was necessarily a big deal.' The DI looked unhappy. 'I wanted to come out and see her right away but she had to get off — date night with her husband — told me she'd call round at the station on Friday but never showed. I figured she must've got held up here, what with Christmas being so busy for them.'

'Don't beat yourself up, mate,' Knevitt told his DI quietly. 'I'd have thought the same.' Then to the others: 'We'll be checking in with Charles Esdaile tomorrow.' The DCI took over. 'Gave every impression of being in bits, but . . .' His shrug was eloquent in its acknowledgement that policemen could never trust to appearances.

'D'you reckon the murderer found out that Dr Esdaile was going to spill the beans about something . . . maybe even give the police their name?' Doyle asked. 'So all that about her whacko ideas and a missing prayer book doesn't have anything to do with it?'

Burton looked pained at hearing academic studies described as 'whacko' but held her peace, as interested as the rest to hear the answer.

'There *might* be a connection with Dr Esdaile's research interests,' Knevitt said carefully. 'If so, we've yet to find it.'

'Or the Ricardian stuff could be totally coincidental,' Morrissey pointed out.

'Useful camouflage for the killer, though,' Carruthers observed, 'seeing as it sounds like she got up some people's noses.'

'At any rate, to answer your initial query, Inspector Burton, I suggest we say nothing about the Sullivan case for the time being . . . wait to see if someone mentions it first and take things from there.' Knevitt got to his feet and the others followed suit. 'Now, let's take a quick look at Dr Esdaile's office. I'll have Forensics and autopsy reports for you later, but figure you'd like to see where she was found and get a feel for the woman.'

With that, he led them along the vestibule past other closed doors to a room at the end.

'Who else works down here?' Markham enquired as the DCI lifted the crime scene tape and proceeded to unlock the door.

'Mainly academics on the history side . . . plus the community access and schools people. The conservation and collections teams are dotted around in various towers and crannies.' Knevitt gave a short bark. 'It's a strange world all right . . . like a village—'

'Or Wonderland,' Morrissey put in unexpectedly. 'Beyond the jewels and costumes and suits of armour, there's this whole other population beavering away behind the scenes. Feels like you need a team of Sherpas to get about, and there's around a hundred and fifty people live here.' He noticed Burton's dismayed expression. 'Don't worry,' he said with a wry grin, 'we can rule out most of them on the basis that whoever did this knew Dr Esdaile's routine and left a calling card.'

Intrigued, they filed into the room.

It was a scholar's sanctum all right, Markham thought. Somewhat less luxurious than the chief curators' quarters, its panelling and elegant appointments meant it would have fitted into any Oxbridge Provost's residence. The visitor's eye was immediately drawn to a massive antique framed tapestry above the fireplace.

'Don' reckon much to that,' Noakes muttered, eying it with disfavour. 'Why'd she go for a picture of some big ugly puffin? You'd have thought she'd want a Virgin Queen lookalike with cartwheel ruff an' fancy jewels an' all the rest of it.'

'I think that's a *pelican*, sarge, not a puffin,' Burton murmured. 'It was Elizabeth the First's special emblem . . . something to do with her being a mother to the nation—'

Noakes squinted dubiously. 'How come?'

'Well, there's a legend which says the pelican sacrifices herself to feed her young, so Elizabeth kind of adopted it as her motto.'

'Oh aye.' Her colleague was transparently unimpressed, appearing keener on the more conventional framed prints of assorted medieval worthies in doublet and hose.

Knevitt and Morrissey listened to this exchange with quizzical amusement but said nothing as Markham's team moved around the quaintly carved furniture, bookcases and display cabinets, showing an almost superstitious reluctance to approach the stained leather-topped desk where Margaret Esdaile's body had been found.

'Hey, jus' listen to this,' Noakes exclaimed delightedly as he scrutinized a book of Jacobean recipes open on a reading lectern. '"Take three round balls of horse dung, boil them in a pint of white wine . . . Take a hound's turd an' mix with ointment of earthworm or bats".'

Doyle looked distinctly queasy, as though he regretted those three sausages for breakfast. Carruthers meanwhile was more interested in a display case captioned *The Weaker Vessel in James I's England.*

'Old James didn't like clever women,' he said with a sidelong glance at Burton. 'He said teaching them Latin just made them more cunning.'

Doyle peered in. 'The Elizabethans didn't have much time for women either . . . Just listen to this from some lord or other: "I must a little touch on the feminine commonwealth",' he read out. '"The plotting and malice among them is such that I think envy and hatred hath tied an invisible snake about most of their necks to sting one another to death." *Blimey.*'

It was a delightful room, thought Markham. Full of fascinating curios that made him imagine he would have liked the woman who collected them. But his mind was running on Morrissey's words to them earlier.

'You said the killer left a calling card, Gordon.'

The DI withdrew a plastic envelope from his jacket pocket and laid it down on the desk.

Markham's team gathered round.

It was a creased sheet of A4 paper streaked with rust-coloured blotches bearing two images: the first showed a cloven-hoofed, horned demon dragging a woman along by her hair while underneath was a skull and crossbones with the menacing words *Death shall dissolve.*

'What are they?' Doyle asked blankly.

'Magnified engravings from something called the Lennox or Darnley jewel associated with Mary Queen of Scots,' Knevitt told them. 'It's kept at the Palace of Holyroodhouse in Edinburgh. Dr Esdaile was making notes for an article she'd been asked to write about it for *History Today.*'

'Are those smudges blood?' Burton asked hesitantly.

Morrissey nodded grimly. 'Yes. The forensics people found the sheet of paper folded and tucked into Dr Esdaile's sleeve. Dr Locke identified it as having been most likely removed from a wallet in that cardboard filing system next to the desk . . . she preferred boxes to those oak drawers over by the window.'

Markham's keen eyes roamed the room. 'How many people knew where to find it?'

'Very few . . . really only her immediate circle or personnel based down here on the historical side.' Knevitt endeavoured to sound upbeat. 'Narrows the pool of suspects down somewhat,' he told them.

There was a sudden noise beyond the window.

Markham crossed the room in a few strides. 'Nothing doing,' he said. 'Just a little cellar area and some bins.'

'Most likely one of the warders' cats,' Morrissey commented with an uneasy glance at his superior.

What were they keeping back, Markham wondered as he met Noakes's eye.

But before anyone had a chance to ask further questions, the Tower Bridge detectives were marshalling them from the room.

'We've got permission to use the Council Chamber upstairs,' Knevitt told them. 'That's where they interrogated Guy Fawkes.'

'Should concentrate a few minds,' Noakes said with a wolfish grin.

'Morrissey'll take you across to the chief yeoman warder's office so you can meet the Beefeaters, sarge,' the DCI told him. 'And there's a driver waiting out front to take DS Doyle and DS Carruthers over to Hampton Court. Then after the interviews are finished, you can have the guided tour. A full debrief can wait till tomorrow when we compare notes back here.'

Again, Markham had the feeling that Knevitt's briskness disguised an anxiety that not all the heartiness in the world could dispel.

Whatever was going on in this strange — what had Morrissey called it? — Wonderland, the DI sensed there were further revelations still to come.

CHAPTER 4: FORTRESS VILLAGE

'So what was it like then, Gil, with the moonlight ramble and everything?'

Olivia put the question eagerly as she lay stretched out on the king size bed in their bedroom at the Tower Hotel overlooking St Katharine Docks. Replete after a lavish room-service supper of chicken and ham hock pie with triple-cooked chips, they had avoided the subject of Markham's investigation until every last crumb was polished off and they were settled with coffee.

Taking his cup across to the picture window with Tower Bridge in the background, Markham contemplated his partner, swaddled in an outsize towelling robe as she waited for his account of the day. She had been delighted with his gift shop offerings of glass paperweight inscribed with an engraving of the Tower and an Anne Boleyn initial necklace, and now looked at him expectantly, like a ten-year-old eager for her bedtime story, he thought indulgently.

Where to begin, he wondered, sinking into the leather armchair and setting his drink down on a side table.

'It all felt pretty surreal,' he said finally.

'Spooky?' Olivia asked hopefully.

'Well, at night with everywhere flood-lit, it was incredibly atmospheric . . . but uncanny too, almost as if we were intruders who had no right to be there,' he observed sombrely. 'As if after nightfall, the place rightfully belonged to *them*: all the people who suffered and died there, left to rot . . . or executed and then buried in that sinister little church under a load of quicklime — such a *squalid* end.'

His partner was taken aback at the pity in his voice.

'Oh, you mean the Chapel of St Peter ad Vincula . . . I seem to remember some famous historian called it the saddest place on earth.' She regarded him thoughtfully. 'Was that the highlight then?'

He smiled apologetically. 'Oh, our guide was thorough — mad keen on all the bells and whistles — but somehow it went by in a blur. I just had this impression of medieval cobblestones, with evil and danger lurking behind ramparts and doorways and courtyards . . . everywhere really,' he finished lamely, conscious this wasn't entirely what she had expected to hear.

'Evil?' she said uneasily. 'Even in the church?'

'Yes, there most of all . . . even though it's a working parish church with regular Sunday services and all the rest of it.' He sipped his coffee before continuing. 'The crypt was particularly claustrophobic — low arched ceilings, flagged stone floor and clammy white plasterwork . . . cold and dank, like it was oozing with dead men's sweat. There was something — hard to put into words, Liv — something *wretched* about it despite the flower arrangements and candles. There were rows of shiny black tablets too—' he shivered involuntarily — 'with the names of people whose remains had been taken out from under the nave and reinterred behind the walls . . . boxes of bones all jumbled together.'

'I wonder if that means Thomas Cromwell ended up next to Thomas More,' Olivia laughed, trying to lighten the mood. 'Satan's agent snuggling up to the saint.'

Markham smiled back at her, shifting in the chair as though to shake off a spectral hand that rested on his shoulder. 'Is that what they called Cromwell?' he asked.

'Oh yes, spawn of Satan all right . . . just before being executed, he owned up to a "great heap of sins".'

The tactic had worked, she noted with relief as the shadow lifted from her partner's face.

'So what else is down in the crypt?' she continued, her tone deliberately light.

'A little shrine to Thomas More . . . Well, it's really just an alcove with kneelers, candles and a portrait bust.'

'No tomb then?' Olivia sounded disappointed.

'There's a large chest inscribed with an epitaph, but the guide said it's probably just a memorial and More's remains are most likely sealed up somewhere else in the crypt, apart from the head which ended up in Canterbury.' Markham was clearly uncomfortable with the subject of interments and sepulchres. 'We were very privileged to be taken down there,' he went on matter-of-factly, 'because it's not on the regular tourist trail. And you have to book with a warder if you want to see inside the church, though with so many grave markers, it was more like a mausoleum,' he concluded.

Olivia decided there had been enough talk of death. 'What did George make of it all?' she enquired.

Markham chuckled, immediately looking less careworn.

'Noakesy was desperate to see the ravens,' he told her. 'Only they were tucked up for the night . . . But he loved the carved graffiti and the cells where they kept Thomas More and John Fisher, couldn't get over what they must have suffered from the damp. Told the yeoman warder he was surprised arthritis didn't do for the pair of them long before they got their heads cut off.'

Olivia grinned broadly. 'Not quite so antipapist as usual then.'

'Far from it. He was seriously impressed by how spartan it was . . . And of course he insisted on seeing the staircase leading to the chapel in the White Tower where they found the remains of Richard the Third's nephews.' Markham proffered this information hesitantly, scanning his partner's face for signs of discomfort with the subject of murdered children, but Olivia's expression remained untroubled.

'Any vibes?' she joked. 'As in historical ESP?'

'It was just a staircase, though obviously Noakesy lingered, sniffing the air like a species of cadaver dog. Our guide took it all in his stride, though.'

Olivia giggled. 'How did the Beefeaters react to George?'

'Like he was a brother in arms.' Markham smiled at the recollection. 'The minute he met the Yeoman Gaoler, they were swapping army stories. And by the time we were in the warders' pub, there was no stopping him.' He broke into a mischievous approximation of his friend's dour Yorkshire accent. '"You gotta be able to trust the blokes on your flanks, mate . . . It's a matter of life an' death."'

Olivia clapped her hands delightedly.

'I'm not sure Doyle and Carruthers were quite so enthralled,' Markham added wryly. 'But everyone was fairly benign once we were a few drinks in.' He chuckled again. 'The head honcho got all confidential with me . . . some long rigmarole about his missus having to give up bingo when she started getting blotto . . . But they shooed us out in time for the Ceremony of the Keys. Incredible to think that's been going on for more than seven hundred years.'

'Did you extract any gossip about the case?'

'Noakesy told me he'd heard some stuff about a prowler and some weirdo targeting children . . . We're going to unpack that when we see Knevitt and Morrissey in the morning,' he said vaguely.

She could tell he was fobbing her off, but let it pass.

'Any joy with the suspects?' she wanted to know. 'Are there lots of stuffy academic types? And how've you been able to narrow them down? I read somewhere that a hundred and fifty people live in the Tower, so it must be like hunting a needle in a haystack.'

'The killer left a calling card,' Markham said before proceeding to tell her about the paper with its magnified engravings from the Lennox jewel. 'There's only a small number of people who would have known about Dr Esdaile's research on the jewel and where she kept her notes — essentially the chief curators, her intern, the events manager, conservation officer and chaplain,' he rattled off. 'Possibly her current partner and the ex-husband too.'

'What about the warders? Would any of *them* know about her research?'

'We can't discount them, though it seems pretty unlikely. Noakes scored a hit there, so he may be able to winkle that out. Apparently Dr Esdaile clashed with one of them, John Whittingham, accused him of being slapdash when it came to learning the Tower story — that's the spiel they memorize for visitors — and a bit handsy with some students. But according to Noakes, his army record's stellar and he's got a string of medals—'

'Oh *well*, that clinches it. He's in the clear then,' Olivia said with heavy sarcasm.

Markham rolled his eyes at her tone. 'I know what you mean, Liv, but to be honest the guy seemed on the level — big, bearded, jolly type with a booming laugh . . . maybe a bit brash, but well-meaning enough. His colleagues seem to rate him.'

'But he's the sort who might rub a prickly female academic up the wrong way?'

'Well, Daniel Locke and Benedict Ryan — they're the joint chief curators — never had any run-ins with him, but—'

'It might be different with a woman,' Olivia interrupted.

'Quite possibly,' Markham conceded. 'But more likely they belong to the "anything for a quiet life" school of thought,' he added wryly.

Olivia chucked a pillow at him. 'Typical male,' she laughed. Then: 'So what are the boss men like?'

Markham knew his partner relished humorous comparisons. 'Hmm let me see, Locke's the pompous type, short on empathy and humour, wavy silver hair, gimlet eyes and toothbrush moustache . . . rather put me in mind of Enoch Powell. Ryan's an older version of Prince William, but with none of the warmth or charm . . . oh, and he's got a lisp, which rather detracts from the donnishness.'

'What about the chaplain?'

'Dark and haggard, could do with a square meal . . . sort of Rory Stewart lookalike,' Markham said, referring to the emaciated-looking former government minister and ex-soldier turned broadcaster. 'A bit precious, but he's got presence and a beautiful speaking voice.'

'Same surname as your sergeant,' she pointed out.

'But there the resemblance ends,' Markham replied, thinking of his easy-going subordinate. 'There's something tormented about the Reverend Father Bernard, as he asked us to call him.'

'Heathcliffe gone wrong?'

He grinned. 'Hardly that, though apparently he and Locke were both admirers of Dr Esdaile—'

'Only she found the whole Tower setup just too incestuous for words.'

'Well, she met her first husband Dr Steven Winders when he was based there. He works at Hampton Court now along with his wife Lucy who's the HR manager.'

'See what I mean about incestuous.' Olivia liked to have the last word.

Markham laughed. 'Maybe it *is* a bit hothouse,' he admitted. 'But Charles Esdaile's a businessman, so Margaret broke away in the end.'

And look where that got her. But Olivia bit back the retort.

'What's the husband like?' she asked.

'Distraught . . . We're seeing him tomorrow. Doyle and Carruthers interviewed her ex, but I've yet to hear what they made of him and wife number two.'

'Did you get anywhere with the intern and events manager?'

'Not so as you'd notice,' was the weary reply. Markham recalled his impression of twenty-something-year-old Sophie McGrath: curvaceous with a soft, caressing manner that he was willing to bet would have gone down a storm with his sergeants. The events woman was an altogether tougher proposition, with her sleek brown bob, square jaw and designer specs. 'I had the feeling neither was a fan of Dr Esdaile, but they made all the right noises.'

Olivia sensed his deflation.

'I suppose they all had stonking cast-iron alibis then?' she quipped.

'We'll be reviewing people's whereabouts tomorrow morning,' he replied. 'But so far they've all given a good account of themselves. Nobody stands out . . . except perhaps Elena Rogers. She's the trainee conservator who rattled Dr Esdaile's cage by helping herself to something from a display case without permission—'

'What kind of something?'

'A horoscope from the early 1700s which belonged to a woman convicted of sorcery.'

Olivia sat up straight. 'A *witch*?'

'I *knew* that'd pique your interest, Liv . . . But this was just a wise woman accused of putting a spell on some village children.'

'James the First was obsessed with witches,' she said thoughtfully. 'I mean, that's the reason Shakespeare wrote *Macbeth*.'

'Well, James certainly had no time for learned women. One of the documents on display in Dr Esdaile's office says that when he heard his cousin Arbella Stuart was a marvel of scholarly accomplishment, he just asked, "But can she spin?".'

'*Ouch*!' She thought for a moment. 'Arbella's the one who haunts the Tower, right?'

'Along with any number of others,' was the dry retort. 'Great box office.'

'Did the conservator or whatever she is admit to pinching the horoscope?'

Markham thought back to studious-looking, gently spoken Elena Rogers with her somewhat old-fashioned chignon and modest, almost twee, knitted two-piece. Quietly pretty, she didn't look like anyone's idea of a thief. Absent-minded maybe, but that was hardly a crime.

'She thought she must have taken it out of the cabinet at some point but couldn't recall having done so . . . wasn't sure how it had ended up on her desk. The whole business sounded like a storm in a teacup, only Margaret Esdaile was quite territorial when it came to the exhibits. The upshot was, Elena apologized. With her working between the Tower and Hampton Court, it wasn't as if they were cheek by jowl, so it was all smoothed over in the end.'

'D'you think it was down to an office prankster?' Olivia wondered. 'Or someone trying to freak Dr Esdaile out?'

'Who can say.' The weary note was back. 'There's always mischief-making in a closed community. And viewed from one angle, you could say the Tower's almost a village.'

'As well as a fortress,' Olivia qualified. Seeing his expression cloud over once more, she added lightly, 'I'll be taking a tour myself tomorrow while you're trying to unravel those alibis. Any suggestions as to the best guide?'

'Great idea, Liv,' he said with forced heartiness. 'You might try and catch Andy Campbell. Apparently Campbell's always excellent value — good enough to tread the boards if he'd wanted.' He recalled the woman Noakes had described as looking like a frightened rabbit. 'His wife Justine works in one of the cafés . . . looked shattered by it all.'

'Well, there's always the Rev Fr Bernard available to administer pastoral care,' she pointed out sardonically.

'Hmm . . . not really sure he's got the, er, common touch.'

'How'd he get along with George?'

'Noakesy rocked up just as Kate and I finished interviewing him . . . got straight down to brass tacks, demanding to know why the clergy have ditched Deuteronomy and got God waving the white flag, and where did he stand on *Star Wars* fans listing their religion at the last census as "Jedi".'

'Oh the poor padre.'

'He made himself pretty scarce after that, I can tell you . . . No doubt he'll bear Noakes's preferences in mind when it comes to Dr Esdaile's funeral on Sunday,' Markham added with heavy irony.

Olivia was startled. 'Wow, that's a bit speedy, isn't it.'

'I believe the Esdailes' connections and the fact that St Peter ad Vincula's a chapel royal oiled the wheels,' he said laconically. 'Presumably that's why they also fast-tracked the autopsy.'

'Did George and the others pick up any creepy vibes in the church?' she asked, curious to know if they shared his discomfort.

'They found the crypt oppressive and Noakes said it was like a catacomb. Doyle and Carruthers just looked askance at the stuff about boxes of bones.' Suddenly he grinned. 'Our guide asked if we wanted to say a quick prayer at Thomas More's tomb, which caught them off guard. Cue much shuffling of feet.'

'I'm sure Kate rose to the occasion . . . We know how she loves a guided tour.'

If there was an edge to the remark, he chose to ignore it.

'Oh she said all the right things . . . There was a sticky moment when we got on to the warders' ceremonial dress and Noakesy said the hats made them look like Morris dancers, but other than that the tour went off well.'

Olivia sensed he would have preferred to jettison their guide and explore the Tower on his own. As ever, her partner was the cat that walked by himself.

'Sounds like you may have won over the Beefeaters,' she said lightly.

'The Yeoman Gaoler told me these days they prefer to be called warders — "Beefeaters" carries pejorative overtones apparently. They struck me as a decent lot, with only a couple of women who seemed to be treated as honorary men—'

A giant yawn interrupted his reflections and she noticed with a pang of compunction how wrung out he looked.

'Sorry, Gil, you've had a long day and here I am pestering you with questions.'

'It's been quite therapeutic, sweetheart . . . helped me marshal my impressions into some sort of order.' His lips twisted in a wry smile. 'Knevitt and Morrissey are far more simpatico than Sidney, so I've no need to fear accusations of "feyness" or "letting my imagination run away with me".'

'I should think *not*!' she exclaimed indignantly before winking at him. 'I suppose there's no question of romance after all that Tower treachery and torture . . .'

He needed no second invitation.

* * *

Wednesday 6 December was one of those gloriously sunny, crisp winter days that made unsettling phantoms temporarily recede.

When the team convened in their basement incident room, however, the brightness of the day seemed dimmed for Markham as Noakes spoke of rumours that had bedevilled the Tower community.

'Them warders were a bit cagey to start with,' he told them. 'But they opened up after a while.'

The ex-sergeant was wearing a Tower of London hooded cream sweatshirt — presumably by way of compliment to his hosts — and fawn cargo trousers, both items a size too small for him. Having earlier met up with the Ravenmaster, he was in high good humour, his cheeriness augmented by Knevitt's provision of excellent coffee and bourbon creams to which he did full justice despite having already sampled the Tower Hotel's Full English.

'Turns out every now and again a kid would vanish an' then, jus' when the parents were panicking an' doing their nut, they'd reappear out of nowhere—'

Doyle was puzzled.

'But that's *bound* to happen sometimes,' he interrupted. 'I mean, you get it in shops and museums and those kinds of places all the time . . . tannoy announcements saying look out for a missing child. Everyone knows kids wander off, that's why mums and dads need to have eyes in the back of their head,' he added, complacently aware that he and Kelly were deferring the joys of parenthood for the time being.

'Yeah, but here's the thing.' Noakes patted his paunch portentously. '*These* kids trotted out the same weird story that a ghost took 'em an' said scary things.'

'Scary things?' Carruthers looked highly sceptical.

'Could just have been attention-seeking,' Burton suggested. 'And if the children turned up safe, it doesn't sound like attempted abduction or anything like that.'

'The warders were positive summat were . . . *off*,' Noakes insisted. 'Said you wouldn't get anyone able to make kids disappear into thin air unless . . .'

'They knew every inch of the Tower inside out.' Burton was determined to discount any supernatural explanation.

Knevitt and Morrissey listened attentively. 'Presumably nothing came of it, though,' the DCI said quietly.

'The parents were jus' happy to get their kids back an' didn't want to hear any talk about spooky stuff,' Noakes confirmed. 'So it never went anywhere. Plus, the higher-ups didn't want police sniffing around or owt getting into the papers.' He sniffed disapprovingly. 'Wanted it all squared away nice an' neat an' tidy.'

'But the warders were uneasy?' Morrissey prompted, his and the DCI's expression suggesting to Markham that these revelations weren't entirely news to them and they already suspected something of the kind.

'Whittingham, Andy Campbell an' a couple of others talked about there being a prowler . . . someone turning up in places where they shouldn't have been.'

'*Someone*.' Carruthers was impatient. 'Like who?'

'Look, they were dead embarrassed talking about it,' Noakes shot back, affronted. 'Didn't want me thinking they were big girls' blouses.' Burton winced audibly at this. 'They're all ex-forces, see. Felt a bit like pillocks telling me they were pretty sure someone were snooping around up to no good.'

'One of their own?' Knevitt asked intently. 'Someone on the staff?'

'A couple of 'em *thought* they'd spotted a figure moving around late at night, wearing a dark coat with the hood up . . .

an' one of the female warders fancied she saw torchlight in that little church, but when she checked it out no one was there.'

'Doesn't really amount to much,' was Doyle's verdict.

'Just superstition and folk telling tall tales,' Carruthers agreed. 'As for the stuff about kids doing a disappearing act, that's something and nothing if you ask me.'

'Even so.' Burton looked uncomfortable. 'Historically, there's plenty of children who suffered here,' she mused. 'Not just the Princes in the Tower, but a raft of other youngsters who had a claim to the throne . . . starved, imprisoned, executed or vanished without trace.'

'What are you saying, ma'am,' Doyle cut in, keen to pre-empt a seminar on Plantagenet and Tudor monarchs. 'That all this — Esdaile and the Sullivan kids — is down to some fruitcake who's read too much Jean Plaidy?' He was quite proud of himself for recalling the name of Kelly's favourite author.

Burton frowned as Carruthers tried to conceal a smirk.

'Hardly,' was her wintry response. 'But it's not out of the question that someone might have become psychologically unbalanced from working here . . .'

'Convinced themselves they'd lived before in Tudor times or something . . . pretty nutty,' Doyle hypothesized.

'Or perhaps their surroundings triggered some pre-existing condition,' Morrissey suggested as Burton looked at him gratefully.

'As things stand, there's nothing concrete so far to connect the Esdaile and Sullivan cases,' Markham observed, bringing them back to the point.

'I've arranged for Andy Campbell to walk us through the Beating the Bounds ceremony later,' Knevitt informed them. 'At least that will give you a feel for what happened in 2008.'

'How many of our suspects were around back then?' Carruthers wanted to know.

'Believe it or not, pretty much all of them,' the DCI confirmed wryly.

'What, even Sophie wossname an' that woman they thought nicked stuff from the display case?' Noakes challenged. 'We're talking more'n a dozen years ago, so they'd only have been kids.'

'I believe Sophie's best friend lived in the Tower because her father was a yeoman warder, so she went along with the family that day. She was a teenager in 2008, while Elena Rogers was a university student working as a volunteer in the gift shop, which meant she was around too. Andy'll take us through what went down, but as he tells it, most people could have been in the vicinity one way or another.'

Burton suppressed a groan but tried to sound upbeat, whipping out her notebook.

'In terms of alibis for Dr Esdaile, the pathology report indicates she was killed sometime between nine and midnight on Friday.' The DI scrutinized her list. 'Dr Locke was in his Tower Bridge apartment trying to meet a deadline for the OUP. Dr Ryan was virtuously ensconced with his other half . . . ditto Dr Winders. All but two of the yeoman warders were resident or on duty in the Tower. The events manager Clare Hunter was at home in Kensington nursing a cold. Sophie McGrath had a dinner date. Elena Rogers was at her parents'. Charles Esdaile was working from home and Fr Bernard was holed up in his flat on Water Lane preparing the Sunday sermon.' Burton sighed. 'There's any number of staffers who are based at the Tower: immersive project managers, exhibits organisers, volunteers' coordinators, fundraising assistants, infrastructure analysts, installation specialists . . . you name it, they've got it. But in terms of personnel who would have known about that piece of paper found on Dr Esdaile's body, we can pretty much narrow it down to those names I've read out.'

'What about the yeoman warders?' Noakes clearly didn't like the idea of his new chums being in the frame.

'Doyle and Carruthers can check out their movements — shift patterns etcetera. That's if you're agreeable, sir,' Burton said politely to Knevitt.

'Of course, Inspector.'

'It's unlikely they knew the ins and outs of Dr Esdaile's office,' she went on, 'but anyone who had the Queen's House on their regular beat or spent time with her will warrant a closer look.'

'Any chance the facilities team would have known the layout?' Carruthers hazarded. 'Cleaners, housekeepers, outside contractors, people like that.'

'It's a valid point, Sergeant,' Knevitt said evenly. 'Morrissey went through the maintenance manager's logbook to establish the pattern of traffic through the basement.'

He nodded to his DI who told them, 'The Queen's House isn't open to the public on account of it being the governor's residence, plus you've got warders' houses on either side, so the Green is pretty much a private complex. Access is tightly limited, not least because the curators didn't like anyone touching their papers or moving things.' Deadpan, he added, 'I was told they could go quite psycho when that happened.'

An interesting choice of words, Markham thought, exchanging glances with Burton.

'Maintenance say they only use only tried and trusted people in the Queen's House — folk who've been volunteers, come up through the ranks or know the warders . . . kind of a word-of-mouth approach,' Morrissey continued. 'I've gone through the list, but it looks like none of them ever did more than nod and say hello to the curators.' Something in the stolid inspector's quizzical expression suggested that they would have been regarded as too lowly for anything more in the way of bonhomie. *Below the salt*. But all he said was, 'It's just possible they may have overheard a snippet of conversation about Dr Esdaile's work on the Lennox jewel, but they wouldn't have had a clue where to look for paperwork or that kind of thing.'

'What about the schools' people, you know, education and local authority bods,' Carruthers insisted doggedly. 'Don't they work down here sometimes?'

'A floating population,' Morrissey replied. 'And again, they had little interaction with the curators who weren't into fraternizing.'

'Bloody feudal setup,' Noakes muttered.

'Any chance someone could've discovered Dr Esdaile's body before the cleaner and then maliciously stuck that creepy picture on her as some kind of sick joke?' Doyle asked. 'If she'd had it out on the desk, maybe it was spur of the moment.'

Knevitt shook his head. 'It doesn't feel opportunistic. Dr Esdaile was stabbed multiple times, and I'd say whoever killed her was gripped by some kind of powerful emotion — rage, resentment, personal loathing — which is why they felt driven to leave a message.'

'Like they were *signing* their handiwork,' Burton concluded.

Knevitt's dark eyes rested on her admiringly, and Markham was momentarily winded by a spasm of jealousy.

For God's sake, he told himself despairingly, he was meant to be done with all that. But the harder Kate Burton tried to recalibrate their relationship and keep it on a professional footing, the more he missed their closeness. She could no more heal the scars of his past than a priest could pardon sin, but she somehow had the gift of creating a comforting space to which he felt that his fears and hopes could be safely entrusted. It was something about her — a mixture of vulnerability, stillness and repose — that he periodically craved and his partner could not give him; a kind of artless simplicity that Olivia had somehow mislaid on her travels, though Burton, as the hard-bitten detective, should by rights be the more worldly of the two.

A conundrum that he was as far from understanding as ever.

He became aware that Noakes was observing him with narrowed eyes.

Oh for God's sake, he thought again, that's all I need. Noakesy trying to get inside my head!

Aloud he merely enquired, 'What's the plan for today, Len?'

'I'd like you and DI Burton to sit in while we interview Charles Esdaile,' the DCI replied. 'And I wouldn't mind hearing your impressions of the ex, so we can take a trip out to Hampton Court as well. Then this afternoon, we'll retrace the Sullivan kids' movements on that Beating the Bounds route.' He turned to Carruthers and Doyle. 'I read your email about Steven Winders. It was interesting that you felt that there was unfinished business between him and Dr Esdaile.'

'There was just something grudging about the way he spoke, sir,' Carruthers jumped in, never backward in coming forward, Markham thought with wry amusement. 'He almost made it sound like she was stealing his ideas . . . muscling in on his patch.'

'We didn't know enough about Richard the Third to follow the ins and outs,' Doyle said humbly, oblivious to his colleague's 'speak for yourself' vibes. 'But he definitely implied he'd beaten her to the draw when it came to all that stuff about Richard the Third and his niece plotting to kill the wife.'

'I got the feeling Winders wasn't over her,' Carruthers said. 'He sounded pretty bitter when he started banging on about how she chucked scholarship for mammon and called Charles Esdaile a fully paid-up member of—' he gave an apologetic glance at Burton — 'the Institute of Wankers.'

'How did Lucy Winders come across?' Burton asked, her expression inscrutable.

'Seemed like a nice normal woman,' was Doyle's verdict. 'Quite plain and mousy, though.' Aware how the DI disliked anything that smacked of body fascism, he amended hastily, 'I mean compared to *him*—'

'Winders is striking,' Carruthers came to his colleague's rescue. 'You could imagine him on telly doing *Time Team* or something, but you wouldn't notice *her* in a crowd.'

'Hmm,' was Burton's noncommittal response.

Carruthers resumed his pen picture. 'She said Dr Esdaile was fine if she took a shine to someone but had a tendency to play favourites, nice as pie with junior staff but didn't suffer fools and could be quite brutal with other people if they fell short. Didn't give us any specifics, though . . . wouldn't speak ill of the dead blah-di-blah and anyway there were never any formal complaints about Esdaile.'

'But she alienated people over the fuss she made about that warder . . . John Whittingham,' Burton said thoughtfully.

'Andy Campbell said it were all a fuss about nothing,' Noakes chipped in. 'Would've blown over in no time if that interfering cow Clare Hunter hadn't encouraged Whittingham to feel he was hard done by . . . Sounded to me like she stirred the pot 'cos she were jealous of Esdaile.'

Knevitt turned to the ex-sergeant. 'See if you, Doyle and Carruthers can come up with some background on this Beating the Bounds ritual,' he suggested. 'That's when the Sullivan twins disappeared, and Margaret Esdaile claimed to have information about it . . . so there's *got* to be a link with her murder.'

'I'll take the sky pilot,' Noakes announced. 'Reckon I fancy another dekko at Thomas More's cenotaph whatsit an' all.'

'What about the ravens, sarge?' Doyle asked with a sly wink at Carruthers.

'They ain't going anywhere,' the other said firmly.

'Yes, Charles the Second said a great calamity would befall the kingdom if they ever left the Tower,' Burton reminded them earnestly, leading Carruthers to wonder for the umpteenth time what was the female equivalent of 'mansplaining'.

Calamity.

The word reverberated in Markham's mind was though it was an echo chamber.

The ravens were *in situ*, but something presaged danger and he felt powerless to prevent it.

CHAPTER 5: NOW AND THEN

Charles Esdaile's warehouse apartment in an exclusive mews adjacent to St Katharine Docks was a marvel of sleek minimalist architecture and doubtless worth the better part of two million, Markham thought as the stockbroker admitted them to the airy living room with its panoramic view of the marina.

Despite its impressive aspect, the place felt impersonal like a hotel suite, with an almost antiseptic absence of clutter that surprised the DI, since he had envisioned that Margaret Esdaile's home environment would be full of character and quirkiness: panelled walls, heavy armchairs, old-fashioned prints, books everywhere. But perhaps the very contrast with her crowded burrow of an office was in itself refreshing and she was glad to discard academic trappings in her personal life. Certainly the dark leather sofas with tubular metal frames and sleek, modern chandeliers were a decided contrast with her quarters at the Tower.

Esdaile was impeccably attired in a dark-red pinstripe so thin that it was almost invisible. He certainly looked like a banker, with the well-fed pink complexion of a public schoolboy and silvering brushed-back hair. Markham caught a whiff of alcohol as the bereaved husband welcomed them and politely offered refreshments that were equally politely refused.

It proved difficult to penetrate beneath the man's glossy surface, but his red-rimmed eyes and mechanical, almost glazed delivery certainly spoke of some internal anguish, though the DI was careful not to take such markers at face value having known many a chameleon-like killer adept at ventriloquizing the entire lexicon of grief.

Knevitt and Morrissey were considerate in their handling of Esdaile, and Markham's admiration for the duo ratcheted up a notch as he observed their tactful sensitivity. The stockbroker gave the appearance of being stunned by his wife's murder with little idea who could have wished her ill. 'She liked to forget about work when she got home,' he said, confirming Markham's suspicion that Margaret Esdaile preferred to keep her personal and professional lives separate, perhaps as a reaction to the failure of her first union with a fellow academic. 'Of course, there were the usual rivalries and office politics . . . the old boy network, if you will.'

It takes one to know one, Markham thought sardonically, as he listened to this epitome of clubbishness.

'Of course, Margaret never let that sort of thing get to her . . . stood aloof from it all really. She was well able to deal with the kind of pompous brainiacs who are always making you a present of their opinions, knew how to cut them down to size.' It sounded as though a certain queenishness was one of the qualities that had attracted him.

Reference to the Lennox jewel elicited a blank stare that Markham could have sworn was genuine, and Knevitt's reference to various Tower personalities was met with similar vagueness, though Esdaile recalled his wife being exasperated with the events manager Clare Hunter. 'Margaret said the woman had a tendency to take too much upon herself . . . she put a stop to that pretty sharpish . . . didn't like over-familiarity either,' he said, which suggested that the curator's democratic credentials with junior staff were by no means the whole picture.

When it came to discussion of his wife's relations with her ex-husband, the vagueness felt more studied, and

Markham thought he could tell that Esdaile disliked Steven Winders. 'Little Antonia's a perfect poppet, though,' he said, rather as though his wife's daughter was a toy or puppy. 'Her stepmama's got all the personality of a hat stand, but there were never any difficulties about access. Steven might have been jealous that Margaret was the Tower's rising star — Channel Five approached her about a slot on some documentary — but at least he didn't use the child to get back at her.'

Later, as they walked round the marina, Burton was thoughtful.

'It sounds like Dr Esdaile had to put up with a certain amount of misogyny from Locke and Ryan with a dollop of professional jealousy thrown in for good measure,' she mused.

'Well, Charles Esdaile's not exactly what you'd call a New Man,' Knevitt chuckled.

'On the surface he seems a stand-up bloke, though,' Morrissey put in. 'When you get past the Tim Nice-But-Dim stuff.'

'Oh that's an act,' Burton said acidly. 'He made sure to let us know about his consultancy with the CBI and all those NEDs he's been offered . . . and you don't end up with a gaff like that by being a thick posho.'

'We'll have another crack at Messrs Locke and Ryan in due course,' Knevitt said. 'Along with Clare Hunter, since it's clear she ruffled Dr Esdaile's feathers. As for Steven Winders, we'd better go softly softly for the time being seeing as he's bereaved.'

'Esdaile seemed fond of Antonia,' Morrissey remarked, 'but it was obvious he didn't rate her stepmum . . . Mind you, "blended families" can be tricky.' He uttered this opinion with an emphasis that made Markham wonder if the DI spoke from personal experience.

'Right,' Knevitt said briskly as they exited the docks, 'let's see what the others have got for us.' He smiled at Burton, their resident culture vulture. 'We'll follow the scenic route, so you can take in some more visitor attractions.'

At this, Markham felt another lancing dart of jealousy. As far as he knew, Knevitt was divorced with grown-up children and a reputation for liking the quiet life once away from work. Indeed, the DCI's private life was almost as much of a mystery to his colleagues as Markham's own. There was a clear spark of some sort with Kate Burton, however, that DI Morrissey had also noticed judging from the swift appraising look he shot her. Markham wasn't sure he liked this one bit.

Focus, he told himself. Now was not the time to get sidetracked by his feelings. He had a job to do.

* * *

On their return, they found that business was brisk, the castle precincts crowded with visitors avid for a dose of medieval pomp and pageantry.

As for Markham himself, despite the clear, crisp winter day, he continued to find the thick-walled fortress hauntingly oppressive, unable to shake off the sense that this was in truth a gilded charnel house, its 'parish church' built over a pit from which archaeologists had dragged rotting corpses, literally shovelling up remains and re-interring them in a gruesome parody of shelf-stacking. It made his skin crawl.

Even the ice-light of various presence chambers, oratories and galleries, with December sunlight on pale stone somehow whiting everything out, could not dispel the impression of brooding malevolence.

And yet the tourists milled around happily, seemingly unperturbed by phantasmagoria such as the sickening crunch of axes on flesh, blood-soaked corpses collapsing back on themselves and severed heads rolling in sawdust until they were collected in sopping parcels to be buried between the cadavers' feet.

Having arranged with the team to meet up on Tower Green, it was only a short time before Noakes joined them, with the two sergeants hard on his heels.

Markham's wingman, contrary to expectations, appeared to have thoroughly enjoyed his session with the chaplain who had shown him round Thomas More's memorial chapel before they repaired to his office. Tucked away in a corner of the Bell Tower, this boasted any number of curios and artefacts including a framed reproduction of the *Field of the Cloth of Gold*. Having come across a picture of Henry VIII's famous extravaganza during their previous investigation at an Oxford college, Noakes was able to meet the cultured priest on his own ground. It was clear too that his fancy was tickled by the idea of heaven as a massive garden party — providing, of course, that the Recording Angel didn't make him sit next to any of the high command from Bromgrove CID!

'Seems okay for a sky pilot,' was his verdict on the Reverend Bernard Doyle. 'Full of nonsense an' lofty talk, but basically all right.' From which it could be deduced that the chaplain had avoided the fatal mistake of patronizing Bromgrove's rough diamond. 'I told the padre you were hung up on poor sods who got their heads chopped off an' he said not to fret, God would make the party in heaven so good that they'd forget all about it.'

Markham's lips twitched at this, despite embarrassment at having his private neuroses revealed in such a fashion. He could only hope that Knevitt and Morrissey wouldn't put him down as being the kind of credulous fool who consulted crystal gazers and clairvoyants. As for Sidney, he could almost *hear* the DCI's derisive reaction to his superstitious imaginings. *Seriously, Markham, the next thing we know, you'll be telling me you've lived before in Tudor times or some such nonsense. Well, let me tell you, there's no place on my squad for anyone who gives the time of day to new-age mumbo jumbo.*

At least Noakes's idea of heaven was an antidote to the DI's previous gruesome imaginings, though it briefly crossed his mind to wonder how Anne Boleyn, Thomas More and all those other mangled victims could be transformed into shining promenaders who populated some kind of celestial city. 'You gotta have faith,' his wingman insisted. 'It says in the Bible, "Changed from glory into glory", which has to mean summat pretty special.'

Certainly, Doyle and Carruthers appeared sturdily unaffected by any psychic emanations. They reported that there had been no shortage of personnel willing to brief them about Beating the Bounds and all the other delightfully eccentric Tower customs and, like Noakes, had clearly enjoyed their induction into this strange new world. 'I only came here once, when I was at primary school . . . don't think you really appreciate it at that age, to be honest. We didn't get to do the immersive whatsits like the Gunpowder Plot and Torture at the Tower,' Doyle said wistfully. 'Just had to sit through some arty farty types prancing round in big ruffs and daft hats.' It was an endearing glimpse into the young sergeant's schoolboy past. He dragged his mind back to the investigation. 'But no one we talked to remembered anything especially out of the ordinary.'

'Nothing useful from Dr Locke, I suppose?' Markham enquired, without much hope.

'God, that one's a snooty piece of work,' Doyle said with feeling. 'Looked at me like I was something he'd scraped off his shoe when I asked if he'd seen *The Lost King* . . . I was just trying to make conversation . . . y'know show an interest in all that Wars of the Roses and Richard the Third stuff.'

'It was the way you talked about Alan Partridge being in it that threw him.' Carruthers grinned. 'He didn't have a clue about Steve Coogan — or anything that happened later than the sixteenth century by the look of him.'

'So up until the Sullivan disappearance, there was nothing unusual?' Burton interrupted impatiently.

'Nada.' Doyle shook his head. 'There was the odd bit of talk about a prowler, but that was really just the warders. The curators and most of the admin people we spoke to thought they were just bigging the whole thing up — imagining stuff after doing too many ghost tours — lining themselves up for an appearance on that Channel 5 series *Inside the Tower of London*.'

As they stood pondering the implications of this statement, they were joined by their colleagues and Andy

Campbell, a heavy, thickset warder with rather porcine features, a greying combover and watery, exophthalmic eyes which belied his reputation for thespian brio. He was dressed in civvies to ensure the group attracted less attention.

The man had a fine carrying baritone, however, with only the faint hint of a cockney accent, and as he talked Markham could see Campbell was a natural when it came to capturing his audience's interest — in this case, Knevitt, Morrissey, himself and the gang.

'The first of May 2008 . . . I remember the date like it was yesterday,' he told them. 'The procession happens every three years on Ascension Day, with everyone in their best bib and tucker . . . warders, chaplain, choir, deputy governor, Uncle Tom Cobley and all. We start with a service in the church and finish off back at Tower Green with the "National Anthem" followed by a knees-up in the crypt.'

Doyle looked as though he struggled to imagine the space beneath St Peter ad Vincula as being conducive to any kind of festive atmosphere. But all he said was, 'What about the bit in-between?'

'All in good time, lad, I'm just coming to that.'

It was clear to Markham that the ginger ninja didn't care for this condescension, but his DS maintained an expression of polite interest.

'It all dates back to the Middle Ages when they didn't have ordnance survey or any of that malarkey,' Campbell continued. 'In those days they had to beat boundary posts to mark out the land and make sure the next generation knew where their neighbourhood started and finished.'

'The Tower had its own jurisdiction, didn't it?' Burton chipped in eagerly. 'The Tower Liberties.'

Doyle and Carruthers exchanged eloquent glances.

Campbell was highly gratified, however, bestowing on Burton what he doubtless considered a winning smile but was more of a goaty leer which made her recoil a pace or two.

'That's right, dearie.'

Dearie! Oh my days, Doyle thought delightedly, the head prefect looks like she's swallowed a lemon.

Oblivious of this clanger, the warder continued his recital.

'The choir boys, Tower families and all the local youngsters join in, beating the boundary posts with willow wands.'

Burton's insatiable penchant for pedagogy overcame her irritation with Campbell's *lèse-majesté*.

'Isn't there some sort of mock battle along the way . . . a feud or something?' she asked.

'A re-enactment?' Carruthers preferred something like that to people wafting around waving sticks in the air.

'Well, the All Hallows lot come out to meet us . . . it's to commemorate when they used to fight with our lot over a boundary stone. These days we just have a bit of friendly banter and join up together.'

'Oh.'

Markham suppressed a smile at Carruthers's transparent disappointment that the affair wasn't more full-blooded.

Campbell must have picked up on it too.

'It's a rare old day out and everyone has a good time,' he told the detective he privately thought of as being a stuck-up ponce.

'Like a carnival . . . or the best day out ever,' Noakes rumbled with a meaningful glare at Carruthers. 'I watched it once on telly—'

'Yes, they showed it on *Inside the Tower of London*,' Burton interrupted eagerly. 'The procession even goes through the city . . . stops all the commuters in their tracks.'

'I imagine they prefer it to Extinction Rebellion or the Just Stop Oil zealots,' Markham observed mildly.

'Yeah, who wouldn't prefer you in your red an' gold to Swampy and his mates,' Noakes told the warder, ignoring Burton's frown of disapproval.

'It's a grand day out,' Campbell reiterated decisively. 'A real family occasion.'

A family occasion.

As his words sank in, the detectives thought of two children who had never returned.

'I want you to cast your mind back to that date in 2008 if you would, Andy,' Knevitt said quietly. 'Just tell us what you remember . . . who was around and did anything unusual happen, any deviation from the normal programme . . . anything at all.'

'It was a beautiful mild day,' the warder told them. 'One of those days when you think summer's on the way . . . birdsong and blue skies . . . *perfect*.' For a moment, he didn't speak, lost in agreeable reminiscence. Then he resumed. 'My missus and some of the wives organized a bit of a picnic by the West Gate, even though they were up to their eyes helping out with food for later down in the crypt.'

Markham recalled the washed-out woman who had brought them refreshments in the incident room. 'That would be Justine?' he said courteously.

'Yeah, she never likes to disappoint the kiddies,' the other said sentimentally. 'There's always a real party mood. The tourists go wild for it, snapping everything that moves.'

'I can imagine.' Markham smiled at him, thinking that Campbell had painted a picture that was an agreeable contrast to his own impressions the other night: the palace's flood-lit misty murk, dank black arches and even blacker history. 'Can you recall which staff were around?' he continued, careful not to prompt the warder and keeping his tone as casual as possible. At this stage no one at the Tower (other than their murderer) was aware that Margaret Esdaile had contacted DI Morrissey regarding the Sullivan twins' disappearance, and Markham knew Knevitt preferred to keep it that way. Best not to let on that they were linking the Esdaile and Sullivan cases lest this should scare off potential witnesses — or trigger a killer. Of course, people would have their suspicions, but it seemed politic for the time being to refrain from giving the impression that a kidnapper from 2008 had graduated to homicide. As far as Campbell was concerned, the London detectives and their Northern counterparts were merely dotting the i's and crossing the t's by checking out an abduction that might or might not shed light on their current enquiries. If the Tower community concluded that the police regarded this cold case as being pretty much a dead end, so much the better.

'Well, 2008 was before Dr Esdaile joined us,' Campbell said. 'But Dr Locke and Dr Ryan were both involved in the Wakefield Tower project, so they were definitely around.'

'What project was that?' Carruthers asked.

Self-consciously, Campbell scratched his chin.

'Something to do with Henry the Sixth's murder,' he said uncertainly.

'What, the doolally one?' Noakes asked.

A tiny whimper escaped Kate Burton.

'Some form of schizoaffective disorder, wasn't it?' Markham said easily.

'Down to all that inbreeding,' Noakes interjected helpfully.

Amused, Knevitt entered the fray. 'Well, the Wars of the Roses were probably traumatic enough to tip any monarch over the edge.' He shot a complicitous glance at Burton.

'The Wakefield Tower's where Henry ended up getting his head bashed in.' Campbell had caught his second wind. 'There's an oratory in there and students from Eton come every year to place flowers on the anniversary . . . 'cos he founded their college.'

Doyle experienced intimations of nausea at the reference to head-bashing, not least as he had opted for the fried egg at breakfast that morning.

'So what were Dr Locke and Dr Ryan working on?' he asked faintly, hoping to move Campbell off the subject of ancient bloodletting. 'Relics?'

'I don't rightly remember,' the other admitted. 'Happen it was some kind of exhibition for the tourists. The Wakefield's got a spooky reputation. Henry died there the very same night his wife got locked up in a different part of the Tower — people reckon her ghost walks at night crying for him and their son who was killed in battle.'

Carruthers thought, *God, not more ghosts. It's a bleeding cottage industry.*

As though he suspected what the DS was thinking, Campbell concluded, 'Henry's a big draw . . . I remember someone saying Dr Locke got quite possessive about the whole thing, wanted it done right, what with Henry being the next best thing to a saint on account of he was ever so holy and did lots of miracles after he was killed. Locke even arranged for Fr Bernard to bless the display and everything.'

This gave Markham a natural opening.

'Presumably Fr Bernard had a leading role in Beating the Bounds.'

'I remember he got a nosebleed right in the middle,' Campbell chuckled unexpectedly. 'One of the women tried to mop him up, only it wouldn't stop gushing . . . made a right mess of his surplice. The deputy governor wasn't best pleased, told him he should get back to base and have a clean-up before the reception down in the crypt.' He thought hard for a moment. 'Like I say, him, Dr Locke and Dr Ryan were definitely around.'

'S'pose Dr Esdaile's intern an' the conservation lass weren't knocking about back then,' Noakes remarked disingenuously.

Campbell screwed up his eyes. 'Actually, I'm almost sure I saw both of 'em,' he said. 'That Sophie was with her little mate — she was at school with John Whittingham's kids — and the other one . . . Elena . . . I think she came with a crowd from the gift shop. It was a group of students . . . they got a bit rowdy at one point, just high spirits, but Old Mother Hunter gave them a right rollicking. Then there was a coachload of folk who came over from Hampton Court . . .'

'Was Steven Winders one of them by any chance?' Markham slipped it in casually as if he was simply racking his brain for the names of personnel from the other royal palace.

'I remember Lucy from HR being there . . . yeah that's right, though she was just an admin assistant in those days.' The warder slapped his forehead theatrically. 'And now I come to think of it, Winders was knocking about too. There was a load of them from the Historic England Ph.D.

programme . . . It was quite a surprise when him and Lucy got together. What with him being a curator and having this hotshot CV, everyone thought she was punching above.'

Burton's lips thinned at this.

'Was Winders still married to Dr Esdaile in 2008?' Markham asked.

'It was 2010 when Dr Esdaile started here and they got divorced a year or so after that . . . It must've been 2012 when she married again 'cos that's when they changed her details in the handbook . . . she was Winders up till then, took her husband's surname,' he added approvingly without appearing to notice Burton's disapproval of such unemancipated conventionalism.

It was beginning to look as though no one could definitively be discounted for the Sullivan abduction, Markham thought wearily.

'You mentioned earlier that it was like a family day out,' he said to Campbell. 'Children milling around, that kind of thing.'

Was it his imagination or did the warder's expression turn suddenly wary?

'Yeah, that's right . . . Beating the Bounds is always a big deal. The kids all get a bit hyper. It's funny how the City gents in their posh suits disappear down the Tube when they see us coming. And the pedestrians all make way . . . like the parting of the Red Sea.'

'Do you recall Annie and Dominic Sullivan at all?' Markham asked swiftly, before the warder travelled any further down memory lane. He kept his tone inconsequential, as if he was asking questions by rote without any hope of revelations or startling new intelligence.

Campbell visibly relaxed.

'I remember their mum had to pull them up once or twice when they got over-excited,' he chuckled. 'That's Marie Sullivan . . . her husband's some bigwig fundraiser for Hampton Court . . . a trustee or director, something like that. She's got no airs and graces about her, always happy to get stuck in . . . brought a couple of cakes for the picnic.' The man gulped. 'I'll never forget how she started shrieking fit to raise the dead when she couldn't find her kids after we got back up the hill from Trinity House . . . It was pandemonium after that.'

'What about the other youngsters who were there?' Carruthers demanded. 'Did any of them see the twins slope off by themselves . . . or notice anyone approach them?'

'It was such a crowd,' Campbell shrugged helplessly. 'Their mum only looked away for a few minutes 'cos someone wanted to have a word . . . then when she turned round, there was no sign . . . like the walls had closed over them or something.'

'So that was definitely where they vanished?' Carruthers persisted. 'Back at the Tower?'

'Seemed to be,' the other said uncertainly. 'Leastways, their mum was positive she saw them chasing each other round the Green . . . Whittingham's missus said they were being a bit of a nuisance and told them to stay out of the church. She thought they called out something about going to look at the ravens and a couple of the other wives saw them running towards Coldharbour Gate. The Ravenmaster was positive they never showed up on the South Lawn, but one of the caterers spotted them playing in the moat . . . And then suddenly, they were gone . . . like the earth just opened and swallowed them down.'

An uncomfortable silence followed.

'D'you feel up to retracing the route you took in 2008?' Knevitt asked Campbell finally. 'That'll give us a flavour of the event.' And maybe jog the warder's memory, in case something came back to him about one of his fellow revellers.

There was a feeling of worlds colliding as the warder escorted them through the itinerary, despite there being no halberd, mace, pike or other fancy dress to set tourist cameras clicking.

Tower Gateway, the DLR station, Tower Bridge, Tower Hill, Trinity House . . .

Landmarks went by in a haze of crowds, noise and traffic fumes. The chaos on the pavements must have been even greater in early summer, Markham thought as he tried to imagine that day in 2008, listening with one ear as Andy Campbell talked jovially of scouts and children whacking the boundary markers and each other with their sticks.

Despite the warder conscientiously parading them past each of the thirty-one markers (Doyle muttered under his breath that it felt more like a hundred and thirty-one), the exercise did nothing to unearth any buried memories.

'Nothing comes back to me,' Campbell said apologetically once they arrived back outside the Queen's House. 'Leastways nothing about anyone trying it on with the kids.'

'Could someone mebbe have snuck back in with you?' Noakes asked. 'Tagged along at the back of the procession an' then somehow enticed 'em away when their mum weren't looking?'

'You need a ticket to get into the Tower,' Campbell replied, 'unless you work there or you're covered 'cos you're with staff . . . like the families . . . kids and grandkids . . .'

'What about the All Hallows mob?' Noakes demanded. 'Who vouches for *them*?'

'Oh, the vicar gives out special visitor passes, so it's not a free-for-all with every Tom, Dick and Harry rocking up for free grub.'

Turning the Tower into Party Central sounded like a perfect safeguarding nightmare, Carruthers reflected sourly as he tried to imagine children tearing around the place high on sugar and the exhilaration of bashing each other with sticks, because that's what it boiled down to, no matter the Shakesperean style palaver — 'prithee good neighbours, let us pass in peace' — and all that bollocks.

After Campbell had left them and they were back in the incident room, the DS expressed himself forcefully on the subject.

'I reckon someone could easily have joined in without anyone noticing they didn't belong,' he insisted.

'You mean someone from outside?' Burton asked. 'Someone who stalked the twins and then pounced when their mum got distracted?'

'Exactly.'

The DI shook her head slowly. 'I don't see it,' she said finally. 'Even if security *was* sloppy that day, it would be too big a risk . . . they'd stick out like a sore thumb if they were lurking back at the Green spying on kids.'

'By all accounts, Annie and Dominic were a feisty pair,' Knevitt said. 'Mum was adamant they knew all about stranger danger and there was no way they'd go off with just anyone.'

'It had to have been someone they knew,' Morrissey concurred. 'Someone they *trusted*.'

'Don't forget what the warders said about kids going walkabout and being frightened by a ghost,' Doyle added. '*They* thought it had to be an inside job.'

'The initial police investigation proceeded on the assumption that the twins were snatched and then taken *out of* the Tower,' Knevitt resumed. 'The SIO Tony McKenna insisted it was an opportunistic abduction and they were just in the wrong place at the wrong time.'

Burton was visibly taken aback. 'What, you mean he didn't bother with a proper search or use GPR?'

'He attached quite a lot of weight to those sightings of the kids heading away from the Green,' the DCI replied, not without a certain embarrassment. 'The eyewitness statements seemed very credible at the time.'

And McKenna's bosses would doubtless have issued a fatwa against undue interference with the flow of tourists through one of the capital's top visitor attractions, Markham thought cynically, seeing his own dismay reflected in the others' eyes.

'Again, pretty difficult to imagine a total stranger bundling two nine-year-olds out of the moat,' Burton continued after a pregnant pause. 'Bound to attract attention—'

'Whereas someone on the *inside* would know all the nooks an' crannies an' be able to hide the kids without anyone noticing,' Noakes pointed out, 'mebbe even turn it into a bit of a game, kind of like hide an' seek . . . an' then later on—'

'Chummy came back for them,' Doyle finished bluntly, looking sick.

There was silence as a succession of horrific images flashed through the detectives' minds.

'Tony McKenna got his carriage clock in 2011 and died a year later . . . The Big C . . . poor sod didn't even get to enjoy his retirement,' Knevitt said sadly.

'He was a good copper,' Morrissey put in, 'but there was a lot of pressure to deflect attention away from the Tower.'

'Forensics processed the Green and surrounding precincts,' Knevitt explained, 'but they had all the English Heritage boffins and archaeologist types breathing down their necks the whole time and monitoring every move . . . an absolute bloody nightmare apparently. Then the Tower's constable — he's one up from the governor — got in on the act and began sounding off about sensationalist headlines.' The DCI met their eyes. 'The whole thing was ultimately mishandled.' He took a deep breath and added, 'Whatever happened to those kids, as things stand we don't have access to any physical evidence and the chances of a full-scale forensic recce after all this time are zippo.'

'Even though the Sullivan and Esdaile cases could be linked?' Doyle asked.

'The only evidence for that's circumstantial,' Knevitt said. With a grimace, he added, 'Plus, I don't see arguments about a calling card and sinister emblems cutting any ice with the higher-ups . . . As far as *they're* concerned, a joint investigation just means double trouble. The twins' disappearance is officially a cold case, which really translates as back in the deep freeze.'

Markham turned to the DCI.

'How well did the twins know our suspects?' he asked.

'They'd have come across all of them at one time or another,' the DCI replied. 'Campbell told me that Marie Sullivan came along to all the Tower shindigs — Christmas parties, birthday parties, Easter egg hunts, you name it they were there. Mum felt the kids were a bit too young for exhibitions like Torture at the Tower or the more gory stuff, but they were regulars . . . knew all the warders and pretty much everyone who worked here. Mrs Sullivan's passionate about heritage stuff . . . raised pots of money for the Chapels Royal Foundation—'

'And her husband's a big cheese at Hampton Court,' Doyle cut in. 'So the Sullivans are practically *family*.'

'Precisely,' Knevitt agreed. 'They were bright, outgoing nine-year-olds who'd have come across all the staff in both palaces. But we're not talking the whole world and his dog, because — if we're connecting Margaret Esdaile's murder and the abduction — we can whittle the field down to those people who were familiar enough with Dr Esdaile's research to know all about her work on the Lennox jewel.'

'At least we can be sure Charles Esdaile didn't have anything to do with the abduction,' Doyle opined.

'He was at Trinity House that day, though,' Burton reminded them. 'Speaking at the CBI conference. All done and dusted by lunchtime, so plenty of time for him to nip over to the Tower in the afternoon—'

'He couldn't have got in without a ticket,' Carruthers objected.

'I'm not so sure about that,' Morrissey joined the debate. 'After the Sullivan kids vanished, there was talk about possible security breaches . . . warders waving people through without cross-checking lists properly, swept along by all the excitement . . . Andy Campbell told me everything was tightened up in the aftermath, but there wasn't a hoo-ha about it at the time. With it being a royal palace, the folk in charge wanted to play everything down in case terrorists or nutters fancied their chances—'

'Or they got bad press,' Noakes snorted derisively. 'So if their security was bobbins, that means we can't rule Charlie Boy out.'

'Unfortunately not,' Morrissey conceded, 'though Margaret Esdaile hadn't even started working at the Tower in 2008 and didn't marry Charles Esdaile till 2012 . . . plus we haven't been able to uncover any connection between him and the Sullivans.'

'And the man appeared grief-stricken when we saw him,' Markham observed quietly. 'More a heartbroken widower than kidnapper or killer.'

'Yeah — if that was a performance, he deserves an Oscar,' Morrissey agreed.

'All in all, an unlikely contender for our top spot,' Knevitt agreed.

'Unless Dr Esdaile's murder was a crime of passion and someone else took the kids,' Doyle mused, attracting a thunderous glare from Noakes.

'We can't rule out the possibility that these were two separate crimes,' Knevitt said mildly. 'But Dr Esdaile's phone call to Morrissey is a strong argument in favour of the same person being responsible for both. And that calling card seems to me to lead back to the Tower community . . . the Tower *family*.'

'*Family* . . . It makes them sound like some sort of mafia outfit,' Doyle observed uneasily.

'Well, this place is virtually a shrine to the Tudors and all those medieval gangsters,' Knevitt laughed. 'So it kind of fits.'

'Campbell talked about how Dr Locke got all possessive over the Henry the Sixth whatchamacallit — getting the chaplain to do a blessing and all that,' Doyle ruminated. 'What if working in a place like this turns people screwy . . . unbalanced on account of all that stuff about ghosts and haunted buildings—'

'That's what people meant when they said some of the warders were getting carried away talking about prowlers and seeing torchlight in the church,' Carruthers interrupted eagerly.

'There's this creepy exhibition in the Bell Tower,' Noakes said. 'The sky pilot showed me . . . sketches by the same bloke who did the illustrations for Charles Dickens's books.'

'You mean Cruikshank?' Burton asked interestedly.

'Thass the one . . . did the illustrations for a story about Lady Jane Grey. Proper creepy,' Noakes said with a pleasurable shudder, "specially this one of some woman's skeleton propped up against a dungeon wall. She'd been locked away in the Develin Tower an' left to rot . . . According to the padre, the Tower had practically fallen down in Victorian times, but after the book came out it were top of the pops an' tourists started coming in droves. He said Dr Esdaile seemed quite keen on the exhibition to start with but she went off it later, said the whole thing smacked of a cult or horror porn an' she didn't like that mannequin thingy they stuck on the Green . . . called it unhealthy an' morbid.'

'*Morbid!* She was one to talk, seeing as she was researching the Princes in the Tower!' Doyle exclaimed.

'Yeah well, the chaplain thought it were odd,' Noakes admitted. 'But he said historians could be temperamental — had their fads an' fancies — so he put it down to that.'

Markham noted with amusement how Noakes found it difficult to refer to the priest by his preferred moniker of 'Fr Bernard'. No doubt it was too much for his friend's sturdy Methodism.

'Dr Esdaile may have had a point about the morbid atmosphere,' he remarked. 'Certain individuals are far more sensitive to the spirit of places than others. But no one we've come across so far appears to be exhibiting signs of paranoia about historical personalities,' he added drily.

'In that film *The Lost King*, the drippy woman who's got a thing about Richard the Third keeps seeing his ghost everywhere,' Doyle said unexpectedly. 'Sitting on a bench outside her house and popping up all over the place. She has great long chats with him, only stops seeing him when they dig him up from under that car park.'

'Well, if we catch anyone talking to someone who isn't there, we'll take a closer look.' Knevitt shot another impish glance at Burton, who appeared to appreciate the joke. Doyle, on the other hand, fell into sheepish silence.

At that moment, the telephone on Knevitt's desk rang.

The DCI listened carefully and made a few noncommittal noises before replacing the receiver with an exasperated thud.

'Someone's tipped off the Sullivans that we're reopening the abduction case,' he said without preamble. 'They've chewed my superintendent's ear big style and now he wants us to set up a meeting.'

'And tell them *what* exactly?' Carruthers wanted to know. 'I mean, so far we've got sweet FA.'

'At least we can get a feel for the family dynamics,' Burton said reprovingly. 'And who knows, we might learn more about Dr Esdaile and the setup here.'

'I'll send a car to pick them up,' Knevitt announced. 'In the meantime, let's go through all the ordnance survey maps and those witness statements to see if anything else jumps out.' His expression was bleak as he added, 'I'd lay odds those two children never left this place alive.'

'Or maybe never left at all,' Morrissey murmured softly.

Dungeons and skeletons and ghosts, thought Markham, his head full of empty black eye sockets that stared sightlessly on infinity from somewhere deep within the castle. And behind it all, a shadowy, fugitive figure gliding through the Tower's ancient precincts like something he had dreamed.

Only this was no dream.

CHAPTER 6: HISTORY REPEATING

That evening, as Markham waited for Olivia to emerge from the long bathroom soak that she declared was indispensable after a hard day's sightseeing, he sat at the window of their hotel room gazing out at Tower Bridge but not really registering the view.

Rather, his mind was busy with the day's impressions . . .

After an intensive study of ordnance maps and witness statements yielded nothing, DCI Knevitt had brought in the joint chief curators for a further grilling, followed by the events manager, chaplain and Steven Winders, ending up with a roundtable discussion involving all the key personnel.

Their defences were definitely up, however, and the atmosphere took a distinct downturn as questioning progressed, with Dr Locke (wearing his most important expression) enquiring if a solicitor shouldn't be present. It had taken all Knevitt's emollience to smooth things over.

Matters weren't helped by Noakes disingenuously asking the curators if it was true that Richard III's mum was pregnant with him for two years and he emerged with a full set of teeth and shoulder-length hair. 'Presumably you're not suggesting that the last Plantagenet monarch was in fact a werewolf,' Locke shot back with a dangerous glint in his eye.

'*Ackshually*, thass what Thomas More thought,' Noakes countered loftily, with a sidelong glance at the chaplain who had obviously regaled him with all kinds of folklore during their cosy tête-à-tête in the Bell Tower.

Fr Bernard's discomfort struck Markham as more than just awkwardness in the face of Noakes's mischief-making. The DI could have sworn the clergyman was ill at ease about something, though his demeanour was frank enough as he talked about Beating the Bounds in 2008 and ruefully acknowledged his 'Niagara Falls of a nosebleed' shortly after the procession set out. Asked what he thought had happened to the Sullivan twins, he insisted that abduction by paedophiles was far more likely than an inside job.

'What about them kids who went missing an' then said all that about a ghost coming to get them?' Noakes challenged.

'Look,' the chaplain sighed. 'Some of the warders are inclined to showboat. It's understandable really. They're pretty much onstage all the time, performing for the tourists. It's hardly surprising if they get a bit carried away after spending every day posing for pictures, reciting stories and legends.'

Noakes's eyes narrowed. 'That makes 'em sound like circus clowns,' he said flatly. 'But they've all done at least twenty-two years in the armed forces with a clean service record, so there's no call to think they're making stuff up.'

'Not deliberately,' the chaplain replied hastily. It was obvious he liked Markham's wingman and had no wish to cause offence. 'It's just that they may have been a bit, how shall I put it, *overwilling* to give the rumours airtime when it was really more a case of children giving Mum and Dad the runaround. And anyway,' he concluded somewhat lamely, 'I don't see how a member of staff could disappear two nine-year-olds . . . or have any motive for wanting to harm them.'

Steven Winders was like a brick wall. 'If you think one of us has anything to do with murder or kidnap, you're barking up the wrong tree,' he told them bluntly. 'All of this has really upset Lucy, not to mention Antonia.'

Knevitt forbore from mentioning that Margaret Esdaile's second husband and elderly parents were also bereaved. No point in antagonizing her ex at this stage when they clearly weren't going to get anything useful.

The events manager was even more indignant. 'I don't know what you're insinuating,' Clare Hunter told them frostily. 'But the notion of anyone here being a deviant is frankly offensive . . . And aren't you supposed to be investigating what happened to *Dr Esdaile* rather than raking up a long-gone tragedy?'

There was something brittle and unattractive about the woman, thought Markham, as if over the years she had sharpened her face and voice on an invisible anvil.

'She's got a right chip on her shoulder,' was Morrissey's observation afterwards. 'Jealous of all those academic types with their MAs and PhDs whereas she's just got some diploma in hospitality or business management or whatever it is.'

'I reckon she'd be careful to play up to the likes of Locke and Ryan,' Burton cut in. 'She seems the kind of woman who views other women as competition but doesn't have the same insecurity around men.'

'Probably enjoys patronizing the warders and admin staff because it makes her feel superior,' Doyle observed shrewdly. 'And that's why she took up the cudgels for that warder . . . the one Esdaile reported.'

'Mind you, she's been at the Tower for nearly twenty years,' Knevitt pointed out. 'Came up through the ranks and went to night school to get her qualifications. If Margaret Esdaile pulled the ice maiden number and threw her weight about, it's understandable Hunter might have resented it.'

'It was interesting what she hinted about Sophie McGrath making a play for Charles Esdaile at the carol concert last year,' Carruthers said.

'Subtle as a hang-gliding flasher,' Noakes muttered, much to Knevitt's amusement. 'Anything to get us looking at someone else.'

'Don't reckon there's anything in it,' Doyle spoke up. 'Women like her are always jealous of the younger ones,' he explained with the quiet satisfaction of a man confident in his own partner's pulchritude.

Carruthers laughed. 'Sophie McGrath would flirt with a plank of wood.'

'*You* seemed to enjoy it,' Doyle rejoined with a touch of malice.

His fellow DS chose to ignore the dig. 'At any rate, she couldn't have had anything to do with the Sullivan case, seeing as she was only, what, fourteen or so at the time.'

'It seems unlikely,' Markham agreed. 'And John Whittingham was positive she stuck with his own kids and didn't go wandering off.'

'Whittingham's a wide boy,' Doyle said. Then, as Noakes bristled, he added, 'Sorry, sarge, but he's full of himself . . . like he owns the place.'

'Them warders are sound,' Noakes insisted mulishly. 'It's the army training. When shit goes down, they'd have your back.'

The two sergeants exchanged long-suffering looks of the 'Here we go' variety, leading Markham to interpose, 'The warders are certainly a good advert for the Tower. I can imagine Andy Campbell holding tourists spellbound once he gets started on the likes of Henry the Sixth.'

Noakes grunted. 'His missus — the depressing one with the straggly hair — told me he's always doing stuff for the British Legion . . . stand-up comedy an' all sorts . . . won't take a penny for it neither.'

'Sounds like she's proud of him,' Doyle said, anxious to redeem himself.

'Oh aye.' Noakes wasn't so easily won over, but the angry turkey-cock colour subsided.

'Elena Rogers was a waste of space,' the DS continued, moving on to safer ground. 'D'you reckon she's always that dippy or is it some kind of act?' he wondered. 'I mean, she looked at me like I was talking Swahili when I asked about the day the twins disappeared.'

'She certainly came across as quite dreamy and timid,' Knevitt answered. 'Easily bullied, I'd say.'

'By Margaret Esdaile?' Morrissey probed.

'By anyone really,' Knevitt told him. 'She had a put-upon look about her . . . only really came to life when she talked about the padre and that Christian Union shindig he did for her uni.'

Carruthers yawned, having clearly been underwhelmed by the conservator. 'York, wasn't it . . . History of Art or something like that?'

'Anthropology and History of Art actually,' Burton corrected him. 'She got a First—'

'But it didn't get her anywhere with our ice maiden,' Carruthers said sarcastically, using Knevitt's moniker for Dr Esdaile. 'Doesn't look like they bonded over Tudor artefacts or anything like that.'

'True,' Knevitt said. 'And there was that misunderstanding over the horoscope thing which ended up on her desk . . . but she didn't seem to have any animus against Dr Esdaile—'

'As opposed to Clare Hunter,' Doyle interrupted. 'You could tell Elena really didn't like *her* one bit . . . guess the old witch made her life a misery.'

'Yeah 'cos she's got "victim" written all over her,' Carruthers agreed.

'Any road, didn't seem like Elena remembered owt about Beating the Bounds or the Sullivan kids,' Noakes concluded.

'Only had eyes for the Rev Bernard,' Doyle commented slyly.

'It was the church service that impressed her,' Burton said stiffly as her colleagues exchanged sceptical glances.

Now as Markham sat mulling the roster of suspects, Olivia wandered in barefoot and scented, her long hair wrapped in a towel and a contented expression playing about her lips.

'I take it we'll be opting for room service again,' he said with a grin, thinking that she looked like an odalisque, her grey-green eyes and feline bone structure enhanced by the turban.

She perched on the edge of the bed, smiling apologetically. 'Sorry to be so lazy, Gil, but all that trudging around really took it out of me . . . I'll be up for trying out one of the restaurants tomorrow, though.'

'No worries, sweetheart. I take it the footslog was worth it.'

'Oh definitely.' And she proceeded to regale him with her impressions of the Tower.

'It must have been a bustling place in Tudor times,' she concluded, 'though all anyone seems to care about these days are the dungeons and torture.'

'That's what keeps the Tower in business, Liv,' he said caustically. 'The delicious thrill of imagining the sharpening of steel and the headsman in a hideous black mask advancing with his axe.' Mischievously, he hummed a few bars of the 'Dead March from Saul'.

'Pretty voyeuristic.' She grimaced. 'But the warders did a great job ramping up the horror. One of them told me there's any number of secret subterranean passages and oubliettes that would have been infested with rats and flooded with water. It was the lucky ones like Jane Grey and Walter Raleigh who ended up in the cells, while the rest got chucked away like refuse.'

'Did you do the torture tour then?' he asked. 'Take in the scavenger's daughter and all the other contortionist horrors like Little Ease, the cell where you couldn't stand upright?'

'I wasn't in the mood for all that . . . saw the Crown Jewels and the White Tower, tagged along with a couple of the yeoman warder tours. Apparently you can book a private visit and skip the queues, but I quite enjoyed just drifting around imbibing it all. The twisty-turny staircases were a bit unnerving,' Olivia continued. 'Gave me vertigo when I looked round the White Tower.'

'Did you manage to see the stairs where they found Richard the Third's murdered nephews?'

'That was a bit underwhelming actually — just the remnant in a niche halfway up the external wooden staircase . . . But—' she winked at him — 'I got one of the warders to show me inside the church where all the famous folk are buried.'

'How did you manage that? It's meant to be out of bounds to the public.'

'Bribery and corruption,' she said deadpan. Then, chuckling at his expression, she continued, 'I just happened to mention that you were working a case at the Tower . . . your name was the open sesame that got me in.'

'Hmm. Just so long as Sidney never gets to hear about it.'

'Judas Iscariot'll forgive you anything if you help to crack these cases.'

'Well, we're some way from managing that as yet.'

Olivia could tell from the tension in her partner's shoulders that more chit-chat was required to make him unwind.

'I liked St Peter ad Vincula,' she continued. 'With those white-painted walls and the plain criss-crossed windows down the sides, it felt just like an ordinary parish church . . . intimate, with lots of light and—' she shivered theatrically — 'it was surprisingly warm after freezing my butt off in the White Tower.'

'You weren't spooked by it being the depository of traitors and headless queens?'

She shrugged. 'The warder told me there'd been thousands of burials under the church. It got so congested in Victorian times that the floor began to move and they had to dig it up. He said it's not clear who's actually under the memorial pavement now, but they can be reasonably sure the likes of Anne Boleyn and Jane Grey are knocking around somewhere and that's all the tourists care about . . . a case of not letting truth get in the way of a good story.' She smiled. 'I'd say he gives visitors value for money . . . had this wonderful carrying voice like Brian Blessed or one of those booming thesps.'

'Ah, sounds like it must have been Andy Campbell who showed you round.'

'Yes, based on your recommendation, it was him. I could have listened to him all day . . . I could almost *smell* the congregation from his description.'

Markham chuckled. 'Very salubrious.'

'He really brought everything to life and was pretty funny too . . . talked about how people were fixated on the elevation of the host when they went to Mass, like it was a magical talisman, so then they went dashing round London from altar to altar 'cos they wanted to see as many consecrated hosts as possible, Apparently the priests got totally browned-off when they were in mid-sermon and half the congregation hared off the minute they heard bells somewhere else signalling that there was a consecration going down.'

Markham found he was enjoying this glimpse into six-teenth-century idiosyncrasies.

'Fertile ground for the religious reformers, I imagine,' he observed wryly, 'seeing as that sounds more like voodoo than genuine piety.'

Olivia was pleased to see he was more relaxed.

'Well, it's an alien mindset all right,' she replied. 'I mean, they *were* devout, but everything got mixed up with fearfulness and superstition. Their lives were so hard and short, that you can see why they got hooked on the idea that anyone who witnessed an elevation — the biggest miracle of all — would suffer no hunger or thirst or bad luck that day. Mr Campbell said they really saw it as bringing dead parishioners closer too, because the host made past and present come together.' She broke off laughingly. 'I'm not explaining myself very well, but there was something almost *comforting* about the way Mr Campbell told it.'

Markham's gaze was warm. 'I would like to have heard him,' he murmured. As a lapsed Catholic, he found himself oddly moved by this world she conjured up, not least since he had his own creed of fidelity to the dead whom he always imagined as mingled in a real sense with those still upon earth.

'I even got to see inside the crypt,' Olivia told him.

'What did you make of it?'

'Now that *did* feel sad,' she said. 'I kept thinking of what you said about all those bone chests in the walls. Mr Campbell was in his element, though, banging on about excavations and re-interments and osteoarchaeology till in the end I couldn't wait to get out of there. I know it's a terribly holy place because of Thomas More, but somehow . . .' Her voice trailed off uncertainly. 'I wasn't crazy about that ghastly modernist sculpture on Tower Green commemorating the site of the scaffold with some sort of strange glass lozenge meant to represent a pillow. The actual block's inside the church, but I didn't look too closely. Mr Campbell said if I wanted, he could arrange a visit to More's cell in the Bell Tower but I told him I'd take a rain check. I remembered what you said about George finding it cold and depressing, and I felt I'd had enough of chilly stone rooms for one day.'

'Clearly Mr Campbell took quite a shine to you.'

'Well, I reckon I was a good listener and it made a change from escorting brash Americans,' she retorted. 'Though I felt a bit squeamish about his commentary, especially the story about some poor sixty-seven-year-old woman who wouldn't lie down for the executioner and ended up being chased round the scaffold until she was hacked to death. Her only crime was being in the line of succession or something like that.' She gave a shaky laugh. 'George would have loved it.'

'Talking of Noakesy, I believe we can expect a visit from Muriel at the weekend.'

'Oh God, *no* . . . I can just imagine her mugging up on the Tudors, all ready to dazzle you with historical vignettes, only she's bound to say *vinaigrettes*.' Olivia deliberately over-reacted, seeing how the raillery relaxed him.

'We can take her for afternoon tea,' he suggested.

'It'll have to be somewhere like Fortnum's,' she sighed. 'No way is She Who Must Be Obeyed going to slum it in the New Armouries Café even if their chocolate cake *is* epic.'

'Well, assuming we get a break in the case, there should be time.'

She judged it was all right to broach darker subjects.

'How did it go with the Sullivans?' This was the question she had been burning to ask. Something had held her back from enquiring about the missing youngsters: a mix of squeamishness around the whole subject of child murder combined with the sense of being locked out of her partner's professional concerns. A sudden feeling of resentment slashed at her — Kate Burton would have no difficulty choosing the right moment to speak, whereas Olivia so often felt as though she were treading on eggshells.

He pulled a face. 'It was unfortunate that they had to hear about the cold case investigation from someone else.'

'Who tipped them off?'

'They wouldn't say.' He frowned. 'The husband came across as a bit of a stuffed shirt . . . did lots of name-dropping: "my friend Sir Mark Rowley," that kind of thing, but Marie Sullivan's a class act. Gamine and dainty like that dancer you so admire . . . the one who used to be a judge on *Strictly Come Dancing*.'

As a balletomane and obsessive watcher of the hit TV show, Olivia was intrigued by this description. 'You mean Darcey Bussell?'

'That's the one.' He nodded. 'Apparently Marie was a pupil at the Royal Ballet School, but ankle injuries put paid to a professional career so she retrained as a dance teacher. Very ladylike and poised.' Unexpectedly, he chuckled. 'Doyle was a bit overawed . . . said afterwards it was like having tea with the queen.'

She smiled, imagining the lanky sergeant's discomfiture.

'What did you tell them?'

Markham sighed. 'As little as possible, though it was obvious Marie's fixated on the idea that the kidnapper and Margaret Esdaile's killer are one and the same . . . very bitter that the original SIO treated her like a hysterical nuisance and turned the spotlight away from the Tower, whereas she always felt the answer lay somewhere inside the walls.'

'What about her husband?' Olivia wanted to know. 'Does he see it the same way?'

'As far as the twins are concerned, I'd say he favours the opportunistic snatch theory,' came the reply. 'That's because he can't get his head round the notion of anyone connected with historic palaces doing such a thing . . . to him it would be a *defilement*.'

'So they're not on the same page then?'

'Well, Simon Sullivan may be stodgy and self-satisfied — rather like Charles Esdaile come to think of it — but I'd say he's a caring husband who wants Marie to have some sort of closure.'

'Presumably they think the twins are dead.'

Markham's handsome features suddenly appeared tired and strained. 'Oh yes,' he said softly. 'But they'd like to lay them to rest . . . until then, they're in some ghastly limbo.'

'What were they like, the twins?'

He slipped a picture from his trouser pocket and gave it to her.

Olivia took a long look before handing the snap back. 'Adorable,' she said. 'Little blonde angels.'

'Well, Marie said they had a mischievous streak, but sounds like they were good youngsters . . . and totally devoted to each other. She was positive they'd have screamed blue murder if anyone laid a hand on them.'

'Maybe they were just enticed away,' Olivia suggested. 'Went willingly with someone because they didn't realize the danger.'

'Marie's adamant it couldn't have happened like that,' he said wearily. 'As far as she's concerned, it *had* to have been someone they knew.'

'Did you tell them about Margaret Esdaile's call to the police?'

'Yes,' he said. 'Knevitt felt we owed then that at least, but he stressed it was imperative they kept it to themselves.' Unexpectedly, the chiselled features softened. 'Noakesy came up trumps . . . told Marie all about his exploits on the ball-room dancing circuit. By the time they'd finished discussing reverse fleckerls and scatter chasses, I could tell she'd decided the police weren't all bad.'

At that moment, Olivia's stomach rumbled loudly.

'We should think about supper,' he laughed. 'The others are sampling the delights of Vicinity tonight,' he added, referring to the hotel's principal restaurant. 'I imagine Noakes intends to regale them with further historical gems from Fr Bernard.'

'Funny that George and the chaplain should have hit it off like that,' she commented.

'Oh, they're well on the way to becoming firm friends,' was the dry response. 'Last thing I heard, Noakesy was fulminating about churches being overrun by charismatic types who won't be happy till they have everyone dancing in the aisles and doing the lotus position.'

'I take it there'll be nothing like that at Dr Esdaile's funeral on Sunday.'

'Definitely not. Apparently she was a traditionalist, so it'll be the Book of Common Prayer and old-fashioned hymns like "Jerusalem"—'

'Dark satanic mills and boom, as George calls it,' she chuckled.

Markham joined in. 'Carruthers wasn't too keen on the religious small talk. He told Fr Bernard he didn't go "church shopping" because if you back all the favourites, you're bound to go bust. Noakes was cross about that, said it didn't create the right impression and gave him the cold shoulder for the rest of the afternoon.'

'Oh dear.'

'Well the Good Book says, "Let not the sun go down on your anger," but Noakesy keeps his brightly burning in its rightful place, up in the sky.'

'He'll come off his high horse once he's had a few beers.' Olivia knew their old friend well. 'Besides, he'll want to share his hoard of historical nuggets.'

'He's certainly gleaned plenty of fascinating titbits . . . I had no idea there's a secret passage from the Queen's

House — they call it that, even though technically it's the King's House now — through to Thomas More's cell in the Bell Tower, only accessible to the constable apparently. And I didn't know that they're still unearthing skeletons from under the church . . . a few years ago they dug up the five-hundred-year-old bodies of a middle-aged woman and seven-year-old child—'

'As in prisoners . . . people who'd been executed?'

'No, apparently these were just ordinary folk who died of natural causes and were buried at different times close to the church entrance . . . part of the Tower community.'

She shivered. '*Community* makes it sound all normal and cosy, like a little village. But if Marie Sullivan's right, then someone on the inside kidnapped those children and later murdered Dr Esdaile to stop her telling what she knew.' She paused for a minute. 'Is there going to be a search for the twins' bodies, Gil?'

'Not based on what we've got . . . As things stand, we can't place them with any of our suspects after that last sighting on Tower Green. In fact, if anything, the available witness evidence points to them heading *away* from the inner precincts towards the moat. With the Tower being such a famous monument, there'd be an almighty hoo-ha if we suggested any kind of forensic excavations — assuming we had the slightest clue where to look.'

'So what happens next?' she asked, picking up the room-service menu.

'We'll have another crack at the maintenance people tomorrow morning. Logbooks for 2008 weren't available yesterday — some bonkers system of permissions, you wouldn't *believe* the palaver, like we had designs on the Crown Jewels or something — but the plan is to go through the records with a toothcomb, check for any unusual requests or activity, stuff like that.' Markham exhaled deeply. 'Excuse the vernacular, sweetheart, but to quote Noakesy, at this stage we're pissing in the wind.'

She reached out and took his hand.

'You'll get a break in the case, my love, never fear.'

Our best hope is that the killer tries again. But he didn't say the words out loud.

'Right.' His partner's tone was brisk as she scanned the room-service menu. 'How does veal escalope and fries grab you?'

'Sounds perfect.'

'With blueberry cheesecake for pudding,' she murmured ecstatically. Despite her willowy frame, Olivia ate like a horse.

'I bet Kate Burton won't do justice to Vicinity,' she remarked with a hint of acid. 'I can see it now . . . her going full soya with the pearl barley broth and icky plant-based burger while the others tuck into rump steak.'

Markham clamped down firmly on the indignation this spiteful observation aroused in him, guiltily conscious both of his partner's jealous insecurity and the way it ministered to his own ego. More and more, he was coming to feel that the white-knuckle ride of his relationship with Olivia, fraught with all its complicated emotions, epitomized the law of diminishing returns. It gave him a high — kept him on the edge, where he needed to be — yet at the same time failed to assuage a nagging emptiness at his very core. His feelings for Kate, on the other hand, imparted a comfortable glow that warmed him right through without plunging him into a fever.

None of this internal dialogue showed on his face.

'Oh Kate'll smooth down any ruffled feathers from earlier and lap up Noakes's stories,' he merely said evenly. 'I seem to remember she was keen on the carved graffiti and a costume exhibition in the Jewel House, said getting those Tudor ladies into their clothes must have been like kitting a knight out in his armour, what with the whalebone corsets, huge sleeves, ruffs, cuffs, bum rolls and all the rest of it.'

'Bum rolls?'

'The padding under those bell-shaped sticky-out skirts . . . farthingales I think they're called.'

'Hmm . . . might give that exhibition a look-in,' Olivia said grudgingly as Markham suppressed a smile. If it came to it, she and Burton were both culture vultures of the first order. He wondered if his partner would ever overcome her jealous resentment of Burton, but concluded that this was unlikely. With a pang, he acknowledged to himself that his fellow DI seemed more remote these days, as though aware of the danger posed by unresolved sexual tension. If she decided to take the leap and ask for a transfer, he wouldn't blame her. But he didn't know what he would do without her. Perhaps, he thought with a pang of mistrust, DCI Knevitt would force the issue . . .

He suddenly became aware that Olivia was watching him.

'Sorry, my love,' he said lightly. 'I was lost in a vision of the Elizabethan court . . . Gloriana and her ladies.'

'Bess was pretty creepy towards the end with the bright red wigs and all that white clown make-up.'

'White lead and vinegar to cover up the scars left by small-pox,' he replied promptly. 'There's a theory that's what killed her . . . that or her mercury-tinted lipstick.'

'Some people think Henry the Eighth became paranoid and psychotic from having mercury-based treatment for his syphilis.'

'There you go then. Those medieval apothecaries have a lot to answer for.'

With that, the conversation turned from Tudor quacks to the Tower Hotel's gastronomic delights.

* * *

Thursday 7 December was damp and vaporous, with battle-ments and ramparts enveloped in a thick mist and drizzling shower of rain, turning the banked-up snow to curds and whey.

The team assembled in the Byward Tower warders' office presided over by the Chief Yeoman Warder Ken Dudley, a balding bespectacled stork of a man with a sing-song voice that took some getting used to.

Much to DCI Knevitt's ill-concealed irritation, the maintenance manager was delayed somewhere in the bowels of the castle despite having arranged to meet them at half past eleven.

Dudley was genial and unperturbed. 'Visitors expect the displays to be magical,' he confided. 'Maintenance and Events are really up against it this time of year.'

'An' this is a murder investigation,' Noakes said flatly, clearly grumpy from a hangover courtesy of the previous evening's quality lads' time. Doyle and Carruthers likewise looked somewhat green about the gills, though Kate Burton was as crisply alert as ever, leading Markham to suppose she had left them to it and wisely opted for an early night. He was disconcerted and half-ashamed to feel relief that his colleague had not been with Knevitt.

At least Dudley could be eliminated from their suspect pool, since he had been away at a Royal Navy reunion when Margaret Esdaile was murdered, with any number of service-men able to vouch for him. Despite not being as keen on the Senior Service as on his beloved 'craphats' (aka the British Army), Noakes gradually unbent to the man and they were soon happily swapping tales of mess-room bad lads.

This interlude was interrupted by an agitated clatter of footsteps on the staircase outside preceding the arrival of two yeoman warders, out of breath and distinctly flustered.

'What's up?' their boss enquired.

'A kid's gone missing,' the stouter of the two informed him.

'What kid?'

'The events manager's lass . . . It's Take Your Child to Work Day, so she came in with her mum . . . Only now no one can find her.'

The detectives were on their feet.

'What's her name, how old is she and who saw her last?' Knevitt rapped.

'Maggie, ten but she's got a good head on her shoulders,' the younger warder said. 'Clare got called away to check out a problem with the royal beasts' exhibits — we always do lit-up animals 'cos the Tower used to have its own zoo in Tudor times — and told Maggie she could go over to the café and get a hot chocolate . . . didn't think the installation people would want a kid underfoot . . . It took longer than she expected and when she got back there was no sign of Maggie.'

'Did anyone see her in the café?' Burton asked.

'Yeah, the staff said she had a snack but it looked like she got bored and wandered outside.'

'How long ago was this?' Markham demanded.

'About an hour . . . hour and a half . . . You know what kids are like,' the older man said uneasily, 'but after what happened with Dr Esdaile . . . and that stuff before . . .'

'Right, let's get everyone on it,' Knevitt instructed. 'Two warders apiece and we'll divide the zones between us.'

Dudley pressed the intercom bell on his desk. 'I'm on it, gents . . . and lady,' with an awkward bow in Burton's direction.

Suddenly Markham recalled one of the sayings he had read in Olivia's guidebook. Attributed to the Tower's famous prisoner Walter Raleigh, it read: *Despair bolts up my doors, and I alone speak to dead walls: but they hear not my moan.*

With an icy sense of dread and a clogging sensation in his throat, he wondered if another child's cries had gone unheard within the thick walls of the fortress.

Then the adrenalin rushed into his bloodstream, the air around him ceased to thrum and he was pounding down the winding staircase after Knevitt and Morrissey with just one thought in his mind.

They had to stop history repeating itself.

CHAPTER 7: CAT AND MOUSE

It was some twenty minutes later when the call came through on Markham's walkie-talkie.

Rushing to the Chapel of St Peter ad Vincula, with the team hot on his heels, he arrived on Tower Green to find Knevitt and Morrissey questioning a flustered middle-aged woman whose lanyard and secateurs indicated that she was one of the Tower's volunteers. Justine Campbell appeared to be comforting her, murmuring gentle reassurance that of course she wasn't to blame and nobody could have expected her to keep tabs on everything seeing as she was up to her eyes.

John Whittingham and Andy Campbell came panting up shortly afterwards alongside Ken Dudley. With admirable presence of mind, the chief yeoman warder declared his intention of ensuring every Tom, Dick and Harry didn't come crowding in on top of them, promptly disappearing to round up some colleagues who would keep gawpers and rubberneckers at bay.

'Take your time,' the DCI told the agitated volunteer. 'Mrs Campbell thinks you may have been the last person to see Maggie Hunter, the little girl who's gone missing.'

The woman's kind, plump face puckered in concern.

'She wandered in while I was sorting the altar displays and asked if it was all right to take a look at the crypt . . . I knew who she was and said no problem . . . nice little soul . . . made a change from kids who're only interested in the gory stuff and charge around chucking crisp packets everywhere. Anyway, you get down there through that arched door round the side. I unlocked it and then got back to the flowers.' The woman's voice was full of guilt as she concluded, 'There's all these Christmas services and the funeral on Sunday coming up, so I got distracted and didn't think to go and check on her. It wasn't till Justine came and said everyone was in a panic about her that I realized she was missing. The warders were organizing search parties and all sorts.'

Andy Campbell led the group down the stone stairway into the undercroft with its low arched ceilings, thickly painted white brick walls and the sinister black lozenges that proclaimed it to be a burial site. On the north wall an engraved tablet confirmed that this was the final resting place of those whose bones were originally interred beneath the chancel and nave in the church above. At the west end was Thomas More's shrine — the alcove with its crimson backdrop and pointed ceiling housing a large dark chest atop which sat a portrait bust of the saint flanked by two large candles. The two *prie dieux* in front of the shrine and another one to the left, below two prints of More and his fellow martyr John Fisher, were just the same as when Markham had last seen them and nothing looked to have been disturbed. The chamber was chilly but spotless and tranquil. Again, however, he experienced that disquieting sense of being in a charnel house, almost as though all the butchered Tudor corpses immured there were invisible splotches which might at any second seep through the white brickwork and stain it an indelible red. Gazing around, he imagined great blots of moisture oozing through the stone to assume incredible phantasmagoric shapes . . . demonic, gnome-like and malign.

Markham became aware that Knevitt was watching him with a quizzical expression, but still he could not repress the ripples of apprehension nor stop filling the crypt's interior with imaginary faces and forms. Even though he knew this to be a holy shrine, the pictures he conjured up belonged to a counter-realm of darkness. crowding images of rotting flesh, bleached bones and sightless skulls forced their way into his mind in a dreadful cavalcade, like howls of woe and rage from those poor souls whose murdered remains filled the walls . . .

Then suddenly the howling of woe and rage, the shrill confusion of voices, was gone and he could try to reason clearly.

Thomas More, he thought uneasily, wondering at the power of a surname to evoke a set of circumstances. *Morus* was fool and *Mors* death. Was this some sort of sick joke by a killer . . .

As he gazed round the repository of slaughtered Tudors, Noakes's voice interrupted his thoughts.

'Whassthat then?'

His portly wingman jabbed a thumb at an intricately carved oak cupboard which stood to the right of More's shrine next to a low, sarcophagus-shaped shelf. The wardrobe or cabinet looked oddly domestic and out of place, contrasting weirdly with the macabre memorial plaques and subterranean atmosphere that pervaded the crypt.

The chaplain spoke up. 'Oh, that's a church robing closet from Hampton Court used for liturgical vestments . . . they've dated it and the contents to Henry the Eighth's reign.'

'It weren't here last time we looked,' Noakes pointed out stubbornly.

'I believe someone from the collections care team thought this might be an appropriate place for it,' was the vague reply. The chaplain looked round helplessly.

John Whittingham came to his rescue.

'That's right, padre,' he confirmed. 'Only Dr Locke isn't happy — doesn't reckon it fits — so they're thinking about moving it to John Fisher's cell in the Bell Tower . . . more suitable seeing as he was a bishop. The thing weighs a tonne apparently . . . Maintenance practically gave themselves a hernia lugging it down here.'

'There's an inscription round the top,' Noakes observed, squinting suspiciously at the Tudor artefact.

'"I will open the doors of the prison and reveal unto thee hidden secrets",' the chaplain told them. 'It's a paraphrase of Isaiah,' he continued. 'The medievals were very much influenced by their awareness of Judgement and the Last Things. So there were lots of prayers focusing on the worthlessness of this world and the transience of human existence . . . the idea being that people should fix their eyes on the heavenly city. If you were downtrodden and hungry with virtually nothing, at least it offered the prospect of happiness in the next world.'

'Stands to reason poor folk'd be hoping for summat better once they'd snuffed it.' Noakes always had sympathy for the underdog.

Hidden secrets, Markham thought, with a return of his earlier foreboding as they stood strangely paralysed before the museum piece. Even the cynical Carruthers seemed reluctant to approach it, though he attempted nonchalance. 'The Tudors' answer to Narnia,' he said disparagingly, though his expression was wary.

Burton was struck by something else. 'It seems to be calling the world a prison and God a jailer,' she murmured uncomfortably.

'Kind of fits, though,' Doyle commented, 'seeing how it's ended up in the Tower . . . you know, with all the dungeons and cells and torture stuff.'

Noakes moved closer. 'There's a weird little engraving on the side,' he said. 'A dog on its hind legs . . . looks like it's laughing or something.'

The chaplain cleared his throat. 'Yes, it's a laughing dog,' he confirmed. 'When Thomas More wrote a refutation of Martin Luther, he said, "A dog, when goaded, will usually laugh." Just a stock medieval image really . . . a dig at heretics,' he added observing Noakes's bemused expression.

An unwelcome picture forced itself into Markham's mind.

A killer at bay, teeth bared in a snarl.

Justine Campbell found her voice. 'There's a little hook next to it,' she said shakily. 'With a key.'

Suddenly, she jerked backwards with a terrified expression.

'Maggie's s-so small and s-slight,' she stammered. 'You don't think—'

Big, bearded John Whittingham gave a hollow laugh, 'You've been reading too much crime fiction, Jus.'

Morrissey stepped forward, his arm extended as though to protect a crime scene.

But Andy Campbell was too quick. Dodging the detective with surprising agility, he had the key in his meaty paw and the door flung open in a trice.

'S'okay,' he said, gesturing at clothes stands enveloped in transparent protective covers. 'Just some musty old cloaks.'

'Embroidered copes and albs actually,' Fr Bernard protested in an affronted tone.

'Hold on a sec,' Campbell muttered, 'this one's some sort of mannequin.'

The flower arranger let out a strangled shriek as a dummy at the end of the row appeared to move.

In one fluid movement, Markham had thrust Campbell out of the way and lifted the shrouded figure out of the cabinet. With infinite gentleness, he unzipped the heavy garment cover and pushed aside an ornamented hood to disclose a sweet, pale face with closed eyes and dark hair that fell boyishly straight to the shoulders. The slim frame sagged slightly, prevented from toppling over by heavy retainer straps. Only a slight rise and fall of her chest beneath the heavy alb showed that she was alive. Burton was swiftly down on the stone flags at Markham's side, helping to support his burden.

'It's Maggie Hunter,' Whittingham said hoarsely. 'But what the hell's wrong with her—'

'Apart from being strapped to a dummy and shoved in a wardrobe?' Carruthers interjected sarcastically.

'I mean she looks completely zonked,' the warder growled.

'Right, I want everyone out *now*!' Knevitt barked so forcefully that the two warders jumped. The DCI turned to Doyle and Carruthers. 'I'll need you to get her mother down here pronto and have Tower Green sealed off.'

'We can't evacuate hundreds of tourists just like that,' Campbell protested.

'Whoever did this ain't no tourist,' Noakes declared balefully.

'Agreed.' Knevitt locked eyes with Markham before returning his attention to the rest. 'I want the Green completely off limits, with an exclusion zone from the Bloody Tower to Waterloo Barracks. And not a word about Maggie Hunter leaves this room. *Not a word.* If anything leaks, I'll know where to look,' he added menacingly.

'D'you reckon it's the same nutter who did for the Sullivan kids . . . and Dr Esdaile?'

Andy Campbell's blunt question left the team in no doubt that any hope of playing down a connection between the two investigations had finally gone up in smoke.

'We're following up various leads, but you'll appreciate we can't talk about ongoing investigations,' Knevitt said evenly, aware that this was scant comfort to a community where everyone was now under suspicion.

The chaplain belatedly exerted his authority. 'Let's leave the police to do their job,' he suggested. 'We can assemble in the Byward Tower . . . I'm sure Mr Dudley won't mind us taking over his quarters.'

'Good idea.' Andy Campbell turned to his wife and the woman beside her who was shaking uncontrollably with a hand over her mouth. 'See if you c'n get some hot drinks sorted, Juš . . . or maybe something stronger . . . there's brandy knocking about somewhere.'

Justine Campbell looked shell-shocked but was clearly used to coping in every kind of crisis, Markham thought as he watched her tuck strands of hair into the messy bun that appeared to shed pins with every movement.

'C'mon, Moira,' she said kindly, putting an arm round the other's shoulders. 'You've had an awful shock, but a nice cup of tea and sit down should set you right.'

'I should've made sure to check on her,' her friend wailed. 'None of this would've happened if I'd only kept an eye out.'

'You're not to blame, luv,' Noakes rumbled, slapping her awkwardly on the back. 'It's the world we live in . . . In me grandparents' day, they left their houses unlocked. In me mum an' dad's day, they left their cars unlocked. Now we can't even leave our *churches* unlocked . . . An' they call that *progress*!' Seeing the strained look begin to leave her face, he added firmly, 'You weren't to know the lass were in any danger an' besides, you were helping the padre.' He screwed his battered features into an approximation of respectful admiration. 'It's all about *teamwork*, see . . . I remember, when I were a lad at Sunday school, the teacher promised to give a prize to whoever got the right answer. Well, we all went into a corner an' worked things out till we were sure we'd got it correct, then we came back in, sat down an' shouted the right answer out together . . . That way nobody got left out.' He beamed at her. 'Pulling together. *Beautiful*.'

Carruthers gave an incredulous snort, but the homespun patter had a tranquilizing effect. Incipient hysterics were averted, the two women leaving the crypt without further ado followed by the rest.

Knevitt turned to Markham and Burton who were still supporting Maggie Hunter between them.

'Let's fetch the GP,' the DCI told them. 'He's just across the way at Two Tower Green . . . Once she's fully conscious, we'll need an ambulance on standby to get her to the Royal London. See if there's any evidence of sexual interference,' he added grimly.

'On it, sir.' Carruthers moved away with his walkie-talkie.

'What d'you think's wrong with her?' Doyle asked, unnerved by the inarticulate moans the girl had begun to make.

109

'I'd say someone used chloroform so they could bundle her into that vestment contraption,' Burton answered.

'What was the plan, though?' Doyle continued in bafflement. 'Give her mum a bad scare 'cos they hated her . . . or come back later and . . . *do* stuff to her? I mean, is this some kind of vendetta against Clare Hunter or are we looking for a kiddy fiddler . . . the same person who took the Sullivan twins—'

'Maybe it's just some random sick joker who wanted to put the wind up everyone,' Morrissey interrupted.

'Nothing random about this,' Knevitt said grimly. 'I'm inclined to think Dr Esdaile's killer enjoys toying with us,' he added. 'Playing the police for fools.'

Morus, thought Markham. *Fool.*

Memento Mori. Death.

'I reckon they always planned for us to find Maggie,' Morrissey said after a long pause had elapsed. 'What with the hullabaloo when she disappeared, we were bound to trace her to the crypt.'

'Had to be a pretty cool customer for no one to notice anything,' Doyle observed.

'They must've been stalking the kid,' Morrissey continued. 'Waiting till she'd wandered off by herself and it was the right moment to pounce.'

There was another silence, longer than the first.

'Speculation can wait till later,' Knevitt said finally. 'This crime scene's well and truly compromised, but we still need to secure the area and take statements. Clare Hunter could be in serious danger, so she's our top priority.'

'On it.' Doyle was already heading for the exit.

* * *

Much later that same day, Markham and Kate Burton sat down across from each other at the chief yeoman warder's desk in the Byward Tower.

The tourists had long since departed and it was dark outside, floodlights and various Christmas installations giving the palace more than ever an air of romantic mystery despite the murk and drizzle of a raw winter evening.

'Have a drink, Kate.' Markham pushed the bottle of cognac and a glass towards her. 'I reckon you deserve it after all the drama.'

Clare Hunter had finally been located on the east side of the Lower Wakefield Tower where there was an esplanade with benches from which tourists could view the Tower's excavation project (all part of the 'interactive experience'). Looking somewhat dazed and disorientated, she was nursing a twisted ankle — the result, she said, of having lost her balance when she tried to get a closer look at a newly exposed oubliette.

'Did you believe her story, sir ?'

'I suppose she *could* have faked an accident,' he said slowly. 'But the sprained ankle seemed genuine enough, and she sounded pretty fired up about what happened to Maggie.'

'Wasn't going to accept any share of the blame, though,' Burton commented with unusual asperity. 'And let's face it, she had no business letting a ten-year-old wander off by herself like that.' After a moment's pause, the DI added, 'Noakes was very good at making Maggie open up . . . I'm not sure we'd have got anything out of her otherwise.'

'Well, she certainly enjoyed hearing all about famous prisoners having to hand over gifts to the axeman before they were beheaded,' he observed dryly. 'Plus corpses that went on talking even after their heads were off.'

'And Thomas More asking the executioner not to cut off his beard 'cos it hadn't done anything wrong.' She smiled. 'Not to mention the anecdote about Bishop Fisher's head looking as though it came back to life after he was executed . . . She enjoyed that story best of all.'

Burton turned reflective once more. 'Clare Hunter's a single parent . . . had to claw her way up the career ladder, so perhaps Maggie missed out for want of a father.'

'Could well be.'

They drank companionably before Burton spoke again, her face tinged pink with the warmth of the alcohol.

'You don't think whoever did this was *punishing* Clare Hunter for something, guv?'

'Like what?'

'Something involving Annie and Dominic Sullivan . . . It could have been an accident or something that went wrong between Hunter and those children and now someone knows about it and wants her to pay.'

Markham considered this. 'Where does Margaret Esdaile fit in?'

'Maybe they didn't want Dr Esdaile interfering and spoiling their fun . . . wanted to mete out justice themselves rather than having the police butt in.' Burton knuckled her eyes, smudging her make-up in the process so that she looked even more hollow-eyed.

How was it, he wondered for the umpteenth time, that his colleague's vulnerability invariably gave him the queer sensation they were inextricably linked by some bond that transcended flesh and blood and meant he could not do without her.

She was waiting for his answer.

'I'm not sure about the killer being some sort of vigilante on a mission,' he said thoughtfully, 'but there definitely seems to have been an element of sadistic enjoyment or punishment about this . . . though for what isn't clear.'

She sighed. 'Maggie was positive her attacker was strong, came up from behind and pressed something into her face before she had a chance to cry out, someone wearing a cowl or hood . . . muttering the same words in Latin over and over again like an incantation: *Damnati ac morituri* or something like that.'

Frowning at her notebook, she continued, 'I made sure to double check . . . That was one of Thomas More's favourite epigrams apparently. Fr Bernard said it's on one of the memorial tablets in the church.'

All of us condemned to death and about to die. Whatever else was going on, it was clear the environs of St Peter ad Vincula had a strange hold on their killer's imagination, Markham thought, in much the same way that it had affected himself.

The DI contemplated his colleague. Unbidden, he recalled an overheard sarcastic remark of Doyle's about Burton having an extra vertebra or something, which meant she always sat bolt upright in meetings, like she was a secretary — 'CID's Miss Moneypenny — bum half on and half off the chair . . . taking dictation or something'. The recollection made him feel even more treacherously tender towards her.

They sipped their brandy, Burton's peaky little face gradually softening and relaxing as the cognac took its effect.

'How're things with *you*?' Markham asked after a peaceful interval. 'And before you bristle, I'm asking as a *friend*, not as your goddamned superior officer.'

Self-consciously she tucked a strand of the pageboy behind her ears.

'After Dad died, it's like if anything feels good, I'm somehow betraying him,' she said. 'And I can't stop thinking about all the times when I put the job first, before him and Mum . . . It feels like I somehow can't move on . . . with Nathan or anything . . . stuck in a time warp or something . . .'

'How's your mum doing?'

'Can't reach her somehow,' Burton said sadly. 'Can't seem to reach either of them. I go home and sit in Dad's henhouse, but he doesn't speak to me anymore.'

Markham remembered how, during a previous investigation at one of the Oxford colleges, his colleague had spoken of bonding sessions with her father, when they sat together in that warm shed and she spun him stories about having a riotous time at university, just so the man who had given her everything would never realize the experience had been a woeful let-down from start to finish.

He had known since the wedding boutique case that the world had somehow got out of joint for his colleague after losing her father; with his own wildly dysfunctional upbringing, there were no points of comparison and he felt a stabbing sense of inadequacy as he groped for the words to comfort her.

'Your mum and dad understood your work was all about turning bad to good,' he reminded her. 'And I'm sure you'll hear your dad again, Kate, when the time's right.'

'I'm all ears, guv,' she replied wretchedly. 'But for now we're talking radio silence.'

Markham felt momentarily disgusted with himself for experiencing profound relief that her romantic prospects appeared to be the last thing on his colleague's mind. It was obvious that DCI Knevitt felt more than a passing interest in Kate Burton, but whatever the spark between them, she did not appear inclined to hazard anything in that direction.

He told himself that what mattered now was to say something comforting. A compelling instinct drove him to remember an epitaph from a plaque in Thomas More's shrine.

'There's an inscription on one of those brass plates back there in the crypt,' he said slowly. 'From St Paul: "We many be one bread and one body . . ." It reminded me of something Fr Bernard said about how sixteenth-century Londoners were obsessed with relics and shrines and holy wells, because they had this idea of the city as being not just a physical community but somewhere the living and the departed came together and the souls of the dead watched over the living all the time from eternity. So on big feast days like Corpus Christi, people imagined the streets were filled with angels singing, "Holy, holy, holy!".' Oh God, I'm making a real hash of this, he thought despairingly.

But Burton looked pleased.

'That's beautiful,' she said. 'Dad had a sort of conversion before he died . . . didn't start shoving Bibles at people or anything like that,' she added hastily as Markham suppressed a smile at his painfully right-on friend's horror of anything undignified. 'But he liked it when I got Fr Casey from St Michael's to bring round some holy water and relics . . . said it made him feel part of this special community where everyone belonged and time no longer mattered anymore.' Burton squared her shoulders as though to signal that the moment of weakness was past. 'I guess it's hardly surprising that medieval folk saw angels all over the place,' she commented wryly, 'what with the streets all having holy names: Paternoster Row, Ave Maria Lane and all the rest of it . . .'

Markham sensed she was embarrassed at her brief lapse into personal history and took his cue from her. 'It's an alien mindset for sure,' he said lightly. 'Though Noakesy would have been right at home with all that pre-Reformation heretic-hunting,' he added with a chuckle.

Burton joined in the laughter before turning thoughtful.

'That was an odd spat earlier between Dr Ryan and Elena Rogers,' she said.

'It was indeed,' Markham agreed, his mind flashing back over Benedict Ryan's angry outburst at their conference in the Byward Tower . . .

One of the warders had made a clumsy joke about the Tower being cursed, what with the murder of Margaret Esdaile and now all this stuff with missing children.

Then suddenly out of the blue, Ryan was jabbing a finger at the conservator demanding to know what she'd done with some manuscript or other, a Victorian account of Richard III's tragic Queen Anne Neville or 'Anne Warwick' as the curator called her. Elena flared up indignantly at the accusation in an intriguing transformation from her previously mouse-like demeanour, a reaction which caused Markham to wonder if the woman could be more of a spitfire than he had previously supposed. 'You've no cause to blame me,' she snapped. 'I was assessing the leather binding for repair after Dr Locke asked me to liaise with Archives and take a look . . . Then the book just disappeared off my desk in the Queen's House. I reported it straightaway.'

'You shouldn't have left it unguarded in the first place.' Ryan's lisp was so pronounced that the retort came out as a hiss.

'This is hardly the time or the place.' Daniel Locke intervened in a quelling tone, with an uneasy glance at the detectives. 'We can review our security measures in due course, but the police have an abduction on their hands.'

Now, as they sat mulling the latest developments, Burton frowningly examined her notes. 'All our potential suspects were on site today, sir . . . Steven Winders had an appointment over at the Royal Mint and Lucy came along for the ride apparently, Messrs Ryan and Locke were buzzing in and out of the Queen's House, Fr Bernard was at the Bell Tower for a meeting with Sophie McGrath—'

'Only she failed to show,' Markham pointed out.

'Well, he wanted her to help organize readers and timings for the carol concert tomorrow, but she got delayed outside with Clare Hunter and the events team. It was obvious from the faces she pulled that the session with Hunter hadn't been a bundle of laughs . . . I got the feeling she almost *enjoyed* seeing Elena Rogers cop it over that manuscript 'cos it meant the heat was off *her*.' Burton ran a hand through her bob. 'The missing book's odd, especially considering something similar happened with that horoscope thing of Dr Esdaile's, but it doesn't *have* to be connected to what's going on . . . I mean, precious items *do* get misplaced in places like this . . . there was all that fuss about thefts at the British Museum, and I remember reading that tonnes of stuff go walkabout from the British Library.'

'True.' But Markham disliked coincidences. Knevitt's antennae had likewise twitched at the altercation between Dr Ryan and Elena Rogers, however the DCI had his hands full securing the latest crime scene and interviewing witnesses.

'It's been virtually *impossible* to whittle down the timings, boss,' Burton sighed in exasperation. 'The warders and volunteers and housekeeping people were all scuttling around like mad things. Apparently it's always the same in the run-up to Christmas . . . everyone going hell for leather with their own stuff and not taking much notice what other folk are up to.'

'And all the festive visitors milling around offered perfect cover,' Markham observed with a grimace.

'Yep, pretty much pandemonium,' she agreed. 'Obviously there's CCTV at the Jewel House and all the security cameras, but I doubt we'll be able to recognize anyone following Maggie Hunter. They'd have taken care to put on a hoodie or conceal their face, plus they'd be sure to know all the blind spots.' The DI shivered convulsively. 'The Tower's such a strange place with all its legends and ghosts and relics. That vestment carrier from the crypt had more creepy engravings on the back—'

'Religious emblems?'

'Some of them: a holy water stoup, prayerbook and candlesticks . . . But there was this sinister little monkey tied to a chain next to a weasel and ferret . . . a proper little menagerie. Fr Bernard told Noakes they were all connected with religious fables and folklore, but I thought they were *horrible*.' She hesitated. 'What d'you reckon is going on here, sir? Are we looking for someone who's gone off their rocker being around all this superstitious medieval stuff . . . or are they taking revenge on people . . . *or what*?' She endeavoured to stifle an enormous yawn.

'We should get off now, Kate,' her colleague said gently. 'The main thing is, Maggie Hunter's safe and sound . . . Forensics aim to finish up on the Green by tomorrow afternoon so the carol concert can still go ahead. That's invitation-only, so at least we won't be overrun by hordes of visitors.' He smiled encouragingly. 'I believe Noakesy and co have adjourned to the warders' pub for drinks.'

Burton gave a wan smile. 'Room service back at the hotel for me tonight, boss,' she said apologetically.

Good, Markham thought. That meant she wasn't hooking up with Len Knevitt.

'And maybe for me as well,' he replied. 'Time for more Tudor arcana tomorrow.'

A door clanged in the distance.

A warder doing his rounds preparatory to locking up.

As they descended the stone staircase, Markham thought of all the prisoners immured behind the thick stone walls straining their ears for sounds from the world beyond and uttering desperate pleas for mercy.

But no one answered.

CHAPTER 8: SEASON'S GREETINGS

The Tower of London Christmas carol concert was a more subdued affair than usual, but it went ahead as planned on the afternoon of Friday 8 December. The governor and deputy governor were still away sampling the delights of French hospitality, but a fruity-voiced army general who Markham understood to be the constable of the Tower (hitherto unseen due to ceremonial duties elsewhere) was ushered to the front of St Peter ad Vincula along with his wife and a gaggle of other notables. Muriel Noakes would have swooned in admiration at Mrs Constable's hat, he reflected, as he contemplated the towering millinery that ensured those positioned behind her would have their view of the proceedings totally obscured.

'Don't worry,' Knevitt had told Markham and his team. 'I've briefed Sir Malcolm. He and his family are off to their pile in the country later today . . . I get the feeling he doesn't want to be bothered with murder and mayhem.'

'Not terribly festive,' Morrissey added deadpan.

'All the better for us not to have bigwigs butting in,' Kate Burton said crisply.

She was looking pale but had clearly taken care with her appearance, wearing a softly clinging crimson jersey dress and more make-up than usual. Markham was amused to see Morrissey surreptitiously giving her an appreciative once-over before catching Carruthers' eye and suddenly becoming absorbed in contemplating his shoes.

Kate's manner towards Markham himself was somewhat awkward and self-conscious, but he figured this was a natural result of their heart-to-heart the previous evening. He knew his colleague's father was almost like her secret property, so it was a mark of signal confidence that she had been able to open up. Watching her averted profile, he recalled the time she told him about going through a photograph album and coming across a snap of her father reading to her from a picture book. In the background was a big floppy-eared cuddly toy, like a protective talisman, which 'got the tears going' because she suddenly, desperately wanted to ask why he hadn't been able to protect her from the pain of losing *him*.

Markham's own childhood experiences had been so far removed from the norm, that he was almost cauterized from the feelings Burton described, but her disclosures had touched him nonetheless. It only heightened her appealing vulnerability and gave an extra dimension to their relationship, since he knew Nathan Finlayson had become impatient with what he saw as his partner's failure to take herself in hand and move on.

Catching sight of Marie and Simon Sullivan halfway down the church, it occurred to him that *there* was a couple who would never be able to move on until they learned what had happened to their children all those years ago. No doubt there wasn't a day when they didn't reproach themselves for failing to protect the twins from whatever danger lurked in the Tower.

His thoughts wandered to the crypt below, recently processed by Forensics.

'Thomas More believed in demons,' the chaplain had told him solemnly, 'and in Purgatory and the living presence of the dead.'

Well, the dead certainly weren't weighing in to help *this* investigation, Markham thought ruefully. And, unusually for him, he had none of that sixth sense or awareness of malignity that often visited him on such occasions. Around him the congregation was belting out 'See, amid the Winter's Snow', Doyle and Carruthers cringing at Noakes's lusty bass while Knevitt and Morrissey exchanged amused glances.

Noakes needless to say didn't care two hoots about the potential embarrassment caused by him, as Carruthers lamented, 'doing a Pavarotti' ('If only,' Doyle muttered under his breath). To all such complaints his wingman invariably responded sturdily, 'The Bible says, "Make a joyful noise unto the Lord" an' *thass* what I'm doing.' Unlike the two sergeants, Burton managed not to wince too audibly, but the set of her lips told Markham she would be relieved when the service moved on to the readings.

The church itself looked very fine, he thought, surveying the red and white floral arrangements of roses and trailing stephanotis. The well-scrubbed choirboys assembled to the left of the Cholmondeley Monument, where Sir Richard and his lady slumbered armorially on their alabaster chest, positively radiated festive good cheer while shafts of winter sunshine gently burnished the memorial wall brasses. At such a moment it was almost possible to imagine that the ghosts of murdered Anne Boleyn, Jane Grey and Katharine Howard slept well, their souls floating high above the festering shrouds and those tangled corpses without heads.

Mercifully for Burton's equanimity, the musical part of the programme now being done, it was time for the readings. Markham was pleased that the bill of fare included secular offerings from John Betjeman and William Blake, though he felt a frisson at Blake's injunction: 'Where Mercy, Love and Pity dwell There God is dwelling too'. Would it have any effect on the perpetrator of these crimes, he wondered, or were they so far gone as to be immune to the claims of divine compassion?

He could tell from Noakes's restive grunts that his wingman did not particularly care for the poetry. Despite Olivia's best efforts, their friend still had a resolutely obdurate attitude when it came to the English canon, scandalizing her colleagues at Hope by comparing *The Canterbury Tales* to a CND march and insisting that Keats 'only knew what colour blood was 'cos he failed medicine' before going on to declare that he 'wrote stuff about a Derby winner (Hyperion, Olivia interjected faintly) an' had an iffy girlfriend called Brawny Fanny'. He nursed an especial hatred for 'all them godawful "say it with flowers" poems . . . I mean, "Go, lovely Rose" an' all that. Or "Shall I compare thee to a summer's day". Yeah, long an' sweaty!' Markham would never forget Dr Abernathy's face when Olivia's delightfully eccentric colleague had quoted Alexander Pope's 'I lisped in numbers, for the numbers came', only for Noakes to retort, 'Must've been good at bingo then.' He and Olivia had nearly died laughing at that.

Noakes looked decidedly approving, however, when Fr Bernard invoked the psalmist's prayer: 'Thou hast good Lord made the night and in the night woken all the beasts of the woodland, with the whelps of lions roaring and calling unto God for their meat.'

It was a strange choice of reading, though, Markham reflected. Usually at this time of year it was all about the lion lying down with the lamb or swords being turned to ploughshares as opposed to predators roaring for their meat.

He could understand Noakes's complacency, since his friend's conception of the Almighty pretty much equated to Moloch. But it was nevertheless an unsettling prayer from the Tower's chaplain. An expression of concern? A coded message?

Afterwards, Noakes shook (or rather, vigorously wrung) Fr Bernard's hand. 'Top notch, padre,' he said. 'Not sure 'bout that reading about us being like clay in the potter's hand . . . made heaven sound a bit too much like *The Repair Shop*. But as for the rest . . . *triffic!*'

The chaplain's careworn features (he seemed to have aged in a remarkably short time) softened. 'I'll remember to go easy on Jeremiah next time round, Mr Noakes!'

Markham had been tempted to ask Olivia to join them for the carol service but felt it would be unfair. She'd attended endless such occasions at Hopeless and definitely deserved a break. In any event, she had put up little resistance to his insistence that she scope out Harrods and Harvey Nicks while he saw what pickings could be gleaned from the service in St Peter ad Vincula.

He suspected that she didn't care to be around Kate Burton and felt privately relieved that the love triangle was kept well away from DCI Knevitt's shrewd gaze. Knevitt didn't miss a thing, and Markham cringed inwardly at the bare idea of such complicated threads being up for inspection.

He recalled his thoughts to the investigation.

So far they had 'sweet FA', as Doyle inelegantly but accurately put it. And nothing in the demeanour in any of their suspects suggested a guilty conscience bursting to unburden itself.

The warders and their families were all stolidly present and correct, John Whittingham and Andy Campbell well to the fore, smart in their undress uniform. Daniel Locke and Benedict Ryan looked their usual stuffy selves. Steven Winders and wife Lucy stood with Clare Hunter who understandably appeared quite distracted, at times gazing around wildly as though unsure where she was. Sophie McGrath and Elena Rogers were together, though something about the latter's expression and the way she appeared to be leaning away from her neighbour suggested there was no great amity between them. Markham was surprised to espy Charles Esdaile amongst the worshipers but supposed he might be steeling himself for his wife's funeral on Sunday, treating the carol service as a 'dry run' so to speak. Margaret Esdaile's widower appeared composed and dry-eyed but at the end of the service responded enthusiastically to Andy and Justine Campbell, pressing their hands warmly and talking to them for some time. Markham would have given much to know what was being said but didn't care to look as though he was eavesdropping.

Afterwards, there was mulled wine being served in the New Armouries Café, but Markham decided to skip the meet and greet despite Noakes assuring him there would be mince pies and all kinds of goodies.

'You can have my share, Noakesy,' the DI murmured. 'Just make sure to keep your eyes and ears open, okay?'

'What're *you* up to then, guv?' his friend asked with a hint of guilt in his tone.

'I want to go over those time and motion spreadsheets Kate's drawn up for the business with Maggie Hunter.' The other pulled a face. 'Don't look like that,' Markham reproved. 'It's a question of pinning down all our suspects as far as possible, see if anything feels hinky . . . *not right.*'

'Good luck, boss.' Noakes was clearly keen to get off to the refreshments but, added, 'You ain't forgotten my missus is coming down tomorrow?' he said anxiously.

'Of course not!' The prospect of Muriel Noakes on the horizon was one reason why Markham had felt he couldn't legitimately ask Olivia to come a-wassailing today. 'I've booked afternoon tea at Fortnum's,' he said. 'With your wife's exceptionally high standards, we could hardly patronize anywhere else.' Kate Burton had already cried off, citing the need to review the latest batch of witness statements, swiftly followed by the two sergeants who displayed unwonted enthusiasm for assisting her. 'It'll just be you, Muriel, myself and Olivia . . . the Star Chamber, so to speak.'

'*Champion!*' Noakes was touchingly delighted. 'She's allus bending my ear 'bout that kind of thing . . . doing *genteel* stuff an' the like now I'm in business on me own account.'

Markham felt he almost wanted to cry on hearing this but knew he must do nothing of the sort.

'Well, your lady wife is quite right,' he said decisively. 'If any man ever earned the right to be a Gentleman Who Lunches, that man is you, Noakesy!'

* * *

124

'*OMG*, Gil,' Olivia muttered through gritted teeth as they spotted the Noakeses hovering uncertainly at the entrance of Fortnum's Diamond Jubilee Tea Salon. 'What's she come as?'

'Behave yourself,' he murmured as the couple followed a waiter to their table.

Jumping to his feet and flashing Muriel a dazzling smile, Markham made a great production of seating his friend's wife and whipping out her napkin, waving aside the bemused maître d' with theatrical panache.

Gil's carrying on like bloody Manuel in *Fawlty Towers*, Olivia thought crossly, but Muriel was lapping it up and Noakes appeared delighted at such chivalrous attentions.

As Mrs Noakes oohed and aahed, craning her neck to see if she could spot any celebrities, her small eyes bright with excitement, Olivia gave herself a stern talking-to. She would *not* be catty or disparaging and would try to make it through Scones in the City with a modicum of grace . . .

But why in heaven was Muriel wearing all those monstrous contorted frills and bows that made it look as though she was at a garden party, the get-up already attracting satirical glances from neighbouring tables. As usual, her barnet was lacquered within an inch of its life and would not have moved in a force nine gale, while a ginormous handbag was brandished like body armour before being safely stowed beneath the snowy tablecloth.

The colour scheme of the Tea Salon — all eau de nil and moss green — was meant to be conducive to a soothing experience, but Olivia's thoughts darted hither and thither as a bevy of waiters descended on them with all the ritual and flummery for which Fortnum's was renowned.

Despite her invariable resentment of Muriel's glutinously arch manner towards Markham (which was accompanied by ill-concealed disapproval of his partner for not 'measuring up'), Olivia could not help but be touched by Noakes's transparent pride in his wife's dubious gorgeousness and terrifying social graces. The way he glowed as she whittered on about Fortnum's associations with royalty ('the *dear* late Queen simply *adored* their Earl Grey tea') was something to behold. Even when she bestowed a fearsome scowl on him for embarking on scones and eclairs *before* the finger sandwiches, delicate wedges of anchovy toast and savoury tartlets (a solecism of the first order), he merely looked sheepish and mumbled something apologetic about his sweet tooth. There was a tricky moment when he let a knife clatter noisily on his side plate while sawing through a scone and her expression turned thunderous. Happily, Markham's watchful attentiveness never faltered, an easy stream of conversation about the Tower distracting Muriel from scrutiny of her other half's rapid demolition of the cake stand. There was another dangerous moment when Noakes, having likewise downed his champagne at top speed, appraised a buxom waitress as being 'all meat an' no gravy', but this was deflected by Markham with an amusing anecdote about the then Countess of Wessex's visit to Bromgrove CID (Sidney's boreathons about his favourite royal had their uses).

Watching her partner's efforts, Olivia felt somewhat ashamed, telling herself that Muriel doubtless suffered a thousand inner agonies and insecurities of which the world knew nothing. Markham always insisted the woman's snobbery and quasi-comic struggle for social dominion resulted from a fear of somehow not belonging — of forever being on the outside looking in — which dated back to that unplanned pregnancy when she was a teenager. Of course Natalie's miscarriage must have brought all the early trauma rushing back, Olivia thought, striving to do Muriel justice though she felt that if she lived to be a hundred she would never entirely fathom the Noakeses' marital dynamic.

Actually, she supposed there *was* something endearing about Muriel's unashamed glee at the whole Fortnum's experience and the possibility of spying someone famous (titles preferred obvs) or indeed anyone she had seen in the papers. Listening as the other woman chuntered on about what a pity it was that the custom of *thé dansant* had died out (this consisting, as far as Olivia recalled, of superannuated *Come Dancing* aficionados pushing each other round a dance floor between tea and cakes), she tried for the umpteenth time to imagine the Noakeses' first encounter on the ballroom dancing circuit. And failed.

Privately, Olivia thought the whole afternoon tea palaver was vastly overrated and felt pretty much like a conjuror's assistant as Markham produced all the conversational props in his repertoire, charming Muriel with the old-world courtliness which was as much a tribute to his respect for Noakes as the instinctive gallantry that came so naturally to him.

'Not tempted by any of the petit-fours, Olivia?' An affected trill. 'I don't know, you modern girls and your diets!'

God, she might've known there'd be a dig at her putative anorexia.

'Oh, I follow all the celebrity cooks these days, Muriel. Especially Delia Smith. Didn't she call her book *One Is Fun* as a compliment to Queen Elizabeth? No wonder she ended up getting an OBE.'

Easy, Liv! Markham pressed her foot with his under the table.

But the sarcasm was entirely wasted on Muriel. In fact she appeared almost gratified by the younger woman's deceptively deferential tone.

'Delia Smith . . . such a *lovely* person with none of that vulgar swearing so many of them go in for.'

'I think she writes prayer books as well.'

Olivia had noticed Muriel's disapproving scrutiny throughout the meal, her pursed lips suggesting she considered corduroy knickerbockers and ethnic knitwear akin to some bizarre Cossack ensemble that was hardly suitable for afternoon tea. No doubt the woman was pitying 'poor dear Gilbert' for being stuck with someone who lacked any of the essential social graces. It was a reflection that might have tempted Olivia to empty a teapot over Muriel's head, but happily the conversation was diverted into a discussion of the festive season and childhood Christmases.

'I were right upset one year 'cos I'd asked Santa for a puppy,' Noakes volunteered. 'Me mum an' dad borrowed next door's cat an' told me to put a lead on it . . . pretend it were a dog, like.'

Muriel frowned, clearly of the opinion that this was a revelation too far.

'I imagine the Tower carol service was very *tasteful*,' she said repressively.

'Well, there were a dodgy moment when one of the readers turned over two pages at once by accident,' her husband said with relish. 'Fair hysterical 'cos they switched from the Old Testament to summat of St Paul an' it didn't make any sense at all.'

Hastily, Markham steered the talk into safer waters. 'The service was indeed most impressive,' he assured Muriel, 'with some beautiful singing.' (Though not Noakes's.)

'Gil told me someone read out that lovely John Betjeman poem,' Olivia said, thinking that she really ought to help him out. '"And Christmas-morning bells say 'Come!' Even to shining ones who dwell. Safe in the Dorchester Hotel".'

'Very nice,' Muriel said approvingly. The Dorchester Hotel indeed!

Judging by her expression, it appeared to Olivia that Muriel was satisfied her example of civilized refinement was rubbing off. It was enough to make her grind her teeth, but she was glad to have made a favourable impression for her partner's sake.

'Didn't like the William Blake stuff, though,' Noakes chipped in, incapable of being squelched for long. 'I remember Doc Abernathy from Hopeless filling me in on him. Spent all them years trying to rebuild Solomon's temple in Rochdale an' seeing fairies an' hitting coppers . . . thass when he weren't running about in the nuddy an' living it up.'

Olivia grinned. 'Well, with lots of poets, I guess it's a case of emotion recollected in alcohol,' she quipped.

Muriel closed her eyes briefly as though realizing she had been too hasty in revising her opinion of Olivia and giving her the benefit of the doubt.

'Yeah, Abernathy said half of 'em were junkies . . . high on deadly lampshake an' low on LSD — as in money,' continued the Irrepressible One while Olivia bit the inside of her cheek to keep from laughing.

'I think we need more tea here,' Markham said over-heartily, summoning the waiter while at the same time shooting his partner a warning look.

'Christmas at the Tower's a brilliant experience, Muriel,' she said contritely after an interruption for refills (and more cakes).

Mrs Noakes was determined to be gracious. 'It's a shame there isn't time for me to drop in,' she said. 'But this is just a flying visit . . . I need to be back in Bromgrove for the cathedral carols tomorrow.'

Thank you God. For a moment, Olivia was afraid she had said the words aloud.

Muriel dropped her voice an octave, like an actress in a second-rate melodrama. 'And how is the case going?' she asked, turning towards Markham conspiratorially as though to screen out eavesdroppers. 'Of course I know you can't go into specifics *in public.*'

She's getting well Le Carré-d Away, Olivia groaned inwardly. But Markham's courtesy never faltered as he supplied enough information to make this tiresome interlocutor feel she was in his confidence.

'My goodness, it sounds very much as though you're looking for someone totally unhinged,' she commented at the end of Markham's recital.

No shit, Sherlock, Olivia thought grimly.

'I suppose being around all that *horror* — stories and legends — could unbalance an *unstable* or *histrionic* personality . . . though of course with missing children, it's often a case of attention-seeking isn't it. Parents doing televised appeals asking for their safe return and then it turns out *they* were the ones behind it all.'

Was it Olivia's imagination, or did Muriel nod significantly in her direction at the allusion to instability? Again, she felt that warning pressure from Markham's foot.

'So, what next then?' Mrs Noakes demanded brightly.

'Well, it's Dr Esdaile's funeral tomorrow,' Markham told her.

Muriel turned thoughtful.

At this, Olivia's heart sank. *Oh no, if it's a toss-up between notables in the Tower and the WI at the cathedral, the nobs are bound to win.*

But she was wrong. Muriel gave a gusty sigh expressive of infinite regret. 'Such a *shame* I can't be there to support you, Gilbert . . . it would be *delightful* to see DCI Knevitt again.'

Olivia was fairly certain Knevitt wouldn't return the compliment. But she was so relieved at the prospect of Muriel-free obsequies, that she felt able to be magnanimous. 'The team'll be disappointed to miss you too,' she lied shamelessly.

The other inclined her head in a queenly manner (a pose she'd probably copied from scouring photos of the royals in *Hello!*). 'Please do give my best to Inspector Burton and the other officers,' she added with a provocative simper. 'That young, red-headed sergeant is *such* a sweet boy.'

Olivia tried not to grin as she recalled an epoch when DS Doyle had lived in mortal terror of Natalie Noakes, with the perma-tanned one invariably pursuing him at CID Christmas parties like a heat-seeking missile. But now, irreproachably settled with Kelly, the DS was off limits when it came to amorous advances. Judging from a certain gleam in Muriel's eyes, however, it would seem she hadn't been entirely averse to the idea of Doyle as a potential son-in-law. Instead of which, she was saddled with spivvish Rick Jordan — and his brassy mother (who made Violet Kray look like Jane Austen). With that kind of prospect, Olivia could almost pity her . . .

'Give my best to Natalie,' she said kindly as the interminable meal drew to its conclusion sometime later.

Muriel was all affable condescension. 'Now that she's got her BA, I shouldn't wonder if Natalie mightn't be able to help the investigation with any historical queries . . . Richard the Third and the Plantagenets,' she added vaguely.

With the hour of deliverance at hand, Olivia felt posi-tively buoyant. 'They'll be counting on it,' she said insincerely.

Just before the little party dispersed, as they stood by the taxi that Markham had hailed to whisk their guest off to the station, he gallantly presented Muriel with a beautifully gift-wrapped box, causing her to flush with excitement so that she suddenly looked almost young and pretty. 'By way of apology for keeping your husband away from you,' he told her. 'I'm afraid we just can't do without him. Now that he's an independent operator, CID is greedy for his input.'

Sidney bloody isn't, Olivia thought with a rictus smile that hurt her face. But watching Noakes beam with gratifica-tion, and seeing the answering glow on his wife's face, helped to sugar the pill.

'What did you get her, Gil?' Olivia asked once Noakes had headed back to the Tower after gruffly suggesting that his friends should have a bit of time together.

He grinned. 'Does the word Highgrove give you a clue?'

She burst out laughing. 'King Charles' Duchy Originals range?'

'Yep, organic caramel truffles.'

'Muriel will be in seventh heaven . . . name-dropping all the way home.'

'Talking of home, Liv, I'll be heading up to Bromgrove on Monday with Noakesy.'

She adopted Muriel's affected accents. 'A flying visit?'

'We'll be back first thing Tuesday, but I want to brief Sidney in person.' No need to explain that this was a pre-emptive strike to avert any complaints that Bromgrove's high command weren't in the loop or that he had committed *lèse-majesté* by dodging a face-to-face briefing. 'Knevitt also wants me to consult with the psychological profiling team at the university, seeing as they've done good work for me in the past.'

'Just you and George?'

He knew what she really meant to ask was, what about Kate Burton?

'Just us two,' he said lightly. 'In the meantime, the others are going to drill down into the Hunters and the rest of the Tower community . . . We have to be missing something, but I'm blowed if I know what it is.' In fact, listening to Muriel during tea had planted the seed of an idea in his mind and he wanted to check it out. But it was nothing more than a germ as yet . . . nothing he could fully articulate.

Some of the tension flowed out of Olivia. 'You'll have the chance to ask dear Natalie for some pointers on Tudor history,' she said mischievously.

'*Hmm*.'

'All right if I come to Dr Esdaile's funeral tomorrow?' she asked, her voice warm and concerned.

'I'd like you there,' he said simply. 'And now, how about we do as Noakesy suggested and take a wander round Piccadilly.' He winked at her. 'See if we can't pick up some of those "sweet and silly Christmas things" Betjeman wrote about.'

'You're on.' After a pause. 'It'd better not be bath salts, though!'

* * *

Margaret Esdaile's funeral duly took place on Sunday 10 December, with a private cremation scheduled to follow at the City of London crematorium, that vast sprawling necropolis in Manor Park.

The roses and stephanotis of the carol service were replaced by lily of the valley, gladioli and chrysanthemums, but the choirboys were out on duty once again, their little faces appropriately dimmed to half wattage for the curator's obsequies.

It was a solidly traditional affair, but none the worse for being so. The chaplain did particularly well in his homily, referencing Dr Esdaile's Ricardian interests and her conception of Richard III as a man of intense religious devotion whose Dantesque idea of Purgatory owed more than a little to those medieval castle keeps with their concentric fortifications and moated courtyards.

'He must reign till He has put all enemies under His feet. The last enemy that will be destroyed is death. For He has put all things under His feet.'

Listening to the sonorous readings and stirring antiphons, it occurred to Markham that everything about the service had an almost martial flavour, spanning the bridge between past and present and reminding the congregation of the deceased's antiquarian interests and obsession with the Plantagenet cause.

The greatness of kings, he mused. *Sic transit gloria mundi.*

Noakes thoroughly approved. In particular, he liked how the chaplain concluded proceedings by citing the epitaph that Thomas More had composed for the tomb in Chelsea where he hoped to be buried:

> *That he may not shudder with fear at the thought of encroaching death, but may go to meet it gladly, with longing for Christ and in hopes of finding death not completely an annihilation but rather the gateway to a happier life.*

More might have been a Papist (Noakes had his Protestant face on as he said this), but when all was said and done it was the kind of good solid nourishment folk needed to hear when they went to a funeral.

'George makes it sound like Pedigree Chum,' Olivia giggled when safely out of earshot.

But the chaplain clearly appreciated the compliment, however bizarrely expressed. 'I imagine Mr Noakes is what they call an Acquired Taste,' he said humorously to Markham. 'Not the sort of policeman who'd ask what pronouns you wanted to use . . . not exactly PC, but the kind of man you'd want to have your back.'

'I couldn't have put it better myself,' Markham agreed, the two men exchanging a smile of complicity that showed they perfectly understood one another.

'That priest's okay,' Olivia murmured as they stepped out on to the Green. 'Even if he *does* look as though something's eating him up from the inside . . . like an ulcer or something.'

There was no denying Fr Bernard looked pretty wretched, but Markham suspected there could never have been a time when his pastoral gifts were in such demand, what with murder, abduction and violent crime casting a deep shadow over the Tower.

'Are we going to the eats?' his partner murmured discreetly as the congregation milled around outside, people clearly anxious to leave a decent interval before heading to the funeral buffet in the Wakefield Tower (by special permission of the constable).

'Not if I can help it,' he muttered back. 'No doubt Sir Malcolm felt guilty about hightailing it to his country seat straight after the carol service, which is why he was so amenable about letting Esdaile have the wake here.'

She grinned. 'Presumably George can, er, represent the police.'

'While hoovering up every edible in sight.' Markham sighed. 'He, Doyle and Carruthers will be on point duty in there with Kate while I have a brainstorm with Knevitt and Morrissey to see if we can make any sense of the Tower's maps and logbooks . . . though there's precious little chance of English Heritage allowing us to do anything that impinges on their precious conservation remit.'

He noticed she tensed slightly at the mention of Kate Burton, having adroitly managed to avoid any meaningful interaction with his colleague. Somehow he suspected that Burton's makeover — smoky eye shadow and a curve-flattering ensemble — hadn't gone unnoticed, but she swerved further comment. 'One of those nice warders offered to show me round the famous graffiti in the Beauchamp Tower,' she told him. 'He wasn't bothered about the eats, so think I'll take him up on it.'

Markham smiled, thinking she had no reason to be jealous of Kate Burton's personal attributes, her own willowy pre-Raphaelite allure having attracted many an admiring glance. Even the constable had paused to appraise the tall striking redhead whose dramatic bone structure, translucent pallor and witchy grey-green eyes almost gave her the air of a creature from another world, an impression enhanced by her jade, shawl-collar dress topped with a pashmina of the same shade.

'Let's circulate for ten minutes or so, and then we can make our escape,' he murmured.

'Once more into the fray,' she sighed under her breath, smiling so radiantly at an elderly surpliced cleric that he was quite dazzled.

In fact, it was some half an hour later that Markham managed to extricate himself from a contingent of behatted Tower wives who weren't about to pass up the chance of hobnobbing with a real live detective inspector. He was poised to make his getaway when there was a sudden commotion nearby.

Charles Esdaile had been standing at the head of a receiving line which snaked round the Green as people came up to offer their condolences, but now he appeared agitated as he spoke to Steven and Lucy Winders.

'I can't see Antonia.' Esdaile's eyes swept the assembled mourners. 'Wasn't she supposed to be with you?'

'I'm sure it's nothing to worry about, Charles,' Markham heard Lucy say pacifically, with the air of one who knew allowances must be made for the bereaved. 'You know what's she's like . . . a great one for wandering off. She'll be back any minute full of her latest adventure.'

Esdaile's expression was thunderous.

'How are you not worried? Given what happened to that other kid. Remember? The one who was kidnapped and turned up in a cupboard.'

'Take it easy, Charles.' Steven Winders was visibly nettled. 'She won't have gone far.'

'The three of us got separated in that crush coming out of the service,' Lucy said defensively. 'Then Steven said he needed a minute, so we slipped across to the Queen's House. I used the Ladies to freshen up and he had a bit of a wander—'

'Must have been longer than we realized,' Winders muttered by way of half-hearted apology. 'Everything kind of got to us back there in the chapel. We just assumed Toni would show up when she was ready.'

Markham joined the trio, anxiety twisting his gut. He recalled having seen the Winders couple with a pretty little blonde girl inside the church, but there was no sign of her now.

'I couldn't help overhearing that Antonia may have gone walkabout,' he said.

'It's nothing to worry about.' Winders cast an uneasy glance at his wife. 'She'll have found some nook or cranny to investigate.'

Esdaile balled his fists.

'Don't you *get* it?' he hissed, angry colour rising in his cheeks. 'She's only eight years old and there's a *nutter* on the loose.'

He took a breath — clearly preparing to let the pair have it — but Markham laid a restraining hand on his arm.

'Leave this with us, sir,' he instructed. 'You have other things to think about,' he added firmly as the funeral director began rounding up mourners for the journey to the crematorium. Turning to the other couple, he said in a tone that brooked no opposition, 'Dr Winders, I suggest you accompany Mr Esdaile while Mrs Winders attends the wake.' Watching the couple closely, he added, 'I'll arrange for one of the warders to keep a look out on the Green in case she makes her way back here.'

'We never wanted her at the cremation anyway,' Winders muttered sullenly as Esdaile stalked off. 'No place for a child.'

Markham held his gaze and the other man followed Esdaile without another word.

The DI caught Noakes's eye.

'We have another missing child.' He kept his voice low. 'We need to alert Knevitt and Morrissey, and then round up the warders for a search party.' He pivoted to Antonia's flustered-looking stepmother whose straggling updo was coming loose and hanging in lank strands about her face. 'You should go on to the wake, Mrs Winders.'

'You don't think she's come to any harm do you, Inspector?' The woman's voice was squeaky with apprehension that Markham could have sworn was unfeigned. 'I mean, she's a sensible child . . . knows not to go off with anyone. We didn't say anything about Maggie Hunter. Didn't want to frighten her. But all the same, she's pretty streetwise. I mean, they have to be these days.'

She was starting to babble.

'Leave it to the 'spector, luv,' Noakes said kindly, though the look he shot Markham suggested that he had jumped to the same conclusion as Charles Esdaile.

If we don't move fast, the kid's a goner.

John Whittingham and Andy Campbell had already gone ahead to the Wakefield Tower but a contingent of warders was now hovering nearby, so the DI told them to stay put and clear the area before dispatching Olivia to her rendezvous at the Beauchamp Tower and posting a Beefeater to stand guard over the Green.

In no time at all, the crowd, including Lucy Winders, had been shepherded towards the buffet.

But Markham was not unobserved. A burning gaze rested on the tall detective as he headed to find his colleagues. And a sibilant warning followed him like a malediction.

Try all you like, Inspector. You'll never catch me.

* * *

Markham and Noakes had scarcely exited Tower Green when piercing screams stopped them in their tracks.

As they hesitated, trying to work out the direction of the noise, footsteps came pounding towards them from the Jewel

House. Seconds later two overalled middle-aged women exploded into the little square in a state of high panic.

'*Woah*, take it easy, luv,' Noakes said to the older of the two as she gesticulated and gibbered incoherently. 'C'mon, deep breaths now.'

'There's this little girl in the café toilets,' she eventually spluttered.

Markham's stomach knotted at the expression on her face — which had turned floury-white with horror. Instinctively he knew this story didn't end well.

'Looks like someone had a go at her. She's in a terrible state,' the other woman told them.

'But that ain't the worst of it,' her friend resumed between juddering gasps. 'Mrs Hernan's dead.'

'That's our supervisor, see.' The younger woman twisted her pinny back and forth on itself with trembling fingers. 'She must've been doing her rounds and walked in on them.'

The two men exchanged a long, level look.

Markham turned to the group of warders who had converged on the women, alerted by the commotion. 'Please escort these ladies to the Byward Tower while we check out the New Armouries.'

'These gents'll sort you with a cuppa. Lots of sugar for the shock.' Noakes gestured awkwardly. 'Your Mrs Hernan were doing her job an' now we're gonna do ours an' make sure whoever hurt her *pays*.'

The sight which they encountered in the café toilets, however, left Markham and Noakes shaken, inured as they were to scenes of violence.

Antonia Winders was hunched on the floor in front of the washbasins rocking backwards and forwards as a cleaner crouched next to her murmuring words of comfort. With a shaking finger, the woman pointed to the disabled cubicle, whose door was wide open.

The café supervisor, a stout grey-haired woman, lay on her back with one arm twisted beneath her. Even at first glance, her injuries were obvious. Blood pooled around her head — surrounding it like a crimson halo. The result of a crushing blow to the back of the head . . . Her neck looked disjointed, as if it might be broken, while her glassy eyes stared into space.

Careful not to touch anything, Markham and Noakes supported the disorientated child between them and, with the cleaner's help, manoeuvred her into the café.

'She's not making any kind of sense,' the woman volunteered anxiously as the fair-haired little girl moaned and muttered inarticulately. 'Just keeps saying there was this grey figure and then next minute everything went dark. I reckon she took a knock to the head or something.'

More likely chloroform, Markham thought grimly, remembering Maggie Hunter.

'Did she see the body?' Noakes asked gruffly.

'I hope to God she didn't . . . I came looking for Mrs Hernan to ask about the stock check and that's when I found the two of them. I recognized the little girl as being Dr Esdaile's daughter and realized she must've wandered off from her mum's funeral — probably a bit overcome or something, poor little mite. She was doubled over on the floor and mumbling to herself, just like you saw, not making any sense 'cept for that bit about seeing someone in grey and then everything turning black—' She broke off, on the verge of tears.

Markham reached for his mobile. 'You've been very helpful,' he told the wiry little woman. 'We're going to get this area secured and have Antonia taken to hospital. You can go with her,' he added. 'I'd like you checked over for shock. We need to get hold of Lucy Winders too,' he instructed Noakes. While no one had yet been ruled out as suspects in the Sullivan and Esdaile investigations and a cloud of suspicion enveloped the entire Tower community, it was unthinkable that Antonia's parents and Charles Esdaile could be involved in this latest horrifying development. In any event, they could not interview the child without an appropriate adult in attendance and Lucy Winders was the closest at hand.

It was beginning to feel as though *nobody* was safe, the DI thought grimly. Whatever kind of malignant entity was masquerading at the Tower in the guise of a normal human being, it looked like the genie was now well and truly out of the bottle.

The stakes couldn't be higher.

CHAPTER 9: RESET

'What the fuck was that kid doing in the café toilets?' Carruthers asked as the team sat huddled in the Queen's House on Sunday afternoon, mulling over the latest tragedy to hit the Tower. Belatedly recalling Markham's distaste for the 'language of the gutter', he added swiftly, 'I mean, shouldn't her father and stepmother have been keeping an eye out given everything that's happened?'

'More to the point, how did that poor woman end up in a pool of blood with her head staved in?' Doyle shuddered.

'I reckon she blundered in on someone who was up to no good with Antonia an' then they panicked an' had to shut her up,' Noakes said.

'The time frame for someone to ambush Antonia was so narrow,' Knevitt mused. 'That window immediately after the funeral and before the family had to leave for the cremation.'

'Attacked on the same day as her mother's funeral.' The distress in Burton's voice was palpable. 'And then that *bloodbath* . . .'

'The pathologist says Mrs Hernan were unconscious for most of it,' Noakes mumbled with clumsy sympathy. 'They hit her so hard with that disinfectant container thingy, she had no chance. Would've been in a coma with brain damage an' all sorts if she'd survived.'

Markham's mind flashed back to the woman's pallid face and the cries of her devastated husband. 'I was planning a cruise next year for when she retired,' he had confided. 'She'd worked so hard all her life and I wanted it to be a treat. Give her the works.'

Morrissey's words called his mind back to the present. 'Who d'you reckon attacked Antonia?' he said. 'The prowler or kiddy snatcher or whichever freak it is haunts this place?'

'The problem being, she doesn't remember any of it,' Doyle lamented. 'Just some figure with a hood over its head and then the sound of Mrs Hernan shouting.'

'According to the hospital, there'd been a partial attempt at chloroforming her,' Markham said. 'It looks as though she was somehow lured into the toilets—'

'An' then Mrs H. came barging in an' spoiled the fun,' Noakes growled.

'Wasn't the killer taking a massive risk?' Doyle asked in puzzlement. 'I mean, *anyone* could've walked in when they were slipping the kid a Mickey Finn.'

'They got careless,' Carruthers said. 'Just saw a kid and couldn't help themselves. The red mist came down and that was it.'

Burton nodded. 'Whoever we're looking for, they must have the most incredible ability to compartmentalize,' she said. 'Their mind is travelling down all kinds of sick byways while somehow they manage to come across as perfectly normal.'

'A Jekyll and Hyde character,' Knevitt said. 'The kind who helps little old ladies cross the road, while in private they've got a disfigured personality driving them to do terrible things. An act like that must be exhausting. It's a wonder to me how they can possibly manage it.'

'That's just it, sir,' Burton replied eagerly. 'The mask has been slipping. They can't hold it together anymore.'

'So they're taking risks,' Carruthers concluded.

'Her dad an' stepmum were in a right state,' Noakes observed. 'An' Esdaile were livid. Screaming to high heaven about how they weren't fit to look after Antonia an' she's gonna be traumatized for life.'

'Any of those three could've done it, though,' Carruthers pointed out. 'Lucy and Steven had time out. Nipped over to the Queen's House, took a gander before showing up at the Green. Plus, according to the chaplain, Esdaile disappeared before doing his shaking hands bit. The padre wasn't sure where he'd got to but didn't like to ask . . . assumed he needed to be on his own before getting his game face on.'

'For that matter, unless we can be absolutely positive about people's movements, *nobody* can be ruled out,' Burton said soberly. 'It was such a melee after the service. Anyone could have followed Antonia and sloped off to the café unnoticed— Judging from the expression on her face, it was clear she found the idea of family members' involvement absolutely abhorrent.

'The café was closed to the public on account of the funeral,' Carruthers said thoughtfully. 'So Antonia wouldn't have been looking to get a snack or anything like that.'

'According to Steven Winders, she most likely wanted to have a play on the new Barbie smartphone they'd given her.' Burton's tone was studiously neutral, but Markham suspected she didn't at all approve of an eight-year-old having such an accessory. 'She wanted to get away from all the adults and most likely the funeral was all a bit much for her,' she added with some compunction. 'Understandable if she fancied hiding in the loos for a bit.'

'How'd she get in if the place was closed?' Doyle wanted to know.

'It wasn't locked,' Morrissey explained. 'Open to Tower staff but not to tourists.'

They digested this in silence, visualizing a phantom assailant looming over Antonia Winders and then the mayhem that followed as Mrs Hernan interrupted proceedings.

Knevitt turned to Markham. 'I believe you and Noakes are off to Bromgrove tomorrow for a meeting with your DCI.'

'There's no avoiding it, I'm afraid,' the other said heavily. 'Sidney insists on being updated in person.'

'Don' want us hogging the glory,' Noakes added, before Markham shot him a withering glance.

'We'll be fine here,' Knevitt reassured them. 'Mrs Hernan's PM is tomorrow and then we'll zero in on witnesses and alibis.' He did his best to sound sanguine, but Markham wasn't deceived.

'Hopefully we'll catch a break, sir,' Burton echoed. *Before anyone else dies.*

* * *

Noakes was pleased to have a change of scene, settling contentedly into the first-class compartment of their LNER train on Monday morning and perusing the breakfast menu with every sign of satisfaction. 'It says they do a full English with streaky bacon an' everything,' he exclaimed gleefully. 'An' Burton not coming with us means I don' have to watch her slurping Greek yoghurt or berry compote or any of that birdseed vegan rubbish.'

'Actually, I rather fancy the cinnamon porridge with pumpkin granola,' Markham told him with a grin. 'So you get to watch *me* chowing down on an organic breakfast instead. But don't let that put you off your grease-fest,' he added kindly.

Noakes squirmed self-consciously but, as instructed, didn't let it deter him from sampling the full service offered by attentive stewardesses.

'*Ackshually*, Burton ain't the worst,' he conceded, through a mouthful of toast and Dundee marmalade, having made short work of the scrambled eggs, bacon, sausages, mushrooms, baked beans and hash browns. 'Reckon it'll be weird when she moves to London.'

Markham carefully set down his cup of black coffee.

'I didn't know she was contemplating a transfer,' he said levelly.

'Well, don' quote me, boss, but I know Shippers is keen . . . he told me she were coming round to the idea.' His eyes carefully didn't meet Markham's. 'Fresh start kinda thing.'

The DI felt a queer clutch at his heart, and something unhappy and uncertain flickered across the handsome features but so quickly as to be almost unnoticeable.

Noakes's gaze now slid across their table, his expression that of a dog at a rabbit hole. Markham's expression was unreadable, however. 'I'd be very sad to see Kate leave us,' he said quietly, 'but it wouldn't be fair to hold her back.'

It was only as Markham surreptitiously let out a long breath that he realized he had been holding it in.

'Well, she were proper shook up when her dad died,' Noakes went on in his best casual voice, apparently satisfied that there was no threat to Olivia's pre-eminence. 'Shippers said it weren't healthy the way she kept beating herself up over him . . . saying she never spent enough time with him an' weren't grateful enough. Mind you,' his tone turned confidential, 'I remember after me dad dropped dead from that heart attack, I found a load of stuff he must've got off some mail order club . . . *Kings an' Queens of England*, all these posh shiny picture books that I don' remember ever looking at but he saved up for 'cos he wanted to give me a head start at school kind of thing . . .' Suddenly, Noakes's expression was misty and something clicked in his throat. 'I never won prizes or anything like that to make him proud . . . too busy playing footie with me mates.'

Markham wasn't sure how to respond to this expression of regret for missed opportunities.

'Well, you're certainly a bit of a history buff these days, Noakesy,' he said finally. 'So I reckon your dad would be pleased about that.'

It was the right thing to say. The cloud lifted from Noakes's face. 'Reckon he would an' all . . . Burton's more Bamber Gascoigne, so can't imagine *her* folks being disappointed in how *she* turned out.'

'Maybe like you, Kate only fully appreciated her dad's care for her — all the sacrifices he made — when he died.'

'An' it were too late to say it to him,' the other said mournfully. '''Course, they'll clear that up between 'em in heaven,' he maintained stoutly, for he was nothing if not a good churchman. 'But it'd be good to have a proper chat about it down here when all's said an' done,' he added wistfully.

As so often with his friend, Markham was torn between tears and laughter.

Something of this must have shown in his face, because Noakes cleared his throat, apparently deciding that this kind of talk was letting the side down. 'Any road,' he concluded firmly, 'Burton's a believer, so she knows "Death is swallowed up in victory" an' all that. Which means her dad would want her to crack on an' stop moping.'

'Bracing talk, Noakesy. I'm sure Shippers agreed with you,' Markham said diplomatically. Despite the psychologist's undeniable resemblance to Harold Shipman, he felt he really *shouldn't* encourage use of the unflattering nickname. But then, Noakes enjoyed coming up with acid sobriquets for just about *everyone* — not least because of his notorious inability to remember names — so it would be mean-spirited to spoil his friend's fun. Moreover, Markham had little time for cultural snobs in the higher reaches of Bromgrove society who looked down on the ex-DS for his ungrammatical speech, Yorkshire patois and other idiosyncrasies. As Olivia said, it told you more about his detractors than Noakes himself who was somehow above and beyond such pettiness. The DI suspected that such denigration of Noakes was all too often driven by jealousy of someone who was entirely his own man and never followed the herd.

Jealousy was a dreadful thing, the DI reflected soberly, recalling his own experiences with DCI Sidney and the fact that Olivia had encountered it many times during her teaching career. 'Malice and spite are strictly equal ops, Gil,' she had told him once. 'Sure you come across bitchy covens, but the men can be just as bad . . . worse sometimes if they're insecure about themselves or dislike strong women. Some male heads are real "Little Hitlers".'

Now he wondered, was jealousy also a factor in Margaret Esdaile's murder? Were the curator's professional status, achievements and contented personal life an unbearable goad to someone at the Tower?

He had fallen into a brown study that was interrupted by Noakes's voice.

'If Burton an' Shippers move down to London, it'll take her mind off things . . . an' then they c'n get married an' start a family.' He grinned evilly. 'Jus' imagine it . . . a tribe of little boffins.'

Markham was irritated by the twinge of sadness, almost disappointment, he felt as Noakes conjured this domestic idyll for Kate Burton. With an unpleasant jolt, it occurred to him that such a move would also bring her once more within Len Knevitt's orbit.

He felt annoyed at himself. What right or reason did he have to feel upset about Burton's private life? It should be none of his business, he told himself angrily. It would be sheer dog-in-the-manger chauvinism if he allowed his own feelings to get in the way of her building a new life down south. Then suddenly, he recalled a quotation from Olivia's favourite text *Jane Eyre* where the hero (or anti-hero depending on your point of view) spoke of bleeding internally if a cord of communion was snapped. *That* was how he felt about Kate Burton, but he knew the situation was untenable in the long-term and it behoved him to get a grip.

'Shippers says it's a *phase* an' she has to stop being morbid,' Noakes said decisively. 'Apparently, the other day she were wittering on about how one day of the year has to be the date of your death, only it's hidden amongst all the other days so you never notice it . . . banging on about how come we don't realize it or feel anything . . . like we should know by ESP or summat. Shippers had no time for that kind of talk . . . closed her down pretty sharpish.'

'Sounds like you and Nathan have had a few heart-to-hearts,' Markham observed drily.

'Well, I had the feeling he was glad to get stuff off his chest an' all. Happen he thought I'd be able to straighten her out,' Noakes added complacently.

Strange that, about one day of the year being the date of your death, Markham thought as Noakes concentrated on polishing off the DI's unwanted toast. He remembered Olivia saying something similar when talking about anniversaries and birthdays. Only in his partner's case, it was in the context of some high-flown literary discussion about poetry or Thomas Hardy or something like that. He was struck by the disconcerting thought that Olivia and Kate Burton were in many respects mirror images each of the other . . .

With an effort, abruptly aware of Noakes's beady gaze, he said, 'It'll be a loss to the unit if Kate moves to London, but I'm sure she'll always be one of us in spirit.'

He wasn't sure that his friend was entirely happy with this Jesuitical response, but it was the best he could come up with in the circumstances.

Outside the tinted windows of their locomotive, the air was suddenly thick with swirling snowflakes under a blue-grey shield of cloud. Both men felt the agreeable contrast between the coldly austere winter weather and their train's cosily warm interior.

'It's nice like this,' Noakes observed after a time, 'with the snow like cotton wool an' all fluffy. But then it gets dirty an' cruddy an' slushy . . . depressing really.'

Markham knew what his friend meant. These days, with the early fading of light and everything ghost-grey, there was an atmosphere that somehow leached the vital force out of one's bones and sucked energy from every enterprise.

We can't be having that, he thought.

By tacit consent they had avoided discussion of the latest developments at the Tower, but now he said, 'I'm wondering, Noakesy, if there mightn't be an element of Munchausen Syndrome by Proxy somewhere in all of this.'

His wingman was instantly alert.

'You mean like them nurses . . . that make up fake symptoms? Even when the kid's healthy?'

Markham could see Noakes struggling to slot this latest piece into the jigsaw of their Tower investigation.

'That's right,' Markham said. 'Actually it was something Muriel said that started me wondering if some kind of delusional disorder might be in play . . . an impulse to gain attention and sympathy by harming children. The modern imagination tends to associate it with nurses, but there are variant aetiologies.'

Much gratified that Muriel had shone a light on the subject, Noakes was all ears.

'MSP seemed a possible element in the spate of enticements and abortive abductions,' Markham continued, 'with Maggie Hunter and Antonia Winders the latest children falling victim to an emotionally disturbed adult.

'Attention-seeking,' Noakes repeated thoughtfully. 'An' making up stories.'

The DI nodded gravely. 'An overwhelming addiction to drama,' he clarified. 'You see, Muriel talked about parents doing televised appeals asking for their children's safe return and then it turned out they were the ones behind it all. Which prompted me to consider whether MSP could be somewhere in the mix.'

In truth, the idea had brushed through the back of his mind so gently that he had barely processed it . . . just the unnerving hint of a thought that there might be a sufferer from Munchausen's or some other factitious disorder behind those rumours of a prowler at the Tower targeting children. It might even be that the chronic need for attention had somehow fused with a strange compulsion to hurt or punish children, letting loose some sort of demon which had got nastier and more lethal over time.

Of course, he could just imagine the disdain with which Sidney would react to such psychological theorizing, so he wouldn't be giving the DCI the slightest whiff of such speculation until there'd been time to consult with the university profilers.

Noakes must have read his mind.

'I don' see Slimy Sid buying it,' he said doubtfully. 'He ain't that keen on personality disorder stuff . . . at least not unless Burton presents it to him wrapped up all neat an' tidy with a bow on it.'

'Actually, Kate gave me some notes, so I've been mugging up on the subject,' Markham said casually.

Noakes scratched his chin. 'With this attention-seeking stuff, are you thinking what happened with the Sullivan kids started out as a *stunt* — some kind of nutty scheme to get notice — only then it went wrong somehow an' chummy ended up killing 'em?'

'That's possible. Or if we're talking an acute form of MSP, there could have been intent to kill from the outset. Possibly it wasn't enough for them to derive a sense of power from being at the centre of things. They might have needed the fact of *physical possession* . . . needed to have control over the victims. By way of compensation for feelings of powerlessness in their own life, perhaps.

'Blimey.' Noake took some moments to digest this.

'An' Margaret Esdaile found out summat, so our own angel of death had to sort her?'

'I'm not sure that's an appropriate moniker for our killer, Noakesy,' Markham admonished with a faint smile, 'but yes, I presume Dr Esdaile became suspicious for some reason.'

'There's a hole in your MSP thingy, though,' Noakes went on with gloomy relish.

'And what's that?'

'Well, if we're saying whoever's behind the creepy stuff with kids gets off on being the centre of attention an' prancing around in the thick of things, then how come no one knows who it is? I mean, there ain't no point skulking around in a hoodie an' hiding your face if you want everyone to notice you.'

'That's why I talked about "variant aetiologies", Noakesy,' came the prompt retort. 'Mr or Ms X may simply derive some kind of vicarious satisfaction from being caught up in the hue and cry surrounding these attempted abductions and then afterwards pawing them over with people who have no idea they're talking to the actual *perpetrator*.'

'I c'n see how it'd make 'em feel superior,' Noakes said slowly. 'Like they've got this special secret they're hugging to thesselves while the rest are jus' morons running around chasing their tails.'

'The "morons" including Tower Bridge CID,' Markham added tartly . 'I don't say it fits the standard model for MSP — the epidemiology still isn't fully understood and there are all kinds of theories — but it's consistent with certain aspects.'

'Does it mean we're looking for a woman?' Noakes asked.

'Not necessarily . . . According to the literature, I believe the principal coefficients relate to childhood loss and deprivation, physical and mental abuse.' His own dysfunctional experiences in that regard were behind Markham's deep-seated relief that Olivia was unable to have children. Knowing Noakes's shrewdness, he was pretty sure his friend intuited the existence of this hang-up, but it was part of their curious unspoken pact that such matters were never alluded to between them.

'None of 'em at the Tower comes across as 'specially screwy,' Noakes ruminated. 'Well, the curators an' that Hunter woman are well up thesselves, but the rest seem okay.'

'Whoever it is must be well versed in deception and concealing their neuroses,' Markham replied grimly. 'Extremely cunning.'

There was briefly silence while this sank in.

'So you reckon it's all about 'em having this Munchkin thing?'

Markham's lips twitched. 'Munchausen Syndrome by Proxy, Noakesy . . . For God's sake don't call it "Munchkin"

when we're in with Sidney otherwise he'll think you're having a go at the disabled or some other minority . . . definitely *not* what we need right now. Just stick to the acronym MSP.'
Or better still, let me do the talking, he thought.

Noakes grinned unrepentantly.

'D'you think there's anything else at the bottom of it apart from having a grotty childhood that sent them bats?' he enquired. 'I mean, mebbe they really had it in for the doc an' the Sullivans an' the rest . . . mebbe had a grudge or some reason to hate 'em.'

'Yes,' Markham said slowly, recalling his previous meditation on the evils of jealousy. 'I think we'll find there's quite a maelstrom of complex emotions.'

He recalled reading of Beverely Allitt, the nurse convicted of killing four infants in 1991, that she had been dragged through life by her personality disorder like a cart by a runaway horse, a curiously arresting image. However, in Allitt's case there were plenty of signs available for those who cared to read them, whereas none of the Tower suspects appeared to fit the bill.

Outside, the day had turned still darker, though it was still early morning, and the flurries were heavier as though in a shaken snow globe.

'Proper Christmassy,' Noakes said, watching approvingly as the countryside was gradually transformed into a sculpted white landscape.

He wouldn't be saying that when their hometown resumed its usual grey and gritty aspect as the traditionally dismal January weather kicked in and the gutters were clogged with dirty packed snow, Markham thought with an inward smile. Bromgrove was enough to suck the life out of anyone with its cold and clammy welcome to the new year, as residents coughed and wheezed their way through the daily grind. But in the meantime, who was he to cavil at Noakes's childlike delight in seasonal magic.

'The missus says our bin men are heroes this time of year,' Noakes volunteered unexpectedly.

'Indeed.' Markham wasn't sure where this was going.

'I reckon one of 'em has a crush on Mu,' his friend confided.

Taken aback at the diminutive which was hard to reconcile with the lady in question. Markham hardly knew how to respond, but the other took his silence for respectful admiration.

'Yeah,' he continued happily, as though the DI had said as much. 'He allus pushes our purple bin right up to the side door an' then bolts away . . . like he can't bear to be thanked 'cos he's shy round the missus . . . don' trust hisself round her or summat . . . ever so modest.'

Markham knew all too well in what light Olivia would view this revelation, but he knew equally it was information he would never share. Something about Noakes's conviction that his wife was a *femme fatale* touched him deeply and he felt he could somehow hardly bear this chord to be pressed clumsily or in derision.

'I can well imagine Muriel having a powerful effect on people generally,' he said awkwardly, feeling somewhat of a heel as he observed the delight which irradiated his friend's face.

'She were a bit annoyed with me the other week,' Noakes confided.

'*Oh*?' Markham wondered which was the latest offence on the marital bill of indictment that Muriel doubtless kept regularly updated.

'We were watching *Antiques Roadshow* an' afterwards I took some of her china out of the cabinet an' pretended I were checking the hallmark whatsit on the back to see if it were worth anything . . . jus' for a laugh, like.' He looked crestfallen now. 'But she didn't see the funny side.'

Markham strove with difficulty to maintain an expression of immutable gravity. This was a gem he *would* share with Olivia, knowing how she delighted in human foibles.

'Your wife's high standards put the rest of us to shame,' he murmured, hardly knowing what exactly he meant by this but anxious to reassure.

However inadequate the platitude, it worked. 'Whass the plan once we get home, boss?' Noakes asked cheerfully as yet another station flashed by. 'Do we have to tackle Sidney first thing?'

Markham made a sudden decision.

'No,' he replied firmly with a glance at their holdalls in the luggage rack. 'We'll swing by the gym and give ourselves a workout . . . loosen up after sitting still for so long.' After that they would be ready to face Sidney.

* * *

Bromgrove Police Boxing Gym to which Markham and Noakes repaired a short time later was an unofficial CID haunt that was utterly deplored by DCI Sidney and the station's senior personnel, item number one in their list of grievances being the proprietor himself.

Doggie was ex-army, a fact which of itself was sufficient to endear him to Noakes who delighted in shouting '*Barrack shun!*' whenever they encountered each other. Markham suspected his military record didn't bear close inspection (viz. the queasily suggestive 'pet name') but was nonetheless fond of the disreputable major-domo and amused by the way he regularly re-invented himself.

In days gone by, Doggie's 'brand', so to speak, consisted of the Long John Silver look with Wild West overtones of Doc Holliday, his funereal frock coat, horsehair wig, yellow snaggle-toothed leer and eye patch the absolute antithesis of what one might expect from a health club manager. Nor did his hangdog features, unsteady gait and an enveloping pungent aroma of Johnnie Walker (the last two traits doubtless connected) inspire confidence in the salubrity of the premises; indeed, its owner existed in a state of more or less constant internecine warfare with Environmental Health.

Then there had come Doggie's cabbalistic phase when he was heavily influenced by one Marlene ('Mystic Meg' as Noakes had dubbed her) and floated around the place looking like Gandalf or a demented astrologer. With the demise of Marlene and advent of fiancée Evelyn ('Evie') — a redoubtable lady whose daughter Clare had a certain amount in common with Natalie Noakes — he had got his teeth fixed and discarded the eye patch, the prosthesis underneath it a useful reminder of his hard man credentials. Even the horse-hair wig had gone, a mohawk mullet bisecting his bald pate — though DI Chris Carstairs (another habitué of the gym) declared the effect was less American frontiersman and more Squirrel Nutkin on the rampage. The frockcoats and kaftans were but a distant memory, the old villain now more likely to be found wearing tracksuits and fleeces that at least suggested a passing acquaintance with physical exercise (though this wholesome impression was somewhat undermined by a scent of booze and the carpet slippers that were his preferred footwear).

The fact that Doggie was rumoured to have been involved in any number of unsavoury enterprises — such dodges drastically curtailed now that he was respectably affianced — did nothing to impair his popularity with Bromgrove CID many of whom happily resorted to the dingy little outfit in Marsh Lane where they slugged it out in the ring side by side with the local criminal fraternity, both sides seeing nothing untoward in observing a sporting amnesty while on the premises before resuming their accustomed skirmishes once back out on the streets.

For all Doggie's sleaziness and local notoriety, nothing divulged by Markham and Noakes had ever left the gym, the proprietor's own code of honour ensuring that he never betrayed their confidence ('What's said here stays here, Mr Markham'). The DI, with his air of grave courtesy and appearance of being interested in Doggie's anecdotes, enjoyed the dubious honour of being his 'fav'rite 'spector' while Noakes and Doggie shared a resolutely un-PC world view that would have had Kate Burton reaching for her smelling salts (were they not too Victorian an accessory for such an indefatigably right-on officer).

Lurching into the re-grouted 'Premium Locker Room', which boasted a sauna (of sorts) and showers which could occasionally be counted on for hot *as well as* cold water, Doggie greeted them enthusiastically and the trio were soon deep in discussion about the Tower investigation.

'I remember going on a trip when I were at junior school,' Doggie told them. 'There was this *ace* warder who made it feel like you were stepping back in time, described how they stuck traitors' heads on Tower Bridge . . . all boiled and tarred an' left up on the drawbridge to rot.' Markham could well imagine the relish with which a juvenile Doggie had absorbed such gory details. 'An' there was this funny little exhibition of painted statues they stuck on top of coffins for funerals of important folk . . . incredibly lifelike. There were horoscopes an' stuff like that too . . . the Beefeater bloke said if the king wanted to get rid of someone, he could say it was written in the stars an' get away with it 'cos everyone was dead superstitious back then.'

It was quite a testament to the Tower guides that Doggie retained such vivid memories of his visit, Markham thought, amused by the keen attention Noakes paid to the various anecdotes related by this most surprising of armchair historians. His friend was particularly struck by the story of Thomas More on the scaffold at Tower Hill telling Henry VIII's spymaster to 'see me safe up, and as for coming down let me shift for myself', admiration for such soldierly stoicism in the face of death overcoming his mistrust of More's Papist antecedents.

'There were some right brave people ended up in the Tower,' Doggie concluded his recital. 'Some earl or other even got his portrait painted there . . . his cat was in it an' all 'cos it went down a chimney to find him.'

Doggie was fascinated by Markham's MSP thesis, regaling the two men with knowledge acquired from his recent viewing of *The Good Nurse* about the infamous serial killer Charles Cullen. 'That Eddie Redmayne was dead convincing as a sicko,' he told them solemnly. 'It was another nurse who shopped him, y'know, once the cops convinced her it had to be him killing people. He had a terrible time as a kid but, ' with a virtuous sniff, 'even if you've been *dragged up* cos your parents are scuzzballs, there ain't no call to go round taking it out on folk in hospital.' The emphasis Doggie put on the words 'dragged up' suggested that his own childhood had been decidedly chequered and made Markham feel a sudden wave of sympathy for the gym's patron.

Doggie was equally intrigued by the historical backdrop and, like Doyle, had seen *The Lost King*. 'They think that Philippa Langley woman got so hung up on King Richard an' his nevvies, she went round the twist,' he said, with Noakes's louring expression eloquent in its conviction that anything was possible where academics were concerned. 'You could go a bit loopy hanging around a place where folk were poisoned an' got their heads chopped off an' things,' he added, almost as though the Tower harboured some sort of deadly infection that you were bound to catch after too much time there.

'Thass what my missus thinks,' Noakes agreed. 'A case of the screaming abdabs,' he added for the avoidance of doubt.

'The problem being that none of our suspects exactly stands out as being mentally deranged, nor inclined to kidnap and homicide for that matter,' Markham retorted.

'Yeah well, the warders are top blokes being ex-army,' Noakes said defiantly as though daring anyone to challenge him, Doggie's mohawk bobbing up and down in enthusiastic corroboration.

'The padre's a bit of a . . . *sensitive* type . . . a bit *intense*, but basically all right,' Noakes continued. 'The curators are stuck-up tossers an' the rest of then jus' your usual museum crowd,' he concluded with magnificent dismissiveness.

'What about the woman whose kid ended up under the church?' Doggie asked, squinting at them rheumily. 'Could she have stage-managed the whole kidnap thing?'

'Hard to tell, Dogs,' Markham replied, 'though she certainly didn't come across as anyone's favourite colleague . . . bossy and an office tyrant but not necessarily a—'

157

'Psycho,' Noakes finished the sentence.

'Quite . . . though she could of course be adept at concealing her true personality.' With a thoughtful frown, the DI added, 'I'm inclined to assume that whoever attacked Maggie Hunter went on to attack Antonia Winders, though somehow it's hard to imagine a *mother* being responsible for that.'

'Yeah, but parents *do* kill their kids sometimes,' Doggie pronounced with the confidence of one addicted to *Deadliest Mums & Dads*. 'Whatcha going to tell Slimy Sid?' he added, only too well aware of Markham's travails over the years, including the fact that Sidney regarded the DI's loyalty to his own establishment as by no means the least of his deficiencies.

'Oh we'll cobble something together, Dogs.' Markham only wished he could believe it.

'He won't like you being toast of the town with the London mob,' Doggie said shrewdly.

'I'm sure he won't object just so long as he gets his share of the glory,' Markham pointed out.

Doggie wheezed appreciatively.

'I better let you gents crack on,' he said, mindful of the duties of hospitality. 'Mr Carstairs is giving Benny Squint a pasting out there, so he'll be warmed up nicely.'

After Doggie had shuffled off to his office (and the bottle in the top drawer of his filing cabinet), Markham stripped off ready for battle, leaving Noakes to reflect for the umpteenth time on the unfairness of a malign fate which had spared Markham any hint of middle-aged decrepitude while his own silhouette grew more ample with every passing year. It was all down to the genes, he thought glumly, in which case he owed his parents a definite grudge.

'Lead on, Macduff,' Markham exhorted.

It was their private joke and one which never failed to raise a smile.

'I'll take Benny Squint,' Noakes said, not without a hint of malevolent satisfaction. 'If Carstairs has given him a drubbing, it'll be easy pickings . . . Besides, he called me Porker when we were in last, so I reckon it's payback time.'

And with that, the two men headed for the ring and their cathartic pummelling.

* * *

It was late afternoon by the time Markham and Noakes presented themselves before Sidney's PA whose piled dyed hair (now an improbable ash blonde) positively quivered with disapproval at the sight of CID's former *bête noire*. By the looks of her, thought Markham, she was still a long way from forgiving his wingman's derisive outburst when he heard her describing football penalties as 'kickouts'. Mind you, that was comparatively harmless when compared to his ribbing of her policeman son: 'Get on *Crimewatch*. Study hard. Your big feet might make the Yard.' The fact that said offspring wore outsize clodhoppers did nothing to appease her outrage. Still less was this dragon lady enamoured of the un-PC limericks with which Noakes liked to accost assorted secretaries. And she hadn't exactly been convulsed when, in answer to her beady enquiry if Noakes could let her have a current CV, he replied, 'My firm don' give 'em. You have to bring a packed lunch.'

Today, however, her least popular civilian consultant (whom she privately designated Piltdown Man) sat meekly next to the DI in the waiting room while Markham laid on the charm (basically a reprise of his tactics with Muriel Noakes). By the time he had finished, she had softened sufficiently for the indignant bristle to abate, while the pink spots on her heavily powdered cheeks lost some of their ferocity and the sarcastic edge to her voice disappeared completely. By the time she disappeared into the inner sanctum to inform Sidney of their arrival, the silly bint was practically *purring*, Noakes thought sourly.

Kate Burton had amply repaid Markham's faith in her, providing them with a manila folder brim-full of information on MSP and a range of other disorders. Certainly there was enough to blindside the DCI. While they waited to be summoned into Sidney's presence, the DI recalled his conversation with Kate Burton before leaving London . . .

Burton had smiled gravely when Markham discussed the mission to butter up Slimy Sid.

'He's not so bad these days, you know,' was her observation. 'There's even talk of a possible reconciliation with his wife . . . though,' her eyes crinkled roguishly, 'he might have blotted his copybook after that event for the North-West Police Benevolent Fund.'

Markham was intrigued. 'How so?' he asked.

'Well, after his talk was over, there was a kind of receiving line where everyone queued up meet the speaker. Apparently, Sidney was so pumped up and adrenalized that he didn't recognize Mrs Sidney . . . just shook hands with her like she was a stranger. Of course, they laughed it off afterwards but my spies tell me Mrs S wasn't best pleased.'

Markham felt a wave of compassion for his boss on hearing this. Speechifying was a challenge at the best of times and he knew Sidney was desperate to break into the media after he retired, so it was hardly surprising if it took him some time to come back to earth after such a baptism of fire.

'How did his speech go down?' Noakes wanted to know on hearing this revelation.

'Well, apparently the jokes were a bit laboured but it could have been worse.'

'It's all in the timing,' the former DS told her complacently. 'Happen I c'n give him a few tips if it comes to that.' Meeting Burton's eyes, Markham knew she would pay good money to witness *that* particular exchange.

Now the dragon lady was back ushering them into Sidney's office.

On this occasion Noakes was as good as gold, offering no suggestions as to how Sidney might improve his prospects as a budding media pundit. The DCI was clearly mollified by the show of deference and listened attentively as Markham described their Tower experiences to date. It was strange, the DI thought, how the Tower of London somehow caught the imagination of personalities as disparate as Noakes, Doggie and Sidney. Certainly the DCI looked almost wistful on hearing about the various landmarks and treasures, though Markham was careful to keep it brief lest the investigation appeared altogether too much of a junket. Kate might well be right about Sidney having mellowed, but he didn't want to push their luck.

Briefing Sidney in person had clearly worked well. The DCI's adenoidal honk was distinctly attenuated and there was no sign of the eczema that was apt to flare up alarmingly at the merest glimpse of Markham's sidekick.

'I take it you'll be looking at the mother of this child who was abducted and found in the crypt,' he said finally. 'The events woman.'

'She's certainly a person of interest, sir,' Markham answered carefully, thinking as he did so that he sounded like a CIA operative. 'However, it's a stretch to imagine she could have attacked her own daughter, let alone Antonia Winders.'

'Ties of blood are no guarantee where you're dealing with a maniac,' Sidney said portentously. 'I don't need to remind you that those in the family circle are most often guilty.'

'Thass why you c'n count on us to give Steven an' Lucy Winders an' Charles Esdaile the third degree,' Noakes said with sunny innocence.

'I believe DCI Knevitt and the team are doing a deep dive as we speak,' Markham interjected hastily, seeing Sidney's expression cloud over at the thought of Noakes's likely interrogative style. God, what was it about these sessions with Sidney that always ended up with him vomiting meaningless corporate gobbledygook.

'Deep dive, yeah,' Noakes echoed with a completely straight face, leaving their boss with the impression that there might well be a prime suspect in prospect.

'That went okay,' his wingman said afterwards. 'An' he latched on to the MSP stuff like he really thought there could be summat in it.'

'*Hmm.*' Seeing Noakes try to suppress a yawn, the DI smiled. 'Let's head back to the Sweepstakes and order in a takeaway, Noakesy.'

'Can I stay at yours tonight, guv . . . I don' want to disturb the missus.' Who doubtless wouldn't appreciate him rolling in at all hours after a Chicken Vindaloo or whatever other gastronomic reward Noakes had in mind for himself.

'Of course.'

All things considered, the DI felt they were making progress, though the psychological profile could turn out to be a blind alley.

'Whoever did for those Sullivan kids, the doc an' Mrs H., we'll nail 'em, boss.' He could tell that behind all the roister-doister banter, Noakes was strongly affected by the fate that had befallen all those innocents.

A maimed character, Markham mused as they headed for his flat.

Someone dragged through life by a personality disorder as surely as those poor wretches dragged from the Tower on a hurdle to be hanged, drawn and quartered in punishment for their crimes.

Who are you? he asked himself uneasily in the small hours until sleep finally claimed him and the insistent voice was silenced.

CHAPTER 10: SECRETS AND LIES

'So you gave Judas Iscariot some red meat then?' Olivia asked after listening to Markham's account of the flying visit to Bromgrove as they sat with Noakes in the Tower Hotel's Coffee Lounge on Tuesday afternoon.

The afternoon was bitterly cold and snow coming down heavily, transforming the iron tracery of Tower Bridge into delicate filigree as swollen clouds scudded overhead, with the promise of more to come. Indoors, however, the trio were snugly settled in opulent comfort, their surroundings reminiscent of an exclusive country club with a great deal of rustic wood panelling, exposed brickwork and tasteful black and white prints of the capital.

'He seemed happy enough with it,' Markham observed, some instinct telling him to avoid any mention of Kate Burton's input, 'though I'm not sure he'll be convinced by my idea about MSP.'

'He's a psychology graduate though, isn't he,' Olivia pointed out. 'So he's bound to give it houseroom.'

Markham frowned. 'His favourite diagnosis is "Mad, Bad and Dangerous to Know" rather than anything too obscure or controversial . . . and MSP isn't all that well understood.'

'But we gave him a prime suspect in the Hunter woman,' Noakes chipped in, prodding the gooey marshmallows on his mug of hot chocolate. 'All gift-wrapped with a ribbon on top,' he added cynically. 'You could tell he were dead keen on *that*.'

Olivia assumed a mock innocent expression. 'Presumably it was enough to head him off from asking awkward questions about your expense account and demanding to know why the taxpayer should be expected to fund unnecessary CID jollies?'

Noakes guffawed appreciatively. 'This case is dead *glamorous*, luv,' he said. 'Sidney prob'ly sees hisself ending up with a slot on that TV programme *Inside the Tower of London* . . . or mebbe even meeting King Charles an' Camilla if we manage to crack a murder *an'* the missing kids.'

'Won't DCI Knevitt and DI Morrissey have something to say about that, George?' she asked quizzically. 'As in wanting their share of fame.'

'*Nah*,' Noakes said emphatically. 'Them two are like his nibs here.' Now it was Markham's turn to raise a quizzical eyebrow. 'Old-fashioned "thief-taker" types . . . not like Sidders and Ebury-Clarke who jus' ride a desk an' then steal other folks' glory.'

'I'm not sure that's entirely fair, Noakesy,' Markham demurred. 'Sidney's been unexpectedly helpful on a few occasions of late.'

'Oh *come on*, Gil,' Olivia snorted. 'That man's lower than a snake's hips and you know it.'

Noakes spluttered again as a mouthful of hot chocolate went down the wrong way. 'The super's just as bad,' he said once he had recovered. 'Deffo on the spectrum.' Turning to Markham, he confided, 'Apparently when his PA's mum passed away, Ebury-Clarke told her he knew how she felt 'cos it were the same for him when their cat died . . . a *cat*, for God's sake!'

Markham grinned. 'The man's tin-eared, no doubt about it,' he agreed, thinking with an inward sigh that said paragon of tact and sensitivity would doubtless ere long be taking over from Sidney as the unit's new boss. Out of the frying pan and all that.

'I can't *believe* the two of you sloped off to Doggie's,' Olivia commented, closing down any further talk about Markham's superiors, since discussion of the gruesome two-some invariably put her in a bad mood. 'This hotel has a fantastic spa with a swimming pool and jacuzzi if you wanted to chillax . . . as opposed to catching something dreadful at Germ Central.'

'Stop winding us up, Liv,' Markham said easily. 'Thrashing Chris Carstairs hands down was the best therapy I could've had.' Tactfully, he didn't allude to the outcome of Noakes's bout with Benny Squint.

'Dogs got all misty-eyed about the Tower,' Noakes chipped in before Olivia could ask about his own performance in the ring. 'Proper starstruck about some warder who laid on stories about blood and gore during a school trip . . . quite sweet really.'

'I'm not sure I would ever describe Doggie Dickerson as *sweet*,' Olivia remarked with a shudder, 'but it's true about the Tower having a unique atmosphere. The warders bring it to life so you can almost imagine being back in Tudor England.' She was misty-eyed with the romance of it all. 'Taverns and tenements crammed close together on Tower Bridge, so that the top floors leaned across the streets and you could reach out from an upstairs window and touch the building opposite; images of saints and coats of arms everywhere; hundreds of steeples and towers rising above the rooftops; and all those churches with their votive candles flickering and strange plaster figures of saints paralysed in unnatural positions—'

'An' folk stuck in the pillory while folk pelted 'em with rotten eggs before they got their ears lopped off,' Noakes observed with relish.

Olivia wrinkled her nose. 'Thanks for that, George. I was thinking in more *picturesque* terms actually.'

Their friend stopped in consternation while privately admiring the starry eyes and animated features that were to his mind as fine and delicate as one of those medieval carvings in St Peter ad Vincula. 'Well, if you were bottom of the pile, it weren't 'xactly a laugh a minute,' he muttered sheepishly.

Olivia laughed. 'True,' she admitted. 'Life for so many was brutish and short . . . even if you belonged to the nobility. I really felt that when Andy Campbell showed me round the Tower.' Softly she murmured, '"Never send to know for whom the bell tolls; it tolls for thee." I guess we're all under sentence of death, aren't we.'

Noakes was uneasy, not at all sure how to respond and thinking she sounded almost as morbid as Kate Burton with all that talk about not knowing when your time was up.

Seeing his concern, Olivia shook herself.

'I'm getting carried away.' She smiled. 'But it's like another race of people . . . that obsession with relics — apparently one time they even paraded St George's *leg* round the city — and those weird cults . . . the Holy Name of Jesus and the Five Wounds of Christ . . . not to mention their strange talismans . . . the rituals and bede rolls—'

'What's one of them?' Noakes interrupted, distracted as she had intended him to be.

'Henry the Eighth had one when he was growing up. Mr Campbell said you can see it in the British Library — a parchment roll with lots of holy emblems and pictures, so when you unfurled it there's this sort of flowchart to help you recite all the right prayers.'

Noakes was pretty scandalized. 'Sounds more like a yoga mat.'

'Well, if you did it all correctly every day, you were guaranteed protection from sudden death by poison, murder or evil spirits.'

'Oh aye.' The other sounded deeply sceptical. 'Bleeding voodoo if you ask me.'

Olivia chuckled. 'Apparently it was good for keeping the demon of lust at bay too,' she continued mischievously.

Noakes shifted uncomfortably at the mention of lust.

'I remember the padre quoted St Paul about that,' he confided after a pregnant pause.

Olivia's eyes were dancing, 'Do tell,' she urged.

'Well, I asked if he didn't think it were better for vicars an' such to be married . . . that way they'd have a better handle on ordinary folk. He quoted that bit from St Paul about it being better to marry than burn with passion.' Lugubriously, Noakes added, 'Which seems a bit bobbins to me . . . like telling someone who's nervous round dynamite to get a job in a quarry.'

Olivia's peals of merriment rang round the lounge, causing curious heads to swivel in their direction and Noakes to turn puce.

'Enough, Liv,' Markham admonished her. 'You're embarrassing Noakesy.'

'Sorry, George,' but she didn't sound particularly contrite.

As his friend's colour subsided, Markham turned their conversation to the investigation.

'So is Clare Hunter *really* your prime suspect then?' Olivia wanted to know. 'D'you honestly reckon she could have attacked the other little girl?' She'd been horror-struck on hearing about Antonia's experience and was clearly struggling to imagine how any parent could have done such a thing.

'She's certainly shaping up to be a contender for the top spot,' Markham replied. 'Doyle emailed me while we were on the train to say there are one or two skeletons in her closet.'

'*Oh*?' Olivia was deeply intrigued.

'Can't go into it here, Liv,' he said warningly, aware that a couple at the adjoining table were now taking rather too close an interest in their conversation.

Her eyes followed his gaze.

'Ah, I'm with you, Gil,' she returned lightly.

'Apparently Carruthers has something of interest for us too.' He sighed. 'So it's still anyone's guess.'

With a sideways glance, Olivia noted with relief that their neighbours' interest had turned to the arrival of food and drink.

'I can see how someone might become unbalanced working in a place like the Tower,' she said thoughtfully. 'Especially if they maybe had mental health issues to start with . . . I mean, you do kind of feel the weight of all that pain and suffering bearing down on you . . . the place is almost *saturated* with it. Possibly a neurotic personality might internalize it all, if they were into reincarnation or transmigration of souls . . . ideas about time travel or some such,' she added self-consciously as Noakes boggled at her.

Markham suppressed a smile at his friend's expression as she gamely ploughed on. 'I remember reading this book years ago when I was a teenager. The title was *Green Darkness* . . . I guess you'd call it pretty much a schlocky bodice ripper, but the heroine is this woman sent round the twist by imagining she's lived before in medieval times.'

'So what happened to her then?' Noakes demanded impatiently. 'Summat nasty?'

'Well, in her past life she was walled up alive for messing around with a priest.'

Noakes pulled a face. 'The woman sounds mad as a broomstick,' was his verdict.

'It's *fiction*, George,' Olivia said defensively. 'But it made quite an impression on me.'

'Princess Di were into all that,' Noakes said thoughtfully.

Olivia was startled. 'What, as in *reincarnation*?'

'Yeah . . . the missus read some biography which said Di went round telling folk she'd been a nun in Elizabethan times or summat daft like that . . . I mean, *a nun*!'

Olivia had recovered her sang-froid. 'Diana spent quite a lot of time with Mother Teresa, didn't she, so I guess it must have rubbed off,' she said, Noakes's response being an eloquent eye roll.

Markham chuckled. 'Game, set and match, Noakesy. You can't argue with a theory that comes *By Royal Appointment*.'

They sat for a while longer, savouring the warmth and comfort as the light faded outside, before Markham resumed the subject. 'Seriously though, there may be something in what Liv says. If you recall, Doyle wondered something similar.'

'You mean all this reincarnation bollocks?' Noakes caught himself up. 'Sorry, luv,' he said to Olivia, 'but I'm thinking it's a good thing we didn't run that idea up the flag-pole with Slimy Sid.' The pouchy face broke into a wicked grin as he turned to Markham. 'Though can you imagine his face if we gave him all that about chummy fancying they'd lived in Tudor times . . . he'd have had us off to occy health in a flash.'

'Indeed.' Markham pursued his train of thought, how-ever, aware of Olivia's slightly wounded expression. 'But I still think Liv may be on to something here.' He didn't men-tion the fact that Kate Burton too had raised the possibility of their killer being affected by echoes from the past. 'I've felt it myself. There's a kind of *terror* about the Tower . . . you can't help but think of all the doubleness and treachery that once swirled about the place. People creeping in the shadows just out of your eyeline . . . whispering in corners . . . troublesome queens and noblewomen hidden from view . . . plots ensuring that if you disappeared into the bowels of the castle, you never came out . . . a sinister game of snakes and ladders . . .'

'Yeah, you c'n bet if old Henry the Eighth offered any-one a guided tour, they didn't take him up on it,' Noakes quipped before turning serious again. 'To be honest, though, it sounds more the way a *woman* would carry on.' Suddenly flustered, he turned to Olivia. 'Not to be sexist, luv,' he resumed.

'Oh, perish the thought,' she replied deadpan.

'But seeing as how women are more, well, *imaginative* an' kinda *sensitive to atmosphere* an' all that . . .'

Markham took pity on him. 'Stop digging, Noakesy,' he advised kindly. 'We know what you mean. Certainly, it's hard to imagine starchy types like Daniel Locke or Benedict Ryan harbouring some kind of superstitious paranoia—'

'Other than worrying that Margaret Esdaile might steal a march on 'em with her research,' Noakes pointed out.

'True. Ditto for Steven Winders,' Markham continued. 'Apart from professional competitiveness, there's nothing to suggest mental instability.'

'What about the chaplain?' Olivia asked. 'Isn't *he* a bit flaky?'

Noakes jumped in quickly. 'He's an okay bloke, not full of hisself like the curators. The warders rate him too. Andy Campbell said he's really kind if you're going through tough times. Apparently when all that business kicked off between John Whittingham an' Dr Esdaile, the padre tried to smooth it over rather than stirring things up. I mean, some folk might've tried to make a big deal of it . . . stage some big kind of pastoral drama so they could ride to the rescue an' make thesselves look important . . .' His voice trailed off uncertainly.

'I know what you mean, George,' Olivia said meditatively. 'I've met people like that . . . busybody meddlers with a saviour complex who just want to promote themselves at the expense of others, the type who swoop in and make everything ten times worse.'

'That's it,' Noakes said gratefully. 'Well, there's a few of 'em like that . . . the intern girl dropped a hint to Doyle that Clare Hunter an' Lucy Winders were the managing kind.'

'I can easily imagine Doyle lending the beauteous Sophie a sympathetic ear,' Markham observed drily.

'I guess you allus get some bullying in places like the Tower, what with all them massive egos,' Noakes remarked philosophically. 'Margaret Esdaile an' Benedict Ryan came down pretty heavy on that poor kid they accused of nicking stuff . . . Old baldy boots got right in her face about it.'

'Knevitt said Elena Rogers liked Fr Bernard, but it was obvious she couldn't stand the others,' Markham mused.

'There you go then.' Noakes was pleased. 'He might be a bit, well, *weedy*, but last time I checked, it weren't a crime.'

'And of course, he does a good sermon too, George,' Olivia teased.

'That an' all.' Where Noakes was partisan, his sympathies were stubbornly hard to shift. 'He gave Dr Esdaile a good send off.'

'Some of it was a bit, well, Hieronymus Bosch,' Olivia ventured. 'Very dark.'

'Well, like he said, Esdaile were a medievalist an' dead interested in the way they saw the world like this massive battle between good an' evil . . . there were that stuff from Thomas More.' Noakes screwed up his eyes trying to remember. 'Yeah I got it,' he exclaimed triumphantly. 'More had a rant about having to fight "gluttony an' the world, an' the world's lord, the devil".' He frowned. 'Mind you, seeing as More wore a hair shirt under his fine togs an' snuck off to flog hisself when he thought no one were looking, don' seem to me like he'd be one for stuffing his face.'

Markham might have known the reference to the sin of gluttony would resonate with his friend. Trying not to laugh, he said, 'It was very evocative all right.' And strangely moving in its way.

'Any road, he ended on a high with that bit about finding new life in heaven,' Noakes declared firmly.

'That's true.' Gently, Olivia added, 'I'm sure it's what Dr Esdaile would have wanted.'

Markham felt increasingly drowsy, cocooned by the comfort and the pleasure of chewing things over with the two who knew him better than anyone else. But it was time to rouse himself and make a move.

'Noakesy and I are going to have to love you and leave you, Liv,' he told his partner reluctantly.

'Go on then.' She pulled a mock reproachful face then winked at Noakes. 'It's too cold for any more sightseeing or shopping, so guess I'll just have to console myself for your absence with a dip in the jacuzzi.'

After they had gone, however, she seemed curiously disinclined to move, some words of Noakes's coming back to her.

The world's lord, the devil, she thought uneasily.

If the world truly resembled a canvas by Hieronymus Bosch, then as far as the Tower investigation was concerned, the forces of evil appeared to be in the ascendant.

* * *

'Where's Burton?' Noakes demanded as he and Markham hunkered down with DCI Knevitt and DI Morrissey in the Queen's House.

'The inspector told Morrissey there were a couple of leads she needed to follow up,' Knevitt told them.

The DCI was looking very tired, Markham thought, the bags under his eyes almost as pronounced as Noakes's.

'Like a breakthrough?' Noakes enquired eagerly.

'She didn't seem excited enough for it to be anything major,' Morrissey answered. 'But I'm guessing she's the cautious type . . . didn't want to get too excited about it.'

'Didn't she tell you *anything*?' Noakes persisted indignantly.

'Just that your two sergeants had clocked some stuff that went on at the wake after Dr Esdaile's funeral, so there were a few things that needed to be checked out.'

'So Batman an' Robin went with her then?' Noakes asked crossly.

Knevitt chuckled. 'Don't know which of them's meant to be the caped crusader but yeah, they've gone too.'

Markham shared the fruits of their trip to Bromgrove, the two Tower Bridge detectives listening attentively as he expounded his theory of an offender in the grip of MSP, drawing on Burton's aide-memoire and notes supplied by Bromgrove University.

'I'm not sure I don't feel somewhat foolish now,' he wound up. 'It was an observation of Noakes's wife which sparked something in my mind.' Noakes sat up straighter at this and tried to look enigmatic. 'But it seemed to me that certain aspects of the condition might explain the repeated "crises" around those attempted abductions of children and then the incidents with Maggie Hunter and Antonia Winders.'

'I don't think it's foolish at all,' Knevitt said, with a courteous bow of acknowledgment to Noakes which reinforced Markham's conviction that the DCI was a real gent.

Morrissey had been listening attentively. 'Maybe our prowler stroke kidnapper is a different person from whoever did the other stuff — the Sullivan twins, Dr Esdaile and Mrs Hernan.'

'You mean two sickos,' Noakes grunted.

'Somehow I see all of it as being on the same trajectory,' Markham said quietly. 'Some dark pathological impulse which lay nascent for a long time after the Sullivan abduction but never entirely subsided—'

'And then things escalated when Dr Esdaile threatened exposure,' Knevitt interjected eagerly.

'Yes,' Markham agreed, 'though I believe Mrs Hernan's murder wasn't premeditated. That was a case of our killer being cornered with their back to the wall.'

'Why target Maggie Hunter and Antonia Winders then?' Morrissey wanted to know. 'A sick prank that went wrong? Some kind of payback for stuff their mothers had done?'

'Quite possibly,' the DI replied mildly. 'Remember, we're dealing with a profoundly disturbed personality here.'

'You c'n say that again,' Noakes muttered.

They sat in frustrated silence for some minutes.

'Doyle emailed me about "skeletons in Clare Hunter's closet",' Markham prompted eventually.

Morrissey was all business once more. 'Well, one of the catering staff told Doyle there was a rumour that Hunter originally trained as a teacher but ended up leaving her course for some reason.'

'Who did she get this from?' Markham wanted to know.

'She couldn't say.'

'Couldn't or wouldn't?'

'She genuinely wasn't sure how it started,' Knevitt told him. 'Apparently the café people went to the Hung, Drawn & Quartered in Tower Hill for a drink with some of the warders on Friday evening.' The pub's name elicited a snigger from Noakes. 'After the whole thing with Maggie, they felt they needed an outing . . . She got fairly pie-eyed by the sound of it, but remembered someone saying Hunter wasn't all that she seemed and then hearing this story about her screwing up as a trainee teacher.'

'It's hardly evidence that she turned into a pathological child-hater or some kind of mad attention-seeker, though.' Markham recalled what Olivia had said about the bitchiness of school environments and vindictive managers with a saviour complex. 'She could just as easily have got on the wrong side of someone and they fixed it so she had to leave the profession.'

'Agreed,' Knevitt said unexpectedly. 'My daughter's a teaching assistant and says you just wouldn't *believe* the sheer nastiness. As she tells it, the psycho headteachers in some schools make our bosses look like *novices*.'

Markham smiled sympathetically, thinking that it rather sounded as though Knevitt had his own equivalent of Superintendent Ebury-Clarke lurking in the wings waiting to pounce on any and every conceivable deficiency.

'Nevertheless, I guess it's a lead of sorts,' he said finally.

'True,' Knevitt agreed. 'We need to get to the bottom of it, but with her being traumatized after what happened with the kid it won't look good if we go in too hard.'

'Fair enough.' Markham could envisage the pitfalls if they were perceived to have behaved oppressively towards the mother of a kidnap victim. On the other hand, he had confidence in Kate Burton's ability to handle the situation.

'Did Doyle's, er, *informant* have anything else useful for us?'

'Just that the catering staff and warders' families think Hunter's a real prima donna . . . But whether that means she'd be capable of staging her own child's disappearance and putting the kid through that, let alone attacking Antonia Winders, who can say.' Knevitt's shrug was eloquent testament to his helplessness.

'When'll the Three Musketeers be back?' Noakes asked sardonically.

As if in answer to his question, there was a knock at the door and Kate Burton appeared. Doyle and Carruthers bobbing behind her in the corridor.

'I think we may have some more pieces of the jigsaw for you, sir,' she told Knevitt, her face brightening as she spied Markham and Noakes. 'Not that it's conclusive, mind you.'

Noakes and Morrissey exchanged glances. See what I meant about her being cautious, the latter's expression seemed to say.

'That's welcome news, Inspector,' Knevitt said. 'Come on in and let's hear what you've got.'

Markham felt his whole body tense.

Could this be it? he asked himself. Were they finally going to get a lead that would recalibrate the entire investigation?

Outside, the snow continued to fall and it grew dark.

Inside, they gathered round, waiting to hear Burton's revelations.

Perhaps at last the demon was going to be vanquished.

CHAPTER 11: THE KEY

In no time at all, they were settled with hot drinks and biscuits brought in by Pam Appleton and Justine Campbell who both looked thoroughly cowed by the impact of recent events, their demeanour subdued notwithstanding Knevitt's kindly attempts to put them at ease with inconsequential chat.

'My colleagues have just returned from Bromgrove where they were enjoying that legendary Northern hospitality,' he said courteously as they served the detectives.

'Oh aye, legendary,' Noakes echoed winking at them. 'Or as they say in Wigan, "without peer".' A chorus of groans greeted this execrable pun, allowing the two women to scuttle out of the room without further ado.

'How were things back at base, sir?' Burton asked Markham eagerly.

'Well, DCI Sidney didn't exactly roll out the welcome mat,' he said drily, 'but it could have been worse.'

'Sidney an' the rest of CID'll be getting their twisters in a nick over MSP,' Noakes opined breezily.

Seeing that Burton was somewhat bewildered by this gnomic pronouncement, Markham summarized the gist of the meeting, amused to see how his colleague's eyes gleamed as he rehearsed the technical details once more.

Noakes noticed it too. Bet she can't wait to get back to them boffin books of hers, he thought with indulgent tolerance, scooping up a couple more chocolate bourbons.

'I gather you've been following up some leads, Kate,' Markham prompted.

His fellow DI snapped to attention, diving into the tan executive briefcase which complemented her chocolate brown trouser suit. Markham noted that she had invested in colourful new eyewear, the fashion specs in vibrant shades of red hinting at a more subversive side to her personality.

'It was Doyle who did some more digging about Clare Hunter,' she told them, always generous in ensuring that junior colleagues got due credit for their work. She nodded to the young sergeant. 'Why don't you give us a recap.'

Clearly pleased at the acknowledgment, Doyle duly obliged.

'I overheard this waitress gossiping about Clare Hunter in the café,' he said, 'name of Eileen Kelleher. When the coast was clear, I got the woman on her own and asked what it was all about. Apparently a group of them from the café went down the pub with some of the warders—'

'Yeah, the Hung, Drawn & Quartered,' Noakes said with ghoulish relish.

'That's the one. Anyway, Eileen thought she heard something about Hunter not finishing her teacher training 'cos she dropped out in the NQT year. She was pretty hazy about it really . . . a bit sheepish about having been sloshed . . .' Aware that this hardly sounded like an ideal witness, the DS continued hastily, 'But then when we interviewed Clare Hunter, she confirmed it.'

'Did she say why she dropped out?' Knevitt pressed.

'It was something to do with being bullied by a colleague . . . plus, senior management never supported her over behaviour policies,' Doyle answered.

'The thing is, there wasn't a teacher misconduct panel or anything like that,' Carruthers chipped in. 'Apparently she just couldn't hack the toxic atmosphere.'

Having listened to Olivia over the years, Markham could well believe it.

Burton consulted her notes. 'I contacted the school, but management were very cagey,' she said. 'Water under the bridge, not their habit to divulge details of past employees, confidentiality yada yada. So no dice really.'

'It was the same with her GP,' Carruthers continued. 'He got pretty bolshie actually . . . more or less told us to back off.'

'Did Ms Kelleher say anything else about Clare Hunter?' Markham asked.

'She had an idea Maggie might've lived with her gran for a time on account of mum having issues . . . But again, she was pretty vague when it came to the specifics.'

'Probably on her tenth vodka tonic at the time,' Carruthers commented sardonically.

'D'you reckon she was *genuinely* confused?' Morrissey probed. 'Or could she have been frightened of landing herself in it if she said too much . . . worried about it getting out that she was a blabbermouth?'

Doyle considered the question carefully. 'Let's just say Eileen's not the sharpest knife in the drawer,' he concluded with a wary glance at Burton who was inclined to disapprove of elitist condescension.

'Suggestible?' Markham asked.

Carruthers was quick to cotton on. 'You mean someone wanted us to find out about Hunter's backstory, so they used Eileen to generate gossip—'

'An' throw sand in our eyes,' Noakes grunted.

'Well, once the rumours gained currency, we were bound to pick up on them eventually,' Knevitt said slowly. 'A useful diversion if our killer was worried that we were getting too close.'

'Are you saying Hunter's off the hook then?' Noakes objected. 'I mean, if she's looney tunes, that fits the profile for MSP, right?'

Knevitt turned to Burton, 'What did you make of Clare Hunter's reaction when you confronted her with all of this, Inspector?'

'Defensive, but that's hardly surprising,' Burton said. 'I'd say she's neurotic — maybe even got a bit of a persecution complex — but she was upfront about having struggled with motherhood.'

'A candidate for MSP?' Carruthers pressed her.

'I don't know,' she admitted with a sigh. 'By all accounts she's quite a hard character with a ruthless streak, which often happens where someone's been a victim of bullying . . . I suppose she *could* have some sort of twisted hang-up about motherhood and children. But I'd say there's genuine affection for Maggie, whatever their past difficulties—'

'Hunter was spitting feathers after the kid was attacked,' Doyle pointed out. 'I honestly thought she was going to take a pop at us.'

'That's because she felt guilty about letting Maggie wander about on her own and wanted to make *us* the scapegoats.' Carruthers had considerably less sympathy for the events manager.

'D'you honestly see her as a killer?' Doyle challenged his fellow sergeant.

'I think she's maybe unbalanced enough to pull people's strings . . . emotional manipulation, that kind of thing,' Carruthers rejoined. 'But I somehow can't see her whizzing round the place nicking horoscopes and leaving coded messages, let alone actually *murdering* anyone.' He twitched the horn-rimmed specs and cleared his throat fussily. '*My* money's on Lucy Winders for that kind of caper.'

Markham leaned forward, the dark eyes intent. 'How so?'

'I got talking to Sophie McGrath at the wake,' Carruthers began.

'Very cosy,' Noakes leered.

The DS ignored this. 'She told me Steven Winders had a thing for his ex . . . along with Daniel Locke and the chaplain

. . . said there was a scene at the opening of the exhibition in the Wakefield Tower when Charles Esdaile had a go at Locke about it, called him a pathetic lapdog.'

Knevitt's eyebrows shot up.

'Sophie thought it was quite funny,' Carruthers went on. 'She said Esdaile was pretty well oiled and that's what set him off.'

'Did she reckon there was any truth in what he said?' Morrissey asked.

'As she tells it, Locke's divorced and repressed and Margaret Esdaile most likely turned him down, which made him all the more bitter when she threatened to outstrip him academically.'

Knevitt whistled. 'No love lost between them then.'

'From what I've seen of Dr Locke, he'd be sure to find other reasons for his attitude than thwarted passion and vindictiveness,' Markham observed caustically, wondering if a compound of sexual disappointment and jealousy, constantly at its weaving work, could have led to murder. Maybe so, but then what of the Sullivan twins? What possible motive would such a man have had for their kidnap and murder? Was it possible that Margaret Esdaile's murder could after all be a crime of passion unconnected with that long-ago tragedy? And then, what about Antonia Winders?

Burton's voice interrupted his thoughts.

'You said your money was on Lucy Winders,' the DI reminded Carruthers. There was a slight edge to her voice as she asked, 'So where does the fair Sophie reckon *Lucy* fits into all of this?'

Unabashed by her sarcastic tone, the DS continued, 'Sophie said Lucy and Steven had arguments . . . Lucy convinced herself he was regretting their marriage and secretly wanted to go back to Margaret. She threw a hissy fit every time he went to see her, though to be fair he could hardly avoid it because of their work.'

'How come Sophie knows so much about their marriage?' Doyle asked curiously.

Carruthers shrugged. 'She notices things.'

'You mean she *snoops*,' Noakes rumbled.

The DS affected not to hear this. 'By the sound of it, the relationship was rocky,' he said coolly.

Suspicion and jealousy again, Markham thought with a sense of foreboding.

'Plus, Winders worried about Lucy being too highly strung,' Carruthers added. 'Apparently she was the neurotic type.'

'Like Clare Hunter,' Burton said flatly.

'God, this all feels like we're going round in circles,' Doyle burst out. 'We've got this psychopath on our hands and nobody has any clue why they're doing it or what they're going to do next. All we've come up with is there's these two unstable women.'

'Steven Winders and Charles Esdaile aren't out of the reckoning,' Burton pointed out. 'Don't forget, with each of them there's time unaccounted for.'

'Yeah, but it sounds like *Lucy's* the unbalanced one,' Carruthers insisted, 'with all kinds of issues around Margaret Esdaile and the state of her marriage.'

'Or maybe Lucy Winders has Munchausen's and all the weird stuff that went on with kids doesn't have anything to do with the Sullivans or Dr Esdaile. And what happened to Antonia was an accident. She had some kind of meltdown . . . some kind of aberration,' Doyle finished lamely.

'You're forgetting the kid was drugged,' Carruthers pointed out.

Noakes scowled at Doyle. 'So we're back to the two sickos theory then.'

Markham felt his head start to throb.

Too many damn possibilities.

'Did you get anything else from the wake?' he asked his team.

'It was only a small affair really,' Burton said. 'Tower staff mainly, but the catering side had laid on a decent spread. The Sullivans stayed for a bit, which was nice of them considering

. . . By and large it was pretty uneventful, though I overheard Benedict Ryan mutter something to Sophie McGrath out of the corner of his mouth.' Burton screwed up her face trying to remember. 'Something about not being so obvious.'

'What did he mean by that exactly?' Morrissey enquired.

'I can't be sure,' Burton replied, ever cautious. 'But she sidled up to Charles Esdaile when he arrived back from the cremation . . . all doe-eyed, flicky hair and her head on one side. She didn't get a very warm reception, though . . . he jerked back like he'd been stung. Whatever he said didn't go down too well. For a moment, she had a face like thunder, but she recovered pretty quickly and started circulating, working the room.'

Knevitt seized on this new line of enquiry 'Could she and Esdaile ever have got up to something . . . had an affair?'

'Well, Dr Ryan and Elena Rogers were giving her the evils,' Burton commented. 'I'd say she's an operator all right.'

'If there *was* something between her and Esdaile, sounds like it's over now at any rate,' Doyle conjectured.

'Gives her a motive for wanting Margaret Esdaile out of the picture,' Carruthers said thoughtfully. 'A woman scorned and all that.'

'Yeah, but what about the Sullivan twins an' the prowler stuff?' Noakes demanded. 'Jessica Rabbit were only a teenager back then an' she don' look the type to get her jollies frisking round doing weirdy stuff to kids.'

Markham could see that Doyle was trying not to laugh as Burton's eyes bulged at Noakes's latest nickname. But he had to admit it suited the curvy, flirtatious intern.

'I can see Sophie McGrath as a *femme fatale*,' he said, 'but I agree it's difficult to imagine her harming children.'

'The problem is, we can't seem to put any of our suspects in the frame for *both* Dr Esdaile's murder *and* the Sullivan abduction.' Knevitt sighed. 'And yet all the evidence suggests the two must be linked.'

'*Circumstantial* evidence.' Carruthers was punctilious about accuracy. Even considerations of rank didn't dent his self-confidence.

DCI Knevitt was secure enough to take the correction from a junior officer.

'True,' he said heavily.

'How about the warders?' Markham asked, doing his best to sound positive. 'Did any of *them* behave out of character?'

'I think Andy Campbell might've tried to goose one of the waitresses,' Doyle said. 'But I reckon that's probably totally *in character* for him.'

Burton's face and tone were tight. 'What makes you think he did that?'

'There was a little pantry thingy set up behind a screen,' Doyle told her. 'With the room being an oratory, I suppose they wanted to keep the kitchen stuff tucked out of sight.' He looked towards Carruthers as though telegraphing a request for help.

'That's right,' the other DS said smoothly. 'Seeing as it's kind of a shrine where they hold that ceremony of the lilies and roses — when students from Eton lay flowers to commemorate Henry the Sixth — they would have wanted everything low-key.'

Burton wasn't to be distracted by historical lore.

'Did you actually see Mr Campbell *assault* one of the caterers?' she asked Doyle flintily.

Oh FFS, lighten up ma'am. But Doyle didn't dare say it.

'It was a split-second thing,' he answered, clearly regretting having ever mentioned the incident. 'This girl just came round from behind the screen with a tray of canapés. She was offering them to Campbell and John Whittingham and then kind of jumped back. Come to think, it could've been either of them . . . she just looked startled is all I'm saying,' he added defensively.

Markham took pity on his floundering subordinate. 'As you say, Doyle, it's probably par for the course.'

'They were most likely jus' being friendly an' she got the wrong end of the stick,' Noakes insisted stubbornly, his face darkening at the aspersion on ex-servicemen.

Burton's expression suggested that she didn't credit her former colleague with having derived much benefit from those CID training courses on sex offenders, but the DI held her peace, mindful that Noakes had a blind spot where his beloved Tommies were concerned. As it didn't appear anyone had complained about the warders' behaviour, best to let sleeping dogs lie.

'The chaplain disappeared from the wake early on,' she said.

'Yeah, he looked quite ill actually.' Doyle was grateful her mind had moved on from delinquent warders.

'Sophie said he was sweet on Margaret Esdaile at one time,' Carruthers volunteered, 'so it probably hit him hard.'

'No, I think there might've been something else,' Burton said reflectively, her brow creasing. 'I looked out of the window and saw him arriving back from Manor Park with Charles Esdaile—'

'Well, he'd hardly be dancing a jig after that,' Noakes interrupted. 'The crem's usually a bit of a downer,' he added sarcastically.

'I saw a young man approach Fr Bernard, sarge,' Burton continued patiently. 'Staggeringly handsome — like a young Jeremy Irons — with an air about him . . . a real standout.'

Doyle and Carruthers looked at each other. It was rare for their buttoned-up DI to rhapsodize dreamily about the opposite sex.

She caught the exchange of glances and flushed slightly. 'It seemed like he knew Fr Bernard, but the padre's body language was a bit off, almost as if he'd been ambushed. He looked round to see if anyone was watching, muttered something and then kind of shooed the guy away . . . I couldn't see where he sloped off to, but it was obvious Fr Bernard was desperate to get rid of him.'

'I wonder,' Knevitt said slowly then broke off.

The others watched him expectantly.

'I wonder if the chaplain could be gay,' he said simply.

'But isn't he supposed to have had a crush on Margaret Esdaile?' Doyle was baffled.

'That might be a convenient fiction,' Morrissey pointed out, 'to hide that part of his private life.'

'Well there ain't no law against it,' Noakes shot back, red-faced.

Morrissey had come to like Markham's irascible sidekick and, moreover, had noticed an unlikely camaraderie between the ex-DS and Tower chaplain that was proof even against Noakes's iconoclasm and dodgy wit (personally, the DI had enjoyed overhearing him tell a credulous American tourist that 'Robert the Burns was famous for telling a spider, "If at first you don't succeed, then bleeding well push off!"'). So his tone was gentle and respectful as he replied, 'No indeed, and thank God we've come a long way from stigmatizing people for their sexuality.' He spoke so earnestly that Noakes visibly relaxed.

'Whatcha mean by him needing a cover story then?' the older man demanded gruffly.

'There are still pockets of prejudice,' Morrissey pointed out reasonably, 'especially in places like this — royal palaces where some people have hidebound attitudes.'

'But nowadays we've got LGBT and trans clergy,' Doyle protested. 'So it's not very realistic if they think the chaplain's gotta be hetero.'

'Quite.' Morrissey smiled thinly. 'But from what I've seen, there are still folk without the cranial capacity to understand different sexualities. I reckon Fr Bernard might've wanted to protect himself from any gossip or vendetta . . . strikes me he wouldn't be up to handling that sort of gameplay.'

'A private man,' Knevitt agreed.

'What are we saying then?' Carruthers invariably liked things cut and dried. 'That Mr Tall Dark and Handsome has something on the padre?'

'You mean like murder and kidnap!' Doyle exclaimed incredulously.

'How about theft of artefacts?' Burton interjected.

They all turned to stare at her.

'If Fr Bernard's being blackmailed by a younger lover, why not that?' she demanded. 'We know Dr Ryan accused Elena Rogers of "misplacing" a valuable Victorian manuscript, but it could just as easily have been the chaplain who took it from her desk. The two of them are friendly, so he'd know what she was working on.'

'Could jus' be he didn't want to be seen with some pretty boy,' Noakes mumbled. 'Like Morrissey said before, he were worried someone might point the finger . . . Jessica Rabbit would *love* a piece of juicy gossip like that.'

'If the bloke's that dishy, she'd probably want a piece of the action,' Doyle said cynically, with an inward shudder as he recalled the predations of Natalie Noakes. No disrespect to sarge, but he reckoned he'd dodged a bullet there!

'You don't seriously think the chaplain's mixed up in murder and kidnap, though, do you ma'am?' he asked Burton, his voice high-pitched with alarm.

'I don't know what to think any more,' she said uncertainly.

'Maybe the chaplain was mixed up in that horoscope business . . . maybe he, Elena Rogers and Mr Tall Dark and Handsome are all involved in it together.'

Burton turned a frosty eye on Carruthers, not caring at all for a certain sly inflexion in his allusion to the mysterious stranger.

'Woah there,' Noakes expostulated. 'We're getting ahead of ourselves . . . like the padre's Raffles or summat.'

'I agree,' Burton said flatly. 'All we've got right now is Fr Bernard in the company of a young man looking furtive and uncomfortable . . . Still—'

'We need to check it out,' Knevitt finished the sentence.

As the detectives sat digesting this latest development, the telephone rang on Knevitt's desk.

He said little, his features giving nothing away. As he replaced the receiver, however, Markham detected a glimmer of hope kindling in the DCI's eyes and felt an answering tingle.

Could they be on the verge of a breakthrough?

'Talk of the devil,' Knevitt said as five pairs of eyes bored into him. 'That was Fr Bernard. Apparently, there's something he wants to tell us.'

'Christ, the padre's going to cough,' Carruthers breathed. Catching Markham's expression of distaste (for the DI deplored blasphemy), the DS hastily amended, 'Something must've happened . . . ten to one it's connected with that young guy.'

'Somehow I don't think we'll be hearing a confession to murder,' Knevitt said.

'Or kidnap,' Morrissey added glumly.

Markham was inclined to agree with their verdict. And yet when the telephone rang, he had felt his heart do a funny little skip and sensed a prickling at the nape of his neck — one of those strange 'twilight zone' moments he often experienced at the climax of a case, when the ordinary and everyday elided into a realm of surreal evil, leaving him feeling almost otherworldly. He was sure Kate Burton felt something too, one hand pressed against her chest as though to calm a racing heart. The two young sergeants simply looked as though they itched to be part of the unfolding drama.

Despite this latest development, none of the detectives seemed inclined to move, almost as though time had slowed to a trickle and some sinister influence laid them under a spell.

Beyond the windows of their incident room, snow shrouded the little courtyard and muffled all sound. The tourists would now have left for the day, Markham realised, leaving the Tower to its ravens and spectres. Suddenly, he recalled Olivia telling him of the dark shadow of an axe that was rumoured to fall upon Tower Green when danger threatened the castle and wondered if it was looming there now as twilight gave way to night. With a cold shiver at the base of his spine, he thought of all those strange Tudor mannequins — Anne Boleyn, Jane Grey, Walter Raleigh and the rest — and imagined them listening, waiting out there in a winter landscape which gleamed blue black under the floodlights.

187

An antique time piece on the fireplace overmantel suddenly chimed five o'clock, breaking the spell.

'How do you want to do this, Len?' Markham asked the DCI, ever conscious that the investigation properly belonged to Knevitt and Morrissey. 'If we all pile in — go in mob-handed — there's a risk Fr Bernard might clam up.'

Knevitt considered this. 'I'm willing to chance it,' he said finally. 'Noakes can take the lead, seeing as he's already got a handle on the man. The rest of us can stay in the background . . . nice and low-key and unthreatening.'

Noakes beamed, transparently delighted to be assigned a starring role, while Markham reflected on the generosity of spirit which meant Knevitt was prepared to take a back seat. Certain glory-hoggers in Bromgrove CID could have learned much from his example.

Making their way from the Queen's House to the chaplain's office, the atmosphere of dreamlike enchantment enveloped them again. The snow had stopped falling, but the air was cold and still, their breath condensing in little plumes as they went.

Outside the Bell Tower they paused, looking up at the thick stone walls which once shut out the hum of life for Thomas More and John Fisher, replacing it with a stillness like that of the grave, the graffiti left by former prisoners mute attestation of man's inhumanity to man.

Somewhere beyond the ramparts a church clock tolled the quarter hour, solemnly like a knell.

Markham's whole body tensed, as if the sound was a signal that the fortress prison was at last ready to unlock its secrets.

All they needed was the key.

CHAPTER 12: BREAKING THE SEAL

The chaplain's office was dominated by its monumental *Field of the Cloth of Gold* depicting glowing turrets, towers, islets, palanquins and gorgeously ornamented tents.

'Incredible the way they threw up them flatpack castles back then,' Noakes said admiringly, for all the world, Carruthers commented afterwards, as if they had blundered into an episode of *Grand Designs* instead of gearing up to confront a potential prime suspect.

Markham, however, knew what his wingman was about.

In his own inimitable way, Noakes was creating a safe space where the haunted looking clergyman would find the confidence to divulge whatever secrets troubled his conscience.

It seemed to work, Fr Bernard's careworn features relaxing into a smile.

'What's with the flying dragon?' Doyle asked in a tone of genuine curiosity, peering at the top left-hand corner of the painting.

'Part of a medieval fireworks display,' the chaplain informed him. 'Though it could symbolize the powers of evil,' he added hesitantly. 'Treason . . . peasants revolting . . .'

'Or revolting peasants, depending on how you look at it,' Noakes quipped pleasantly.

Kate Burton knew that once their fish was baited, Noakes would proceed to reel in the line. Like him, she took an unhurried survey of the impressive room: walls panelled in oak up to halfway and dark ochre above, deep armchairs and sofa in rich crimson leather and matching velvet curtains either side of a leaded window. An array of oil paintings behind the large leather-topped antique desk were what she privately designated 'the doublets and farthingales variety'. The faded carpet was probably beyond price, she reflected, likewise two inlaid mahogany display cabinets flanking a tiled Victorian fireplace. There was no blaze in the grate, but the room was warm thanks to discreetly positioned radiators and an electric fire, while pools of light from antique lamps softened its cavernous dimensions.

'Isn't that John Fisher?' she asked once they were seated, pointing to the portrait of a lugubrious, lantern-jawed cleric in black velvet cap and stole who gazed out at them from a frame noticeably more gilded than the rest.

'Correct.' The chaplain was visibly relieved by the casual enquiry.

Carruthers followed her lead. 'What's that down by his feet?'

'The red cardinal's hat. Pope Paul the Third made him a cardinal the month before he was executed.'

'Bet *that* got up Haz's nose,' Noakes said with satisfaction, having formed no very favourable impression of Henry VIII.

'Visitors are always full of Thomas More,' Fr Bernard told them, 'but Bishop Fisher was just as remarkable.'

'Isn't he the one who used to carry a dead man's skull everywhere — even put it on the table when he was having dinner?'

Trust Burton to be up on all the creepy details, Carruthers thought with grudging admiration. She'd probably been mugging up on Tudor history from the minute they got the green light for this investigation.

'Correct, Inspector.' The chaplain's melancholic features softened still further. 'John Fisher had something of a morbid fixation. When saying Mass, he always put the skull in front of him. It was the same at all his meals.'

'Sounds a right barrel of laughs,' Noakes grunted disparagingly.

'You have to remember, death wasn't quite the chamber of horrors that it is for us, Mr Noakes,' came the quiet response. 'The medievals thought of their dead as being in a real sense mingled with those still on earth . . . all one great family, if you like, connected by an unbreakable bond.' Diffidently he added, 'It's difficult to explain, but I've always found it a comforting concept.'

Hearing him, Markham felt suddenly convinced that the chaplain was innocent of kidnap and murder.

Carruthers too had reached the same conclusion. The man might be a total wet wipe, he thought with the dismissive cruelty of youth, but this wasn't a ruthless killer in front of them.

'Bishop Fisher was famous for speaking truth to power,' the chaplain told Noakes, cannily aware that this was a trait bound to appeal to Markham's sidekick. 'When Henry the Seventh was dying, Fisher never let up, he was so determined to bring him to a "wholesome fear and dread" of his sinfulness, particularly avarice and greed.'

'Nice one.' Noakes thoroughly approved. 'S'pose he wanted to get the king time off Purgatory.' As a rule, the former DS didn't hold with Papist practices but was clearly prepared to meet the chaplain halfway, Markham thought wryly.

'Well, Henry the Seventh made an exemplary death in the best approved fashion,' Fr Bernard replied. Gesturing to the shelves that covered one wall, he added, 'A popular motto in those days was "Learn to die and you shall learn to live". The book *Ars Moriendi*, or *The Craft of Dying*, was a best seller . . . helped people to make a good end.'

Noakes had his opening. 'Dr Esdaile never got to make a good end,' he said gruffly. 'Nor them Sullivan twins an' Mrs Hernan. Look padre—' he leaned forward intently — 'we know *you* ain't mixed up in it, but if there's something you need to tell us, *now's* the time to come clean.'

So Noakes too had concluded that Fr Bernard was innocent of homicide and kidnap, Markham reflected. His friend might not be playing this interview by the book, but the kind, down-to-earth sympathy was almost a guarantee of police integrity.

The chaplain's smile died away, but as Noakes's assurance of trust fell on his ears, it was clear this mark of confidence had changed the lights for him and he was now prepared to tell them everything.

He drew a deep breath.

'Thank you for believing in me,' he said. 'I could never have hurt those children, let alone Mrs Hernan . . . As for Margaret, she was a fine woman with an ardent commitment to the Tower,' he continued.

'You weren't in love with her then,' Noakes prompted, approaching the subject of the other's sexuality with unusual sensitivity.

'She was my friend . . . I guess you might call her a beard.'

Seeing that Doyle was looking nonplussed, he explained awkwardly. 'People here assumed that my feelings for her went deeper than friendship and I didn't correct them . . . it was cover for my being gay.'

'That ain't a crime,' Noakes declared stoutly, winning himself an approving glance from Burton.

'True, Mr Noakes. But,' the other added ruefully, 'I have to wear a poker-player's face here at the Tower. Being a landmark of the British Crown, there's an old guard,' he gave a hollow chuckle, 'almost literally given that the constable and other notables are mostly ex-Guards Regiment with rigid notions about . . . propriety.' Catching sight of Noakes's expression, he said hastily, 'Don't get me wrong, most of the warders and younger guard are a different story — far more empathetic and accepting — but with those at the top of the tree, the tone and style of working are very establishment . . . all about order, gentility and appearances.'

'As in, don't frighten the horses,' Carruthers interjected sardonically.

Fr Bernard nodded vigorously. 'Exactly that, Sergeant.' He bit his lip. 'It makes them sound like caricatures, or a species on the edge of extinction, but I bought into it all and never wanted to rock the boat by letting them know.' With a touch of defiance he added, 'Anyway, I figured it was nobody's business except my own.'

'Did Dr Esdaile know the truth?' Markham asked, recalling Morrissey's previous comments about the Tower's hidebound culture which, in the circumstances, demonstrated considerable insight.

'I think Margaret guessed, but she never pried . . . It was one of the things I liked about her,' the chaplain answered simply.

'Are you, er, in a whatchamacallit *relationship* at the moment?'

It was comical, thought Markham, to see Noakes aiming for a man-of-the-world lightness of touch, despite this falling well and truly outside his comfort zone.

'I am, yes. And that's been my undoing really.' Markham was struck by how haggard the priest looked as he made the admission.

'Tony's much younger than me,' Fr Bernard continued. 'I suppose that's part of the attraction really . . . You see, I was so afraid I might end my days like Tennyson's Mariana, surrounded by dilapidation and decay.'

Noakes fiddled awkwardly with his regimental tie (which, unusually for him, didn't clash too horribly with a fairly respectable brown tweed combo). He was never terribly comfortable when the subject of poetry came up, always insisting to Olivia that 'Kelly an' Sheets' gave him the 'hump' and he 'couldn't be doing with all that about larks an' linnets an' nymphos'. However, he flailed his features into an approximation of deferential commiseration.

'Kind of like a mid-life crisis,' he prompted awkwardly as Carruthers smothered a grin.

The chaplain looked somewhat startled at Noakes's suggestion but, after a brief hesitation, nodded. 'I suppose you could call it that,' he conceded before resuming his account. 'Tony told me he was attracted to older men, but I was always afraid of him falling for someone of his own age . . . And the unpleasantnesses of elderliness meant I was afraid of toppling from my pedestal.'

'Come off it,' Noakes urged in a burst of bonhomie. 'You ain't past it by a long way.'

With a pensive air, the other replied, 'Kind of you to say so, Mr Noakes, but there was an imbalance of power in the relationship.' He started up from his armchair and went over to the window, momentarily forgetting where he was. After an interval, he turned back to them and resumed his seat.

'We c'n see this ain't easy for you, padre,' Noakes said kindly. 'But no one's judging you an' we've all got into messes from time to time.' As indeed they had, Markham thought to himself.

'Tony wasn't well off,' the chaplain resumed, telling his story in a dull, mechanical voice, almost as though it concerned someone else. 'He dabbled in interior design and antiques but wasn't what you'd call successful. As time went on, he was getting restless and started to resent my emotional dependence on him. It was a complication that women were attracted to him — drawn to him like moths to a flame. He had a childlike, grasping side too, but that was probably down to a difficult upbringing . . .' A deep sigh. 'Turgenev said love is never equal. There is always one who loves and one who is loved.'

Oh God, Noakes groaned inwardly. Sounds like he's back on bleeding poetry again. Time to bring him down from the clouds.

'So old Tone was using you to feather his nest,' the former DS said bluntly.

'It sounds terrible when you put it like that, but I think he was after the kind of affair where a young man is kept in style by his wealthy older lover while reserving the right to play the field . . . And I was so in thrall to him. Every time he said, "I can find someone younger than you," I felt I would do anything to keep him.'

Privately, Noakes thought the lad sounded a right little shit. Glancing across at Knevitt and Morrissey, who had determinedly stayed in the background, he could see by their expressions that they felt the same.

Now for the nitty gritty.

'You said you'd do anything to keep him, padre . . . did that include filching stuff . . . valuable manuscripts kind of thing?' Noakes cleared his throat uncomfortably. ''Cos there were that manuscript Dr Ryan got all worked up about . . . the one he thought the conservation lass had nicked—'

'Plus the psalter thingy that went missing from Middleham,' Doyle interrupted eagerly before subsiding at Noakes's warning scowl.

'I know nothing about the psalter,' Fr Bernad said quickly. 'Absolutely nothing,' he repeated with such conviction that it was clear he was telling the truth. 'As for the Anne Warwick manuscript, that was just a moment of craziness, an insane impulse when Elena's back was turned.' His upper lip was beaded with sweat. 'Artefacts *have* occasionally gone missing over the years, though internal audit policies are much tighter these days. Tony kept badgering me to do more for him, but I'm not rich and my stipend only goes so far. Everything you see in here came with the job, none of it belongs to me personally . . .' His voice trailed off miserably.

'With Tone being in the antiques line, you reckoned he'd be able to fence the book an' earn himself a tidy commission into the bargain,' Noakes summed up, thinking that he would very much like to wring the greedy scrote's neck. 'Am I right?'

'Pretty much, yes.' The chaplain passed a shaking hand across his face. 'I don't know what came over me . . . After all that fuss about the horoscope which ended up on Elena's desk, I figured *she* would carry the can for any further misplaced items. Of course I'm ashamed now . . . I know it was a rotten thing to do.' A far-away look came into his eyes. 'I know it sounds weird, but there was something uncanny about that volume . . . it *drew* me somehow, so that I felt almost *compelled* to take it.'

Noakes didn't like the sound of this. Voodoo territory by the sound of it. Hardly surprising, though, given the strain the poor bloke had been under.

'Where's the book now?' he asked.

'In my flat,' came the reply. 'In the end, I just couldn't bring myself to hand it over to Tony.' There was a desperate note of appeal as the chaplain asked, 'If I put it back, does any of this have to come out?'

'There may be a way round it,' Knevitt weighed in. Compassionately, he added, 'None of us is immune from temptation, sir.' Like Noakes, the DCI shied away from 'Father'.

Seeing their interviewee's dejection, Noakes endeavoured to lighten the atmosphere, even eliciting a shaky smile with his well-worn joke about the health facility where a large notice proclaimed *Warning: Security guards operate in this hospital.*

Finally, ever so casually, he prompted, 'There's summat else you wanted to tell us, right?'

The clergyman looked deeply troubled but evidently decided he must "screw his courage to the sticking place".

'I'm friendly with Pat Molloy, one of the Catholic priests over at English Martyrs on Tower Hill. He ministers to the Catholics here.'

Doyle and Carruthers shifted impatiently, clearly apprehensive that this revelation heralded a stream of religious arcana. However, the chaplain surprised them.

'Fr Molloy had concerns about one of his parishioners . . . felt anxious after hearing their confession the other day,' he explained. 'Obviously, being bound by the seal of the confessional, there were limits on what he could tell me. But he felt maybe I ought to know about it in light of Dr Esdaile's murder and everything else that's gone on.'

Noakes's eyes gleamed. 'Did they confess to murder an' kidnap by any chance?' His tone was jokey but the room seemed to hold its breath as the detectives waited for Fr Bernard's answer.

'No, it was nothing like that . . . just a sense that something was badly off-kilter . . . that she needed help.'

She.

'Who're we talking about here?' Noakes pressed. 'I mean, you c'n give us a name, right?'

The chaplain gave an embarrassed laugh. 'I'm probably sending you on a wild goose chase.'

'You let us be the judge of that, sir,' Morrissey said stolidly.

'Fr Pat's known the Campbells for ever, practically from the time he moved to English Martyrs in 2005. They're regulars at his eleven thirty Mass and Justine helps out with the mother and baby group . . . apparently they can always rely on her when it comes to parish events, bring and buys and so forth. Actually, the more I think about it, the harder it is to imagine her having any sort of mental health issues—'

'Were those the words your mate used?' Noakes cut in. 'Mental health issues?'

The other screwed up his face, remembering.

'Yes, I believe that's what he said.'

'Could you contact Fr Molloy for us, please sir,' the DCI spoke up. 'We'd like to talk to him right away.' There was an urgent undercurrent to the request.

Despite the warmth and lamplight, it seemed to the group that the room was suddenly colder and darker, as though the shadow of evil had fallen across it.

'Sergeants,' Knevitt turned to Doyle and Carruthers who sprang to attention, 'I want you to ascertain Mrs Campbell's whereabouts and arrange discreet surveillance. Tower Bridge can give you a couple of undercovers . . . We need to have eyes on her twenty-four seven.'

The chaplain looked dazed at the speed with which events were unfolding. Markham too was surprised by the DCI's intensity of purpose.

Once back in their incident room, with Burton assigned to collect Fr Molloy from his presbytery, he turned to Knevitt, struck by his colleague's expression of grim determination.

'You seem very sure that this is our breakthrough, Len.'

'Back there, I remembered something . . .' Knevitt broke off, looking self-conscious.

'Spit it out then.' Noakes hoped the DCI wasn't going all fey on them. The padre's moonshine about books giving out spooky vibes was bad enough.

Knevitt said, 'One of the cleaners mentioned that Dr Esdaile reacted badly to an art installation, suddenly went and took a dislike to the Lady Jane Grey dummy.'

Noakes scratched his head. 'Yeah, Pam wossname . . . nice kid but maybe a bit airy fairy,' he added warningly. 'Caught up in the romance an' all them legends.' Like half of 'em in this place, he thought dourly.

'That's right, it was Pam Appleton,' Markham mused. 'I recall now . . . she said that Dr Esdaile described the mannequin as a "whey-faced monstrosity". It seemed rather an extreme reaction.'

'I don't know if you've noticed, but the head bears an uncanny resemblance to Justine Campbell,' Knevitt continued slowly. 'The rabbity face and wispy hair . . . same furtive expression. As soon as the chaplain said her name, it flashed through my mind, like a sign or something.'

Now he came to think of it, there *was* something vaguely unsettling about the figure's soft placating expression, Markham reflected, but he had presumed the sculptor was unsure whether to cast the Nine Days Queen as plotter or martyr.

Noakes was looking dubious. 'Not much to go on, though,' he grunted, wondering if lah-di-dah airy fairiness was infectious.

'You remember that volunteer . . . the flower arranger who told us Maggie Hunter was down in the crypt—' Morrissey began.

'What about her?' Noakes demanded impatiently.

'Well, *she* told me it was Justine Campbell who zeroed in on her when everyone was searching for Maggie Hunter and a couple of the warders said Justine made a beeline for the church. What if that's because she knew *exactly* where to find Maggie — because *she'd* put her there — and wanted to be at the centre of the drama . . . wanted to be the one who "rescued" the kid? I heard people calling her a heroine afterwards, and she seemed to like it.'

'Bit of a stretch from wanting some attention to snatching kids an' committing murder,' observed the Greek chorus.

'But attention-seeking fits with the Munchausen profile,' Morrissey pointed out doggedly.

'Look,' Knevitt said briskly, 'it sounds like this Fr Molloy will be able to fill us in on Justine Campbell's background, so we won't have to raise suspicions by asking HR for her personal file . . . *that* would most likely start the rumour mill off, which is the last thing we want.'

'Molloy and the chaplain won't blab,' Morrissey added. 'Clergy confidentiality and all that jazz.'

'Plus, the padre couldn't get his head round the idea of Campbell being involved,' Noakes commented sagely. 'I can't meself to be honest. The idea of that scraggy little creature being the Tower prowler . . . doing for those kids an' then butchering Esdaile . . . bludgeoning Mrs H. an' all. Happen she's a few sarnies short of a picnic, but a cold-blooded killer . . . nah!'

'I'd bet the farm on it being her,' Knevitt said. 'She and Andy are almost part of the Tower furniture. If anyone would've been able to win the Sullivan twins' trust, it was her.'

Noakes frowned. 'Are you thinking Andy was in on it too?' he asked, clearly reluctant to credit the ex-serviceman's complicity.

'We can't rule it out,' Knevitt acknowledged, 'but something tells me he's a straight shooter whereas with *her* . . .'

'You seem very certain about this, Len,' Markham repeated quietly, thinking that it was quite unlike the phlegmatic DCI to rely on intuition or "copper's hunch".

Knevitt grinned ruefully. 'I imagine the likes of Sidney and Ebury-Clarke would give my ESP short shrift, but the hairs rose on the back of my neck as Fr Bernard was talking and I suddenly had this terrifying hint of a thought that Justine Campbell's the key to it all.' Sheepishly he added, 'The Tower's a strange place, so perhaps that's why I'm picking up on all these emanations . . . Inspector Burton told me that Shakespeare calls it a slaughterhouse in one of his plays.'

Par for the bleeding course, Noakes thought moodily (failing to notice that Markham had stiffened at Knevitt's reference to his fellow DI). No doubt she scented a fellow boffin in Knevitt, though the bloke had seemed too sound to be spouting all this stuff about *emanations* an' ESP an' whatnot.

'Let's see what Fr Molloy gives us then,' Markham said quietly. 'You did well getting Fr Bernard to open up, Noakesy,' he added.

'Yeah,' Morrissey agreed. 'I reckon he was in two minds about it to start with . . . but now we've got a lead of sorts.'

Mollified, Noakes turned to Knevitt. 'Ten to one Campbell's jus' some saddo angling for attention from the local *Fleabag* "hot priest".' Markham felt profoundly grateful that Burton wasn't present to hear his friend's breezy denigration. 'But if you're right about her, I owe you twenty quid,' Noakes concluded magnanimously.

* * *

Noakes looked set to lose his bet, Markham thought in their incident room an hour and a half later. Outside, a sharp wind had picked up, whistling and gusting round pitch black ginnels, courtyards and alleyways, but the team paid it no mind as they absorbed the implications of what they had learned.

Fr Molloy hardly resembled the 'hot priest' conjured up by Noakes, being a balding, rubicund, double-chinned figure more reminiscent of Friar Tuck than anyone exotic. However, his manner impelled trust, and what he had told them upped the ante considerably.

'Okay, I'll kick off.' The DCI began his summary of the interview. 'A middle-aged woman trapped in an unhappy marriage, history of miscarriages, didn't fulfil her potential and dropped out of college, jealous of her younger sister who seemed to have it all — doting husband and children, university job, vibrant social life blah blah.' He nodded at Morrissey who took over.

'Difficulties sustaining relationships, possible BPD, tendency to develop obsessive fixations about people and unable to cope with rejection.' The DI paused meaningfully. 'Fr Molloy said Justine was upset when Marie Sullivan rebuffed her attempts to build a friendship, though she seemed to get over it by throwing herself into parish stuff so he didn't attach too much importance to her saying it was karma when the Sullivan kids went missing.'

'Whass BPD?' Noakes disliked acronyms, but this one rang a vague bell.

'Borderline Personality Disorder,' Morrissey replied. 'With Molloy being a qualified counsellor, he'd have clocked the signs quicker than most people.'

'Taking a risk by chumming up with him, wasn't she?' Noakes was puzzled. 'I mean, sounds like she spilled her guts . . . for all she knew, he might've put the men in white coats on to her.'

'He knew her as a devout parishioner,' Markham pointed out. 'It was clear he'd never flagged her as a danger to the public.'

'Until her last confession,' Carruthers interjected.

'Even then, he only spoke about it in the broadest terms,' Markham pointed out.

'Yeah, worried about breaking the seal an' all that,' Noakes said irritably.

'But *that's* when it looks like she tripped up,' Markham went on. 'Let slip something that raised a red flag with Fr Molloy and made him wonder if there could be a connection with the prowler incidents and what happened to Maggie Hunter . . . Margaret Esdaile's murder was nagging at his subconscious as well, though he shied away from seeing Justine as a killer. Marie Sullivan worships at English Martyrs too — quite probably confided to Fr Molloy that we were reopening the Sullivan case — so he'd have been hyper alert to anything iffy involving the Tower.'

'He should've gone to the cop shop,' Noakes growled.

'After the attack on Maggie Hunter, he dropped a strong hint to the chaplain in hopes that Fr Bernard could do some digging which would rule Justine out, since he didn't feel that whatever went down in confession justified him charging in and flinging accusations around,' Markham reasoned.

'Catholics are dead set against "calumny and detraction",' Burton agreed. 'He'd have been in serious trouble with his bosses if he mishandled things. Besides, he couldn't square what he knew with the notion of Justine being a serial killer.'

'Stuff all that nicey-nicey seal of the confessional malarkey,' Noakes groused. 'Molloy should never have kept schtum.'

Now Burton took over. 'Fair point, sarge, but we've got plenty of intel that's useful. In terms of symptoms, there's an obvious overlap between BPD and MSP,' she explained. 'Unstable self-image, mood swings, pronounced fear of rejection and depression. Quite a lot of people suffer from BPD—'

'Didn't Princess Di have it?' Doyle piped up eagerly, feeling himself to be quite up on the subject, what with Kelly being a devoted fan of the late Princess.

Burton, never very keen on discussion of 'slebs', gave a tight smile. 'Well, the jury's still out on that one,' she said, 'but a number of psychiatrists think the Princess may have struggled with the condition . . . Other markers include distrustfulness, attention-seeking, a tendency to see people in black and white and pronounced feelings of victimization.' The DI was in her element as she rattled off the list of indicators.

'Justine had good reason to cast herself as a victim if Molloy was right about her husband being a bully,' Knevitt ruminated. 'What was that phrase he mentioned . . .'

'She told Fr Molloy he was a "street angel and a house devil" and sometimes wished he was dead,' Burton said baldly. 'Mind you, she always rowed back on it afterwards, so he couldn't be sure what was truth and what was fantasy.'

'But he *was* bothered by her fixation on Anne Neville,' Morrissey reminded them. 'Didn't think it was healthy the way she went on about how everyone wronged the woman but she got her revenge on Richard the Third and the rest of them from beyond the grave. Hearing her talk like that gave him the sense everything was getting jumbled in her mind and he worried that she was losing touch with reality.'

Markham recalled how Mrs Noakes had speculated about the possibility of the Tower's unique ambience inducing malign symptoms in an unstable or histrionic personality and, not for the first time, wondered at Muriel's flashes of prescience. Come to think of it, Doggie Dickerson had said something similar — about the Tower's capacity to send people 'round the twist'.

'The Tower community would see Justine Campbell pass and think that a colourless shadow had gone by,' he said slowly. 'It was the perfect camouflage.'

'So you reckon *she* was the prowler?' Noakes demanded.

'Look, she'd been part of the Tower "family" for donkey's years,' Markham continued. 'Knew the castle inside out and did cleaning shifts too—'

'Access All Areas,' Doyle cut in earnestly. 'And if she was spying on Dr Esdaile, she'd have known where to find that piece of paper with the creepy pictures from the Lennox whatsit.'

Morrissey nodded. 'Maintenance said only trusted personnel were assigned to the Queen's House, and with her being married to a long-serving warder it meant she had *carte blanche* to snoop.'

'D'you reckon it was *her* who planted that horoscope on Elena Rogers' desk?' Doyle asked him.

'Most likely yes,' Morrissey replied. 'It suited her to have everyone looking sideways at Elena . . . plus, I think she probably enjoyed making mischief and getting under Dr Esdaile's skin.'

'Margaret Esdaile would've kept Justine at arm's length,' Knevitt surmised. 'I imagine she was probably shrewd enough to intuit that Campbell was unstable. And by all accounts she was great pals with Marie Sullivan—'

'Another twist of the knife, seeing as Marie had rejected Justine's overtures,' Burton finished.

'And then Dr Esdaile found out something about the Sullivan abduction which prompted her to contact the police.' Carruthers picked up the thread. 'Something which potentially implicated *Campbell* . . . which could've explained why she suddenly took against that mannequin, assuming it reminded her of Justine.'

'But Esdaile didn't work in the Tower at the time when the twins disappeared,' Doyle objected.

'She must've been uneasy about Justine,' Carruthers resumed. 'Like Fr Molloy, she couldn't really imagine her to be a kidnapper or killer . . . But there was something that niggled . . . something that bothered her and preyed on her mind . . . an unguarded remark or some interaction that made her want the police to check Justine out, for her own peace of mind.'

Burton looked thoughtful. 'She might have wanted *Andy* Campbell checked out too . . . Perhaps *both* of them worried her for some reason.'

'Esdaile must've been careless and given herself away,' Doyle said, 'else how would Campbell have realized she was suspicious?'

'She could've overheard the phone call to DI Morrissey,' Burton suggested, 'or possibly a change in Dr Esdaile's manner towards her was the giveaway.'

Noakes got in on the act. 'Mebbe Esdaile started sniffing around . . . asking questions about the Campbells an' *that* set the alarm bells going.'

'It was complete overkill, though, the way she went for Esdaile,' Doyle said with a reminiscent shudder. 'The autopsy reports said *multiple stabbings*, right?' His words hung heavily in the air.

'Correct,' Knevitt grimaced.

'It's possible Justine had tried to establish a friendship with Dr Esdaile as well as Marie Sullivan,' Burton hazarded. 'If she was knocked back, it could have plunged her into a downward spiral and triggered feelings of intense animosity towards Dr Esdaile. The fact that Margaret Esdaile and Marie Sullivan were friends would only make the bitterness and sense of abandonment worse.'

Again, Markham saw admiration for Burton in the DCI's eyes and tried to ignore the discontent that lanced through him. He knew he should be glad that others appreciated her worth but felt a gut-twist of sadness at the prospect of losing a colleague who had somehow become his strength and stay, almost as important to him as Noakes.

Careful, he told himself. No need to advertise how he felt, particularly given the ex-DS's disconcerting ability to read his mind.

'That's a very persuasive analysis, Kate,' he said calmly as she blushed with pleasure.

'So Campbell's barking then,' Noakes grunted. 'A total basket case.'

'BPD means someone can appear superficially intact when in reality they're experiencing internal chaos,' Burton replied thoughtfully. 'But it doesn't necessarily follow that they're mad in the conventional sense.'

'Downright wicked, if you ask me,' Doyle spoke up. 'Especially if she's killed those two kids *and* did all the other stuff.' He frowned. 'Could she *really* have done that?' he asked the room at large.

'Oh I think she could,' Knevitt answered. 'Annie and Dominic Sullivan would have trusted her . . . and, if she plotted it over a long time, with her knowledge of the Tower's layout — all its secret hiding places — she would have known how to ensure they were never found. She's small but pretty wiry, so with the advantage of surprise, she could easily get the upper hand.'

'Why'd she go after Maggie Hunter?' Doyle wanted to know. 'Or any of the kids she stalked?'

'That's where the MSP would have kicked in,' Burton argued. 'A desire for attention and urge to be at the centre of things . . . mixed up with some kind of sadistic impulse towards children, most likely because she wasn't able to have her own kids and almost begrudged their existence . . . hated seeing others' happiness.'

'Makes her sound like the witch out of *Hansel and Gretel*,' Doyle observed uneasily.

'Fr Molloy said Justine could be very inconsistent round children,' Markham reminded him. 'Almost smothering them with affection one minute, then teasing and winding them up the next . . . He put it down to the lack of a stable family life.'

'If Justine carried all that psychic baggage, then it could've triggered almost total dissociation from the terrible things she did,' Burton ruminated. 'Let's face it, keeping the demons at bay must have been practically a full-time job, but then there came a point when she was totally detached from the real world.'

'Fr Molloy may have acted like some sort of safety valve,' Carruthers suggested.

'How d'you mean?' Noakes grunted.

'Well, maybe that was the first time she felt accepted for who she truly was,' the young DS said diffidently.

This struck Markham as an empathetic observation, reminding him that there was more to his superficially sardonic subordinate than met the eye.

'So Justine was very close to the edge at Margaret Esdaile's funeral,' Burton resumed. 'It would have stirred up all kinds of resentments and unhealed wounds, and the demons came out so she just couldn't help herself . . . went after Antonia Winders . . . planned on doing something to her, though we don't know precisely what . . . and then Mrs Hernan walked in on them.'

'She was so mousy and insignificant that no one ever suspected her,' Doyle marvelled. 'Like the invisible woman or something.'

'I can't help wondering if that confession, or whatever it was, to Fr Molloy was Justine's way of turning herself in,' Burton said slowly. 'Maybe she desperately *wanted* to be stopped.'

Noakes was becoming impatient with the speculation. 'Where does Andy Campbell come into all of this?' he demanded with a belligerence which again demonstrated his reluctance to believe the warder could have been complicit.

'That's anyone's guess,' Knevitt rejoined wearily. 'Like I said before, my sense of it is that Justine acted alone.'

Noakes's fists unclenched, some of the tension leaving him.

'How're we gonna nail her?' he asked simply. 'Fr Roly Poly ain't given us enough for an arrest . . . reckon he would've told us if she'd actually come right out in confession an' said she were the murderer.'

'Agreed,' Knevitt said. 'But there's sufficient to treat Justine as our new prime suspect.'

No one demurred.

'I think I know how we can do it,' Burton spoke up.

She had their attention now.

'The chaplain owes us,' she said calmly. 'Quid pro quo. We sort the business with that manuscript and he helps us trap a killer.'

'He'd make a total Horlicks of it,' Carruthers retorted scornfully.

'He's our best bet,' Burton insisted. 'With Justine being deeply religious, a clergyman's best placed to make her open up.'

'Won't she smell a rat?' Doyle objected.

'Not if we make sure he presses all the right buttons . . . Fr Molloy seemed to think she was unravelling pretty rapidly, so if we can only apply the right pressure . . .'

'You're on,' Knevitt said decisively. He looked at their weary faces. 'We get some rest, then everyone back here eight o'clock sharp tomorrow morning . . . Justine Campbell's going nowhere, which gives us time to brief Fr Bernard and bait the trap.'

'What if we've got it wrong?' Doyle quavered.

'Not an option, matey, no cock-ups allowed,' Noakes declared as Knevitt shot him a grateful look. ''Sides—' he winked at them — 'this is my big break . . . I c'n see the headline now: *Bromgrove private dick helps city boys crack biggest case in decades* . . . You don' wanna rain on my parade now, do you?' he added winsomely.

And with that, the die was cast.

As the detectives slipped out into the night, nothing stirred in the Tower.

Over in the ravens' enclosure, however, the castle's feathered guardians were unusually restless, shifting and twitching in their roost.

As if they sensed the final chapter was at hand.

CHAPTER 13: REQUIESCANT

The afternoon of Wednesday 13 December found the detectives and Noakes assembled in the Chapel of St John the Evangelist.

On his earlier whistle-stop tour of the White Tower, Markham hadn't truly taken in the soaring beauty of the Romanesque chapel which sat in a semi-circular apse at the south-east corner. It was notable for its stark simplicity, with a tunnel nave and groin-vaulted aisles whose thick piers supported unornamented arches at ground level, surmounted by another row of concentric arches in the curving gallery above. The overall effect put him in mind of early Christian catacombs with their patina of praise and devotion. He knew the shrine had been witness to gruesome scenes, including an archbishop being dragged to his death by a baying mob, but found it difficult to associate the creamy yellow stonework and simple altar cross, softly backlit by the late-afternoon sun, with anything other than an atmosphere of pure and noble spirituality fit for the worship of monarchs down the centuries.

It was both awe-inspiring and intimate, with plain pine pews, just three stained glass windows and a handful of decorative panels in the criss-cross leaded side windows. Looking about him, the DI understood why such surroundings might have felt like sanctuary to troubled souls — as if some unseen presence laid a gentle, cool palm on their brows and temporarily divested them of tormenting thoughts and obsessions. He felt it himself — that stillness as from a caressing hand.

Abruptly, he shook himself free of the strange spell, recalling that there was a job to be done.

'You're positive *this* is where she wants to meet?' Noakes asked the chaplain, clearly less convinced than Markham of the chapel's suitability.

'*She* suggested it,' Fr Bernard replied simply. 'Says it's somewhere she feels she can *breathe*.'

Noakes merely grunted before muttering, ''S'like an aqueduct more'n a church.'

The chaplain led the detectives up spiral stone steps to the viewing gallery, urging them to be careful how they went. Markham recalled Olivia commenting that there was something vertiginous about the Tower's staircases, but concluded that this particular climb was worth it for the sense of peace and tranquillity — of being transported out of one's everyday worries and concerns.

Kate Burton, however, was looking about her in consternation.

'There's nowhere we can set up a lookout,' she said anxiously.

'I've thought of that,' Fr Bernard said. 'We're due to hold a carol service in here on Friday — this one's especially for clergy and choirs attached to the Chapels Royal along with their families . . . there's usually a sprinkling of trustees and notables, and the whole thing's being televised this year. Channel 4.'

Burton was quick to catch on. 'So there's going to be all sorts of cameras and recording equipment up here—'

'Which means an audio or tech booth wouldn't look out of place and arouse Justine's suspicions,' Carruthers finished.

The DCI considered this. 'If we put some sort of Portakabin or soundproofed kiosk down there,' he said, gesturing to the far end of the left-hand tribune where they were standing, 'it would be in keeping with arrangements for the service, right?'

''Course, we'd have to make sure you can't see in or owt like that,' Noakes warned.

'Shouldn't be a problem,' Morrissey told him. 'We just get one of those modular jobbies with opaque film over the windows . . . or we could even go windowless. Maintenance could sort something out for us in a jiffy.'

'Won't people smell a rat if it's usually the TV people who arrange that side of things?' Doyle demurred.

Knevitt thought hard. 'We tell the chief yeoman warder that Channel 4 want to know if the Tower can erect something at short notice . . . talk about a supplier letting them down or some other excuse . . . budget cuts, logistics issues, anything really so long as it sounds reasonably plausible. And we make sure that Justine Campbell hears all about it by getting Ken Dudley to say something in his briefing tomorrow morning. It'll add authenticity if he has a whinge about the TV folk making unreasonable demands . . . throwing their weight about, that kind of thing.'

Noakes grinned. 'According to old Dud, people are always expecting miracles from Maintenance, so it won't take much to get steam coming out of his ears.'

'All the better for us,' Burton said smartly. 'Justine might look cowed and browbeaten, but if we're right about her, she's killed at least three times and attacked two children that we know of . . . not to mention terrorizing other youngsters with her prowler theatrics.'

The words were almost a profanity in the soaring, vaulted spaces of the chapel, the sunlight seeming temporarily dimmed by the DI's bleak denunciation.

'Time's getting short,' Knevitt told them after a pause. 'We need to set wheels in motion with Maintenance asap.'

'I'll see to it,' Burton said promptly.

Markham noticed that her face had paled, a few freckles standing out against the sudden whiteness of her skin like tiny flecks of gold paint.

Carruthers had spotted it too. 'You're looking a bit green around the gills, ma'am,' he said hesitantly. 'You okay with heights?' His voice was gentle and concerned, without its usual sarcastic edge.

She gave a wan smile. 'Not great, to tell you the truth,' she replied.

'It *does* feel a long way up,' Doyle said sympathetically. 'I remember going round the battlements at Caernarfon Castle on a trip when I was in the Juniors . . . came over dizzy and threw up all over one of the teachers . . . ruined my hard man credentials, I can tell you.'

There was something touching about the protective way the two young sergeants hovered over Burton, Markham thought. No matter how irritating they occasionally found her schoolmarm tendencies, Doyle and Carruthers undoubtedly had a soft spot for their punctilious colleague.

Seeing how she stood well back from the stone balustrade, Morrissey said, 'Me and these two'll come down with you . . . We need to check in on the undercovers and see what's happening with the Campbells.'

Despite her discomfort, Burton was still preoccupied with arrangements for the crucial confrontation.

'Where will Fr Bernard and Justine talk?' she asked. 'Surely she won't be comfortable just mooching around the tribune.'

'We'll make sure there's some packing cases or trestles up here for them to sit on,' Knevitt reassured her. 'They won't look out of place with the rest of the TV paraphernalia.'

'We'll give out that the chapel's closed to everyone 'cos of preparations for the carol service,' Morrissey said easily. 'Everyone 'cept the chaplain and essential Tower personnel obviously. It'd look odd if the warders were barred from doing their security sweeps or whatever, but we'll have eyes on Andy Campbell and the rest of them . . . Plus, there'll be undercovers posing as Channel 4 techies downstairs. The padre will be wired up within arm's reach of our lookout, so we can get to him in seconds . . . He'll be wearing a stab vest as an extra precaution,' he added grimly.

Now it was the chaplain's turn to pale as the implications of Knevitt's words sank in.

Markham's dark gaze came to rest on the priest. Noting how leaden his complexion looked, how sunken his eyes with the flesh round them appearing almost bruised, the DI wondered if the man was up to this.

'There's something almost, well, *sacrilegious* about my hearing a confession to *murder* in such a holy place,' Fr Bernard said hoarsely, his throat working with distress.

'Not half as sacrilegious as letting old Jussy get away with bumping off two women an' them kids,' Noakes said firmly. More kindly, he added, 'Look, padre, she needs *stopping* . . . an' I reckon if Fr whatsit's right, then it'll be a relief to get it off her chest. Don' forget it were *her choice* to meet in the chapel. Happen being in here, with the ghosts of all them kings an' queens, will flip the switch an' she'll go batshit.' He gazed around him with lugubrious relish. 'John Whittingham told me some prince fell from the next floor up . . . the clothes line or whatever he were using to escape snapped, so . . . *splat!* Weirdy sounding name . . . summat like the Gruffalo . . .'

'That was the Welshman Gruffudd ap Llywelyn,' Fr Bernard said with a wary eye on Kate Burton who had nervous patches on her throat listening to this anecdote. 'But there's never been anything like that happen in the chapel . . . We'll be perfectly safe.'

Once Burton and the two sergeants had headed back down, Doyle and Carruthers going fore and aft at Noakes's insistence 'in case she had a funny turn', Markham addressed the others. 'Do you really think the unique atmosphere of this place will have enough of an effect on Justine . . . enough to ensure she—'

'Spills her guts?' Noakes finished complacently.

'You took the words right out of my mouth, Noakesy.'

Knevitt darted a searching look at the chaplain. 'Providing the padre here touches all those chords as per Inspector Burton's script, I think we stand a good chance of extracting an admission to murder.'

'We need a BAFTA winning performance from you, padre,' Noakes said beadily. 'No pressure,' he added with menacing jocularity.

There was a tense expectant silence.

'I'll do my best, Mr Noakes.'

'We're counting on it, mate.'

* * *

The chaplain was certainly living up to his side of the bargain, Markham thought the following afternoon as the team eavesdropped on the conversation between the priest and Justine Campbell, with Fr Bernard leading her by imperceptible degrees to the point of irrevocable self-incrimination. Starting by saying that he and Fr Molloy were worried about her, the priest gradually prised open her defences and stared into the chasm beyond.

Slowly but surely, their prime suspect's narcissism and shaky sense of self, along with her bitter resentment of Marie Sullivan and Margaret Esdaile for a series of slights real and imagined, were laid bare by her interlocutor with a gentle ruthlessness that did credit to Kate Burton's patient coaching. Slowly but surely, she brought up all the past in dredges of self-pity that could not disguise a deeply fractured personality and unnerving fluctuation between seeming reasonableness and overt irrationality. Most disturbing of all was the projection of her incapacity on to medieval avatars, as she rambled on disconnectedly about how she identified with Richard III's despised wife Anne Neville for her persecution by a callous, unfaithful spouse who took up with a younger model in the shape of Elizabeth of York. Could it possibly be, Markham wondered, that the woman suspected husband Andy of having a fling with Marie Sullivan or Margaret Esdaile, or possibly both? Certainly, the way in which Justine mingled her marital history with that of a long dead queen and ranted about fate not being mocked — Elizabeth of York, she asserted, 'paid' for her sins with the murder of her brothers, the Princes in the Tower — raised all sorts of alarming possibilities in connection with the Sullivan twins and Dr Esdaile's daughter.

The tipping point when it arrived was nonetheless something of a shock to the detectives.

'I don't judge, Justine,' the priest said softly.

'Not like the rest of them then,' she hissed in a voice that held a world of venom.

The detectives hadn't risked rigging up CCTV, but from long experience in such situations Markham knew just how Justine Campbell must look as she spat out the words, her gaze as black and blank as that of a shark, her eyes empty cavities.

His colleagues were rigid as they sat motionless on the bench that had been squeezed into the Portakabin, almost afraid to breathe.

Markham guessed what they were thinking.

Don't bother with specifics. Confront her with what she's done. Now *before she loses it completely!*

'I know what you're leading up to,' Justine said unexpectedly, her tone as flat and neutral as if they were discussing the weather.

'What?' The chaplain 's voice was steady, but Markham guessed he must be almost faint with nervous anticipation.

'It was me.'

'What do you mean?'

'I killed Margaret Esdaile . . . oh, and Marie Sullivan's brats.' The casually heartless postscript elicited a gasp, hastily suppressed, from Kate Burton. 'I never meant to hurt Antonia, though,' came the ragged admission. 'I was upset after the funeral. Not myself. I just wanted to give her a bit of a scare. But then Mrs Fusspot Hernan appeared from nowhere and started having hysterics.'

'Where are the Sullivan twins, Justine?' Fr Bernard asked, his manner devoid of outrage or censure. Markham knew he was remembering Knevitt's injunction: '*Make her give up the kids, padre. Those parents need closure.*'

'Downstairs, of course,' she sniggered, and Markham felt the hairs rise on the back of his neck.

'Where do you mean, Justine?' The chaplain exhibited none of the horror he must be feeling.

Suddenly she let out a surprised exclamation.

'*Andy!*'

FFS, where did Campbell spring from! Noakes half rose.

But Knevitt signalled. *Wait, we need more.*

Her husband spoke urgently, 'It's all over, Jus.'

'You stay away from me!'

'C'mon luv, you can't go on like this . . . you need *help.*'

Her voice sounded ethereal, disembodied. 'Get away!'

And now Knevitt gave the signal.

But it was too late for Justine Campbell. Grappling with her husband as the detectives exploded from their hiding place and raced towards her, she jerked backwards and somersaulted over the stone balustrade in a sweeping arc — like one of those strange medieval seraphs that defied the laws of gravity — with no sound except a choked little cry.

The sickening thud as she hit the stone flags below was something none of them would ever forget, despite being long hardened to desperate outcomes.

Footsteps thudded up the stairs to the gallery as undercover officers crowded the tribune, but Knevitt gestured to them to stay back.

'It was an accident,' Campbell said, staggering slightly as he collapsed on to a packing case. 'She lost her balance.'

'Which stairs did Justine mean?' The DCI was remorseless, a pulse throbbing at his temple.

'She must've meant our old flat,' the other mumbled, unable to meet Knevitt's hotly accusing gaze. 'Over at the Casemates . . . that's the warders' accommodation on Mint Street by the Outer Ward. They converted our place into a storeroom Christmas 2008, so we had to move into a cottage a few doors down.'

Christmas 2008.

The same year the Sullivan twins vanished, Markham thought, as Campbell's words dropped into the appalled silence. As their import sank in, the DI's feet and gorge rose and his hands felt so cold that they seemed turned to lead. Sweat broke out on his forehead as an image swam before him of empty black eye sockets . Somehow, however, he maintained a calm demeanour.

Knevitt broke the trance-like atmosphere. 'Get him out of here,' he barked at the hovering undercovers who duly hustled Campbell away.

Then the DCI led his colleagues and Fr Bernard down to ground level where the chaplain dropped to his knees next to Justine Campbell's broken body, sprawled upwards across the flagged altar steps. Blood trickled from the corner of her mouth and the blue eyes were filmed over in a vacant stare.

White and quiet, they watched as he prayed: 'Go forth O soul, out of this world in the name of the Father Almighty who created you . . . Dead to the world, O Lord, may she live to Thee, and the sins she has committed in this life, through human frailty, do Thou forgive . . . All creatures are alive in the sight of their King . . .'

More invocations followed, all curiously moving, and of course he knew no sinner was excluded from God's mercy, but Noakes could not help hoping that whatever berth this newly freed soul was allocated in the hereafter, it was nowhere near that of the innocent children and two women she had murdered. He wasn't sure how it worked when you reached the remotest outposts of time and space, but somehow it wouldn't be fair if Justine Campbell was headed for the same place as the Sullivan twins . . .

The chaplain eased himself upright.

'Of course I will reconsecrate the chapel as soon as possible,' he told them, looking fixedly at the plain gold altar cross mounted between two silver candlesticks. 'Anoint everything again.'

Markham wondered if it was possible to *unsee* evil and sacrilege instead of holiness, replace hideousness with beauty. Somehow it seemed to him that every clean pure plane in the ancient shrine was polluted by what had taken place.

'It will be all right,' the chaplain insisted. 'This hasn't killed our chapel.' Looking round at the thick stone piers — twelve for the twelve apostles — he added defiantly, '"Upon this rock I shall build my church and the gates of hell shall not prevail against it."'

Seeing as this was scripture, Noakes stifled his usual alarm at extempore versification.

'Yeah, this place has seen all sorts,' he said gruffly. 'An' once you've given it a proper, er, clean-up, it'll be right as rain.'

The awkward reassurance brought a smile to the other's thin, taut features.

'And of course, the sanctuary was empty,' he declared with relief.

'*Eh?*' Noakes was puzzled.

'There was no reserved Sacrament,' Markham said quietly.

His friend's expression cleared. 'I'm with you now, padre,' he told Fr Bernard. 'Else there'd be a little red lamp burning.' Personally, he wished God had made everyone Protestant, then there wouldn't be all this confusion about lamps and suchlike.

There was a sudden bustle at the back of the chapel and a handsome Nigerian approached them trailed by two paramedics. Introducing himself as the pathologist Dr Charles Obi, he watched compassionately as the chaplain made the sign of the cross over Justine Campbell's crumpled body.

'She's all yours, doc,' Knevitt said finally.

Then the detectives and chaplain filed out of the chapel into the Tower precincts where snow had fallen once more, giving an even quieter hush to the fortress which had been rapidly cleared of tourists and visitors. As they stood at the foot of the White Tower, its cupolas gleaming with an unearthly beauty, they were startled by the piercing song of a winter thrush. It seemed an oddly hopeful sound in the frozen stillness.

Morrissey's voice brought them back to reality.

'We'll be able to excavate the Campbells' old cottage, sir,' he said to Knevitt. 'With it being part of the Outer Ward, English Heritage can't object.'

'I'd like to see them try, seeing as we've had confirmation that it's a gravesite,' was the DCI's forthright response, underlined by an impatient click of the tongue.

With a swift glance at Burton's white, shocked face, Markham said, 'Let's adjourn somewhere warm.'

Meeting Knevitt's eyes, Morrissey concurred. 'Hot drinks all round,' he suggested in a loud, sensible voice. Dominic and Annie Sullivan had lain undisturbed for more than a decade. Soon those little bones would be exhumed and the parents could finally reclaim their children from the Tower.

* * *

Three days after the dramatic denouement of the Tower investigation, Markham and Olivia headed back to Bromgrove by train. With a first-class compartment to themselves and amply supplied with refreshments by solicitous waiters who cast surreptitious glances at Markham when they thought he wasn't looking (he and the rest of his team having been emblazoned, along with Knevitt and Morrissey, across a three-page spread in the *Evening Standard*), it felt like the perfect way to unwind.

Noakes and the two sergeants having lingered for a post-investigation knees-up at Tower Bridge, while Burton chose to take in a couple of art galleries, it felt almost as if she and Markham were playing hooky, Olivia reflected happily. Certainly it would be back to earth with a vengeance when she had to show her face at school, but in the meantime . . .

As he watched his partner work her way through a G & T and assorted snacks, Markham too caught something of the holiday spirit. 'A penny for your thoughts, Gil,' she asked lightly, seeing him smile.

'For once I needn't quail at the prospect of a debrief with Sidney,' he told her. 'He's cock-a-hoop at media coverage of the Tower cases.'

'You were bloody generous giving him so much of the credit,' Olivia grumbled. 'I mean, for heaven's sake, Gil, he practically comes out of it like flaming Perry Mason thanks to all that guff about his "expertise in solving psychologically challenging cases" . . . yeah, too freaking generous by half.'

Markham grinned unrepentantly, the austere features transformed by the warmth of his smile so that she could not help herself smiling back.

'He and Ebury-Clarke are so delighted with CID's new-found fame that it should keep them off my back for some time to come,' he told her. 'And the publicity's bound to do Noakesy's start-up a power of good.'

Her face softened. 'I gather he and the chaplain are going to keep in touch.'

Markham thought back to their farewells at the Tower's West Gate, evening floodlights suffusing the castle with an eerie nimbus. 'Yes, Fr Bernard and Noakes have formed some kind of bond . . . despite the padre's regrettable tendency to quote poetry at the drop of a hat.'

'Doesn't the good book say, "Out of the fullness of the heart the mouth speaks"?' she enquired mischievously.

He chuckled. 'Yes well, I reckon Noakesy could do with less of the sacred eloquence.' Turning serious, he added, 'Fr Bernard came through for us when we needed it. It was really touch and go whether we could break Justine Campbell, but he played his part well.'

Olivia sipped her G & T meditatively. 'You think she was mentally ill then?'

'I would say so, though it's a moot point whether she suffered from BPD or some other disorder . . . SELD, for example.'

'Spare me the acronyms,' she groaned in mock exasperation.

'It stands for Social Emotional Learning Disorder,' he explained. 'Apparently it's a poorly understood condition, but the gist of it is you have a diseased child's mind in an adult's body—'

'Arrested development?'

'Exactly.' Markham recalled his final conversation with Fr Molloy. 'She talked quite a lot to her confessor about when she was a child . . . so much so, that he came to see her as an emotionally twisted preadolescent trapped in the body of a woman.'

Olivia shivered convulsively. 'A *killer child* who developed a sick obsession with children,' she murmured. '*Wow*, makes you wonder whether something happened in her own childhood . . . something traumatic that she repressed.'

'Well I doubt we'll ever know. At least she wasn't destined to see out her days in an institution.' Markham could never recall the Newman Psychiatric Hospital in Bromgrove — the concrete walkways, glass-enclosed booths, air locks, metal detectors, endless yellowish-tan corridors and constant sonic assault of bells and walkie-talkies — without a shudder. He felt obscurely glad that Justine Campbell was not set to moulder in such a place. Endeavouring to speak lightly, he continued, 'At any rate, there was some sort of void within the woman's personality and everything else followed as a consequence, though I don't suppose we'll ever know how she developed that bizarre obsession with Anne Neville and Ricardian history.'

'At least those poor children's remains were recovered.' There was silence and then she burst out, 'Andy Campbell *must've* known or suspected, Gil . . . I mean there had to have been a smell or something.'

'She buried the bodies in the cottage's cellar . . . It was concreted over when the place was converted to a storeroom. Looks like the surveyors slipped up somewhere along the line, but there were various significant archaeological digs underway in 2008 and they had their hands full with that, whereas work on staff accommodation was low priority . . . If he *did* suspect his wife, with being a warder Andy Campbell was well placed to manipulate the process and conceal what she'd done.'

Olivia frowned. 'Is he admitting to anything?'

'No, and unless something comes to light, it's unlikely he can be charged.' Markham sighed.

'How did he even come to be in the chapel?'

'Somehow he made it past the undercovers . . . twigged there was something fishy involving the chaplain and Justine. Word is, he'll most likely opt for early retirement . . . go quietly without any fuss.' Recalling how his partner had gelled with the jovial warder, he didn't mention his suspicion that Campbell might secretly be glad that his wife was dead . . . might even have assisted her fall. Everything had happened so quickly, he could not have said for sure how Justine Campbell came to plummet over that balustrade, but there was no way of proving foul play. Nor were Knevitt and Morrissey ever likely to uncover the whereabouts of the missing psalter or fathom all the circumstances surrounding events at the Tower, since Justine Campbell's jumbled, almost hysterical, outpouring of bile, though abounding in dark allusions to 'revenge' and 'getting her own back', had skirted the malicious pranks and stalking.

There were so many other questions destined to remain unanswered, Markham reflected. What was it, he asked himself, that had raised a red flag with Dr Esdaile and impelled her to contact the police? Justine's bitter assertion that 'the bitch was on to her' left the precise circumstances of her murder shrouded in mystery, so it looked as though they would never identify the precise trigger. He wondered too if the killer had intended to finish off Fr Bernard, only to be thwarted by the arrival of her husband. A pair of scissors found in the pocket of her overall suggested the chaplain had been in some peril . . .

'She was such a colourless ghost of a woman,' Olivia marvelled, interrupting his thoughts. 'I just don't know *how* she managed to make kids trust her.'

'Apparently she had a thing about children,' Markham said sadly. 'Desperately wanted them at the same time as hating it when she saw people playing happy families. Couldn't have any of her own and Andy refused to consider adoption.' Feeling that this might touch a nerve and carefully avoiding her gaze, he continued hastily, 'Somehow it must have added insult to injury when she watched the likes of

Margaret Esdaile and Marie Sullivan enjoying the kind of settled domestic happiness she'd always wanted for herself.'

'You sound sorry for her.'

'I suppose in a way I am, Liv.' Now he looked her straight in the eyes. 'When I heard Fr Bernard asking God to forgive whatever sins she had committed — sealing her five senses away from the world — I found myself joining in. It was quite impressive the way he literally *cannonaded* heaven with prayers for her soul. I've never heard anyone pray like that before.' Nor did he ever want to hear anybody pray like that again, it was such an awesome thing to witness.

'How did George take it when Fr Bernard recited all those prayers for forgiveness?'

'*Hmm.* Let's just say, he has a less benign approach to human frailty.'

She laughed at that. 'D'you ever think about going in with him?' she enquired slyly.

'What, joining Medway Investigations?' Markham replied, startled. 'I'd say I'm probably more use to Noakesy as his eyes and ears in CID.'

She changed tack. 'Any sign of Kate being poached by the Tower Bridge lot?' she asked, her tone colourless.

With a sharp pang, he recalled the pleasure and respect in Knevitt's eyes as the DCI said goodbye to Burton and told her he hoped they would work together again soon. He also remembered having detected a certain answering flutter in his colleague. With a sinking heart, he feared that her days at Bromgrove might be numbered. Perhaps impending separation might lead to a clearing of the air between them — a prospect he secretly desired . . . and dreaded.

Markham became aware that Olivia was watching him closely, her sensitivity to his feelings for Kate Burton as unerring as if they had a shape or colour or smell.

'Who knows what the future will bring,' he told her.

'I want to come back to the Tower some time,' she said softly. 'It was such a surreal experience being there . . . such a strange sense of time outside time.'

'I know what you mean, Liv. Next time, we'll make sure to do Lady Jane and the rest of them full justice.' He reached across the table for her hand. 'In the meantime, there's Christmas presents to think about.'

'George told me Muriel wants a dog,' Olivia confided. 'Knowing her she'll probably call it Feydeau,' spelling out the name with a wicked glint in her eye. 'God help the poor mutt.'

'And what about *you*?'

'A can of mace . . . Let's face it, every teacher should have one.'

Outside the carriage windows, towns and villages flashed by. The snow was melting now, turning the landscape mulchy and waterlogged, but Markham felt a lightening of spirit. Whatever rocks and cross currents lay ahead, he would deal with them.

Bring it on!

THE END

THE JOFFE BOOKS STORY

We began in 2014 when Jasper agreed to publish his mum's much-rejected romance novel and it became a bestseller.

Since then we've grown into the largest independent publisher in the UK. We're extremely proud to publish some of the very best writers in the world, including Joy Ellis, Faith Martin, Caro Ramsay, Helen Forrester, Simon Brett and Robert Goddard. Everyone at Joffe Books loves reading and we never forget that it all begins with the magic of an author telling a story.

We are proud to publish talented first-time authors, as well as established writers whose books we love introducing to a new generation of readers.

We won Trade Publisher of the Year at the Independent Publishing Awards in 2023 and Best Publisher Award in 2024 at the People's Book Prize. We have been shortlisted for Independent Publisher of the Year at the British Book Awards for the last five years, and were shortlisted for the Diversity and Inclusivity Award at the 2022 Independent Publishing Awards. In 2023 we were shortlisted for Publisher of the Year at the RNA Industry Awards, and in 2024 we were short-listed at the CWA Daggers for the Best Crime and Mystery Publisher.

We built this company with your help, and we love to hear from you, so please email us about absolutely anything book-ish at feedback@joffebooks.com.

If you want to receive free books every Friday and hear about all our new releases, join our mailing list here: www.joffe-books.com/freebooks.

And when you tell your friends about us, just remember: it's pronounced Joffe as in coffee or toffee!

Milton Keynes UK
Ingram Content Group UK Ltd.
UKHW040357111224
452348UK00004B/258

9 781835 269091